Garfield ®

UNREALITY TV

BY JIM DAVIS

ROSS RICHIE CEO & Founder • MATT GAGNON Editor-in-Chief • FILIP SABLIK President of Publishing & Marketing • STEPHEN CHRISTY President of Development • LANCE KREITER VP of Licensing & Merchandising
PHIL BARBARO VP of Finance • ARUNE SINGH VP of Marketing • BRYCE CARLSON Managing Editor • MEL CAYLO Marketing Manager • SCOTT NEWMAN Production Design Manager • KATE HENNING Operations Manager
SIERRA HAHN Senior Editor • DAFNA PLEBAN Editor, Talent Development • SHANNON WATTERS Editor • ERIC HARBURN Editor • WHITNEY LEOPARD Editor • JASMINE AMIRI Editor • CHRIS ROSA Associate Editor
ALEX GALER Associate Editor • CAMERON CHITTOCK Associate Editor • MATTHEW LEVINE Assistant Editor • SOPHIE PHILIPS-ROBERTS Assistant Editor • KELSEY DIETERICH Designer • JILLIAN CRAB Production Designer
MICHELLE ANKLEY Production Designer • KARA LEOPARD Production Designer • GRACE PARK Production Design Assistant • ELIZABETH LOUGHRIDGE Accounting Coordinator • STEPHANIE HOCUTT Social Media Coordinator
JOSÉ MEZA Event Coordinator • JAMES ARRIOLA Mailroom Assistant • HOLLY AITCHISON Operations Assistant • MEGAN CHRISTOPHER Operations Assistant • AMBER PARKER Administrative Assistant

kaboom!™

GARFIELD: UNREALITY TV, May 2017. Published by KaBOOM!, a division of Boom Entertainment, Inc. Garfield is © 2017 PAWS, INCORPORATED. ALL RIGHTS RESERVED. "GARFIELD" and the GARFIELD characters are registered and unregistered trademarks of Paws, Inc. KaBOOM!™ and the KaBOOM! logo are trademarks of Boom Entertainment, Inc., registered in various countries and categories. All characters, events, and institutions depicted herein are fictional. Any similarity between any of the names, characters, persons, events, and/or institutions in this publication to actual names, characters, and persons, whether living or dead, events, and/or institutions is unintended and purely coincidental. KaBOOM! does not read or accept unsolicited submissions of ideas, stories, or artwork.

BOOM! Studios, 5670 Wilshire Boulevard, Suite 450, Los Angeles, CA 90036-5679. Printed in China. First Printing.

ISBN: 978-1-60886-975-6, eISBN: 978-1-61398-646-2

CONTENTS

COLORED BY LISA MOORE

COVER BY ANDY HIRSCH

DESIGNER GRACE PARK
ASSOCIATE EDITOR CHRIS ROSA
EDITOR SIERRA HAHN

GARFIELD CREATED BY
JIM DAVIS

SPECIAL THANKS TO JIM DAVIS AND THE ENTIRE PAWS, INC. TEAM.

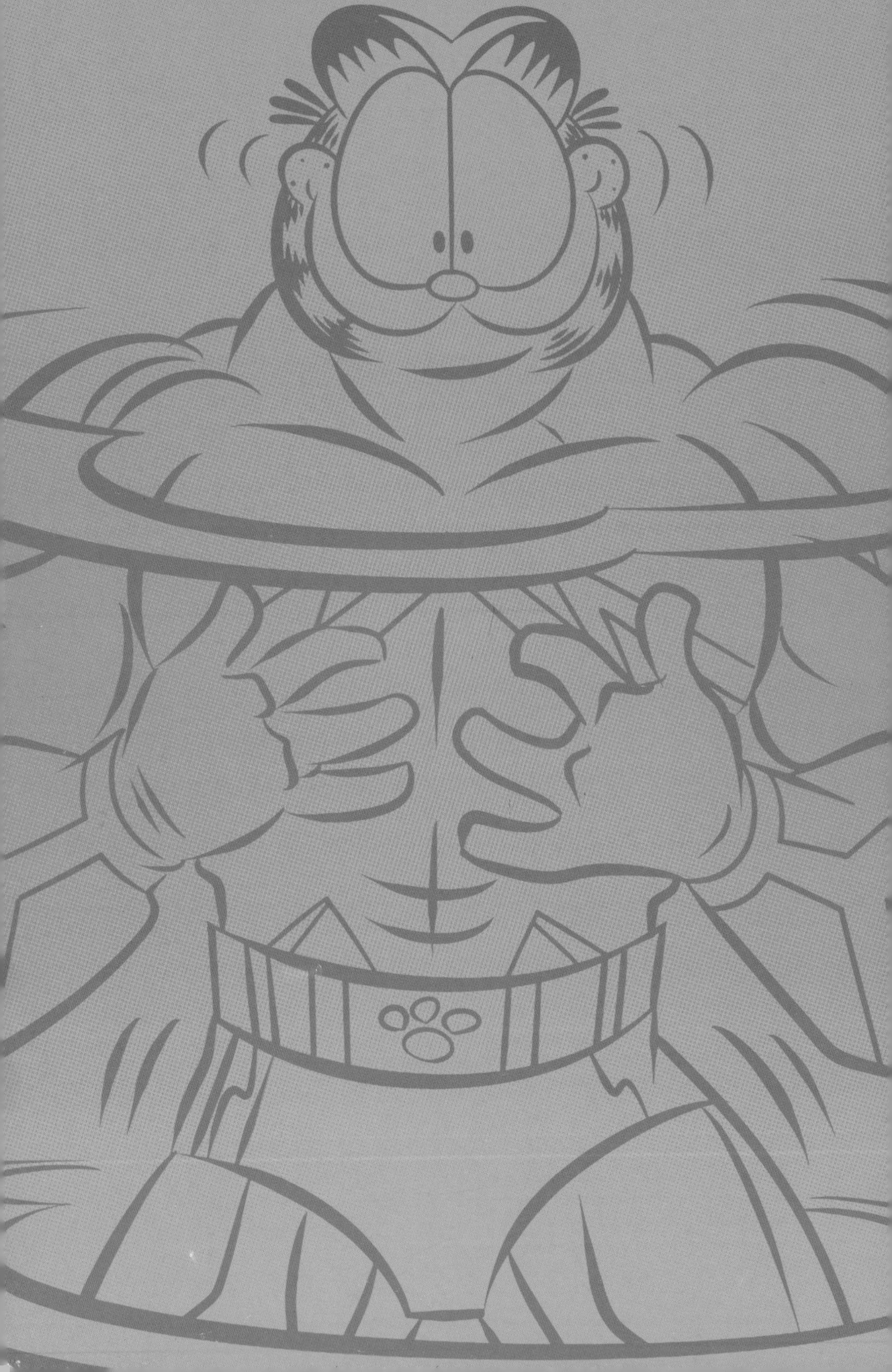

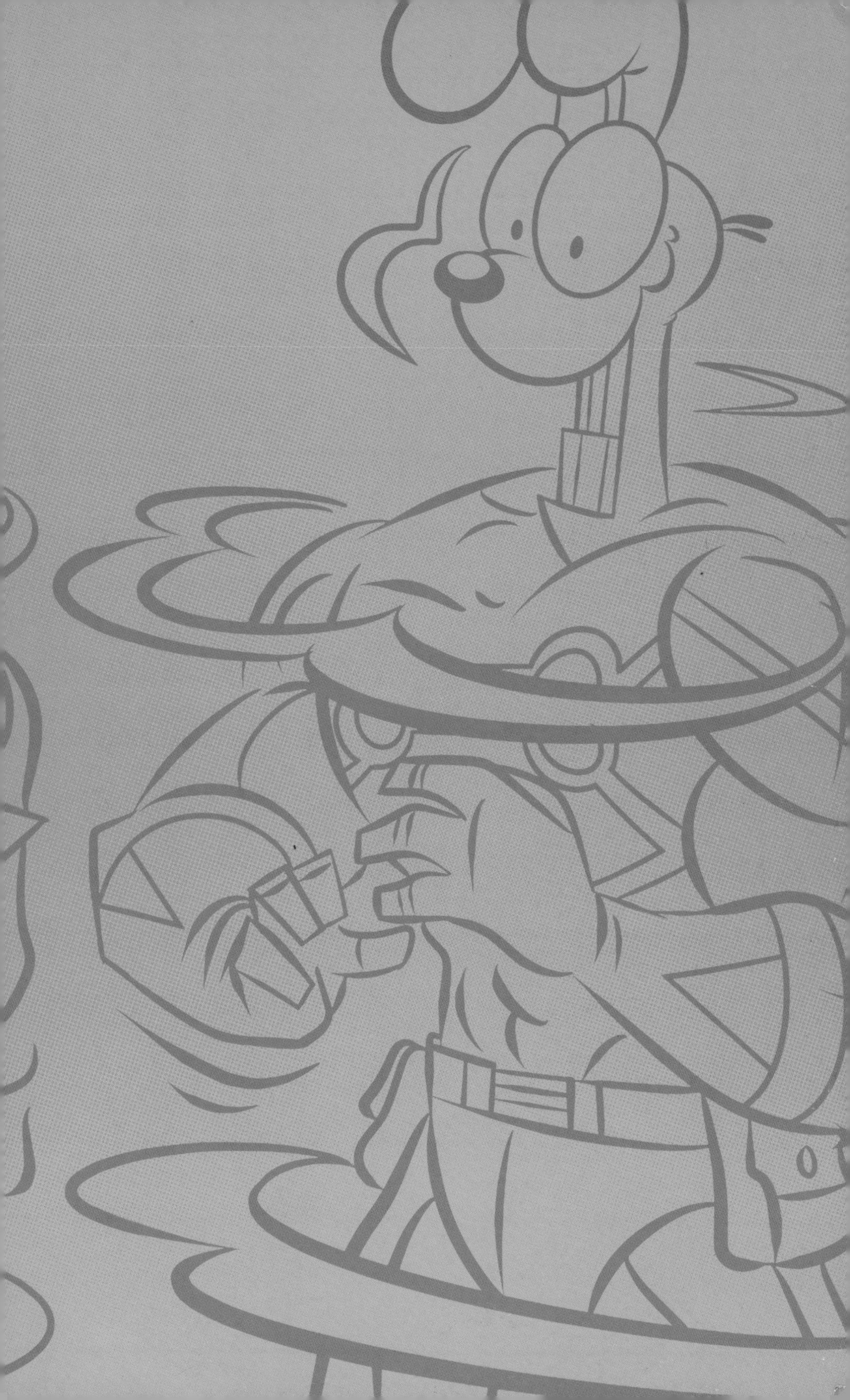

"UNREALITY TV"

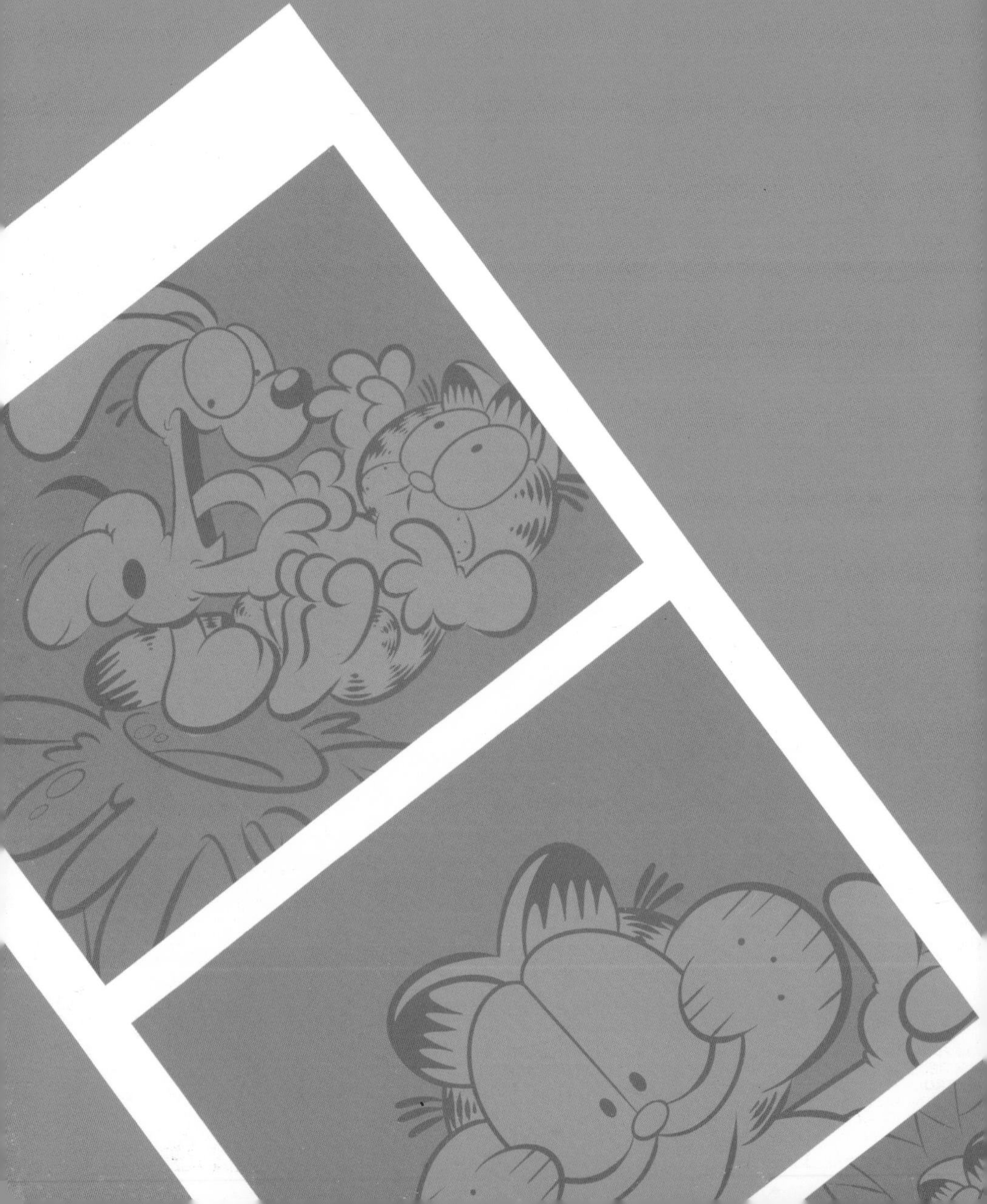

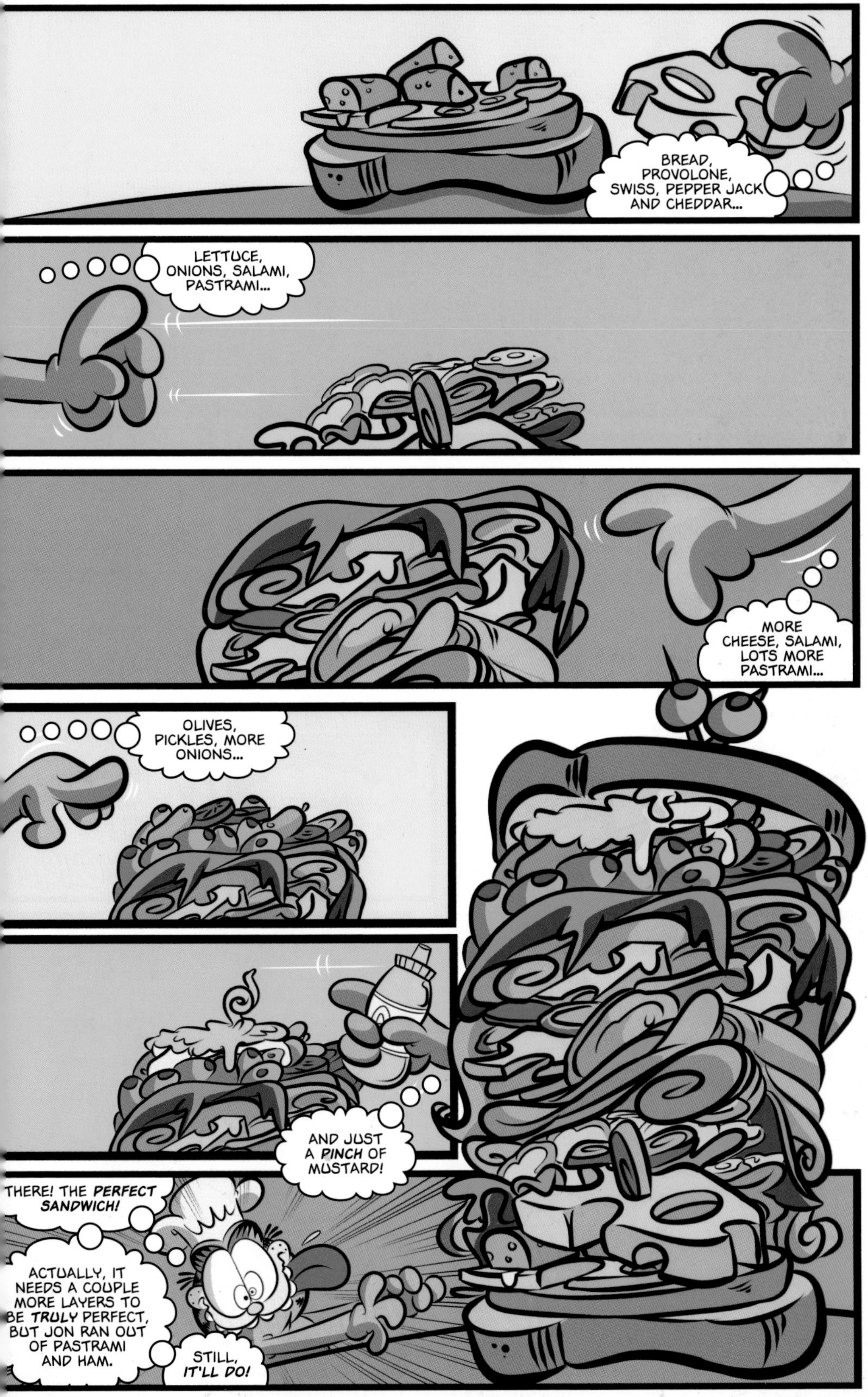
BREAD, PROVOLONE, SWISS, PEPPER JACK AND CHEDDAR...
LETTUCE, ONIONS, SALAMI, PASTRAMI...
MORE CHEESE, SALAMI, LOTS MORE PASTRAMI...
OLIVES, PICKLES, MORE ONIONS...
AND JUST A PINCH OF MUSTARD!
THERE! THE PERFECT SANDWICH!
ACTUALLY, IT NEEDS A COUPLE MORE LAYERS TO BE TRULY PERFECT, BUT JON RAN OUT OF PASTRAMI AND HAM.
STILL, IT'LL DO!

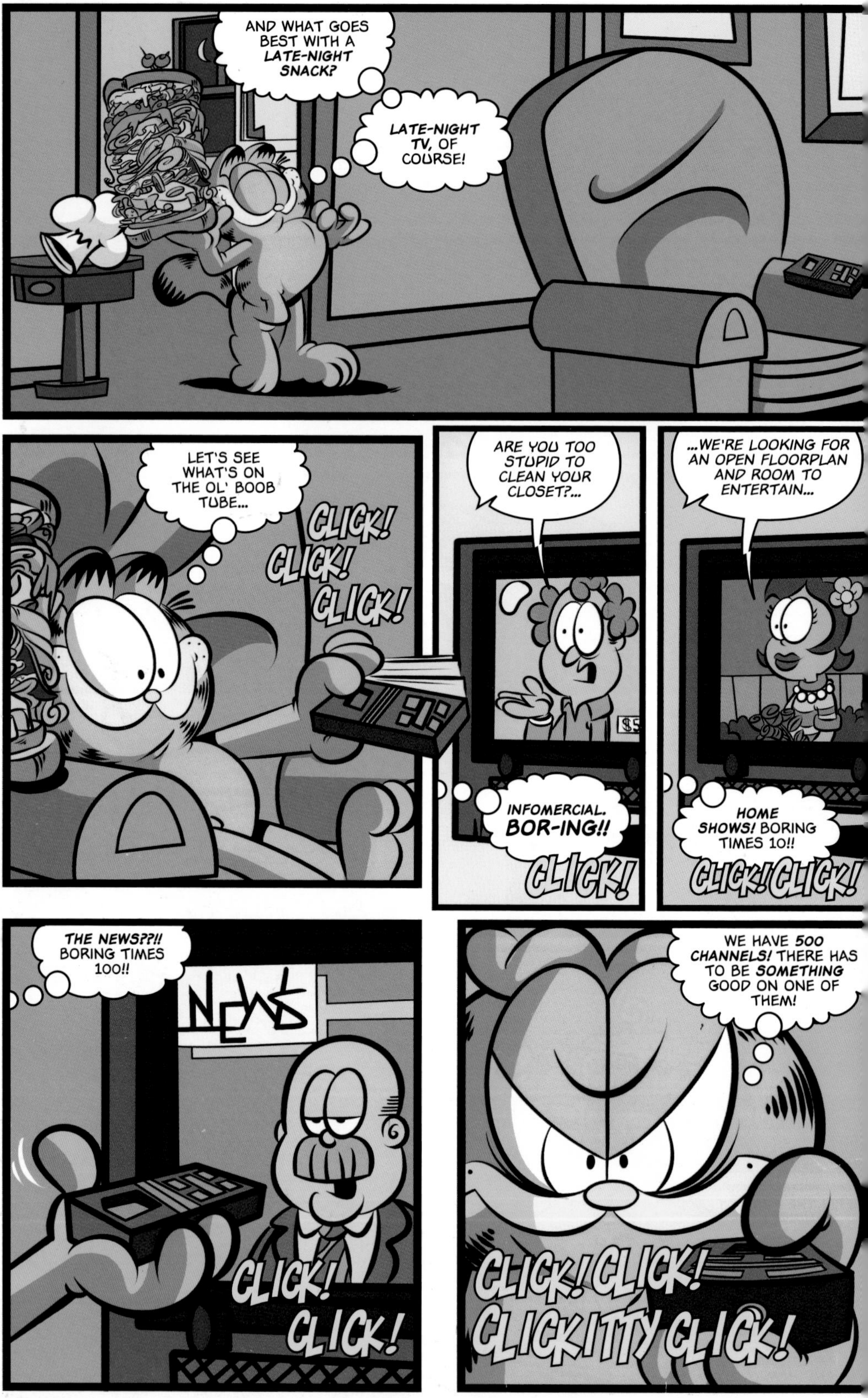
AND WHAT GOES BEST WITH A LATE-NIGHT SNACK?
LATE-NIGHT TV, OF COURSE!
LET'S SEE WHAT'S ON THE OL' BOOB TUBE...
CLICK! CLICK! CLICK!
ARE YOU TOO STUPID TO CLEAN YOUR CLOSET?...
INFOMERCIAL. BOR-ING!!
CLICK!
...WE'RE LOOKING FOR AN OPEN FLOORPLAN AND ROOM TO ENTERTAIN...
HOME SHOWS! BORING TIMES 10!!
CLICK! CLICK!
THE NEWS??!! BORING TIMES 100!!
NEWS
CLICK! CLICK!
WE HAVE 500 CHANNELS! THERE HAS TO BE SOMETHING GOOD ON ONE OF THEM!
CLICK! CLICK! CLICKITTY CLICK!

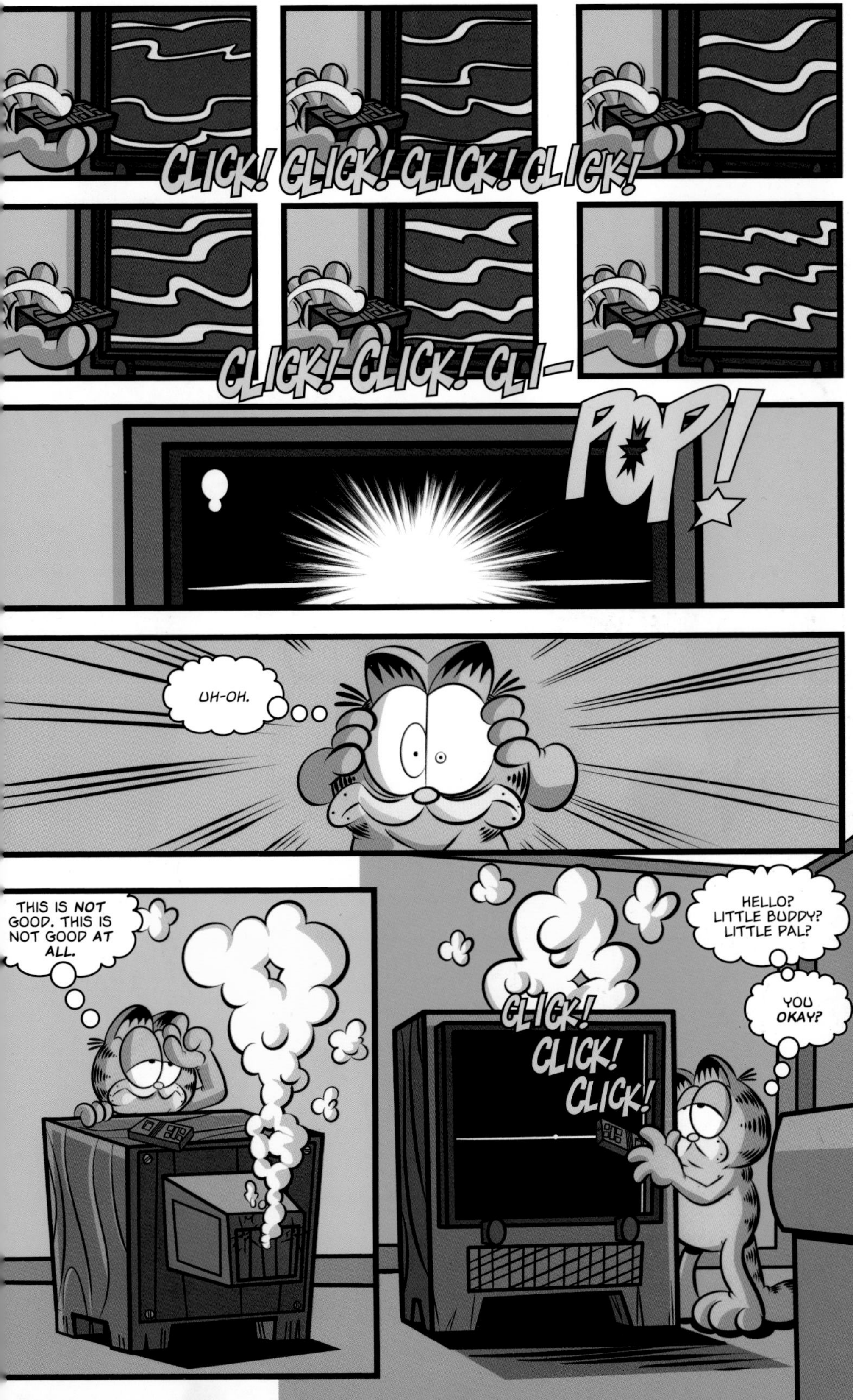
CLICK! CLICK! CLICK! CLICK!
CLICK! CLICK! CLI-
POP!
UH-OH.
THIS IS NOT GOOD. THIS IS NOT GOOD AT ALL.
CLICK! CLICK! CLICK!
HELLO? LITTLE BUDDY? LITTLE PAL?
YOU OKAY?

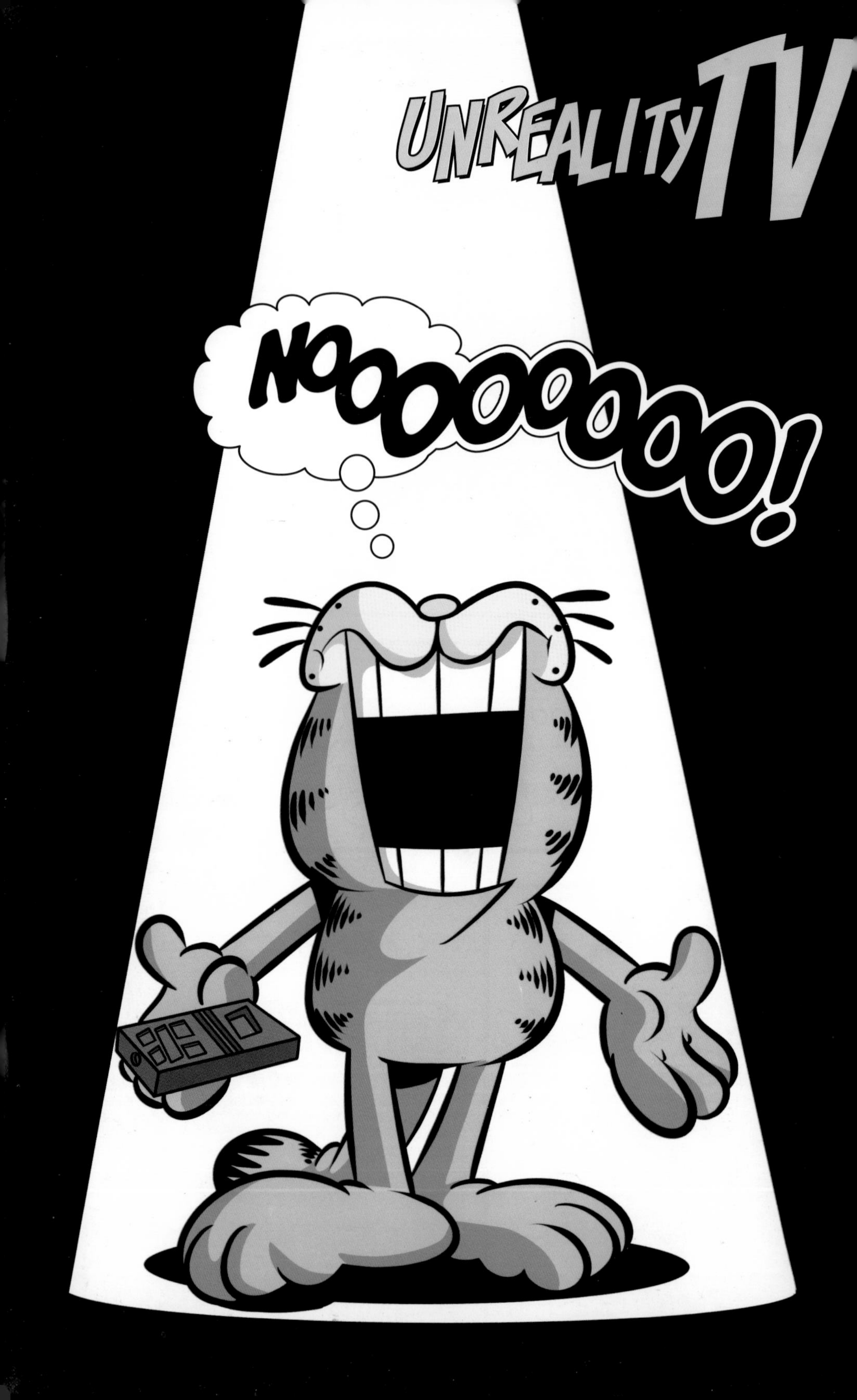
UNREALITY TV
NOOOOOOOO!

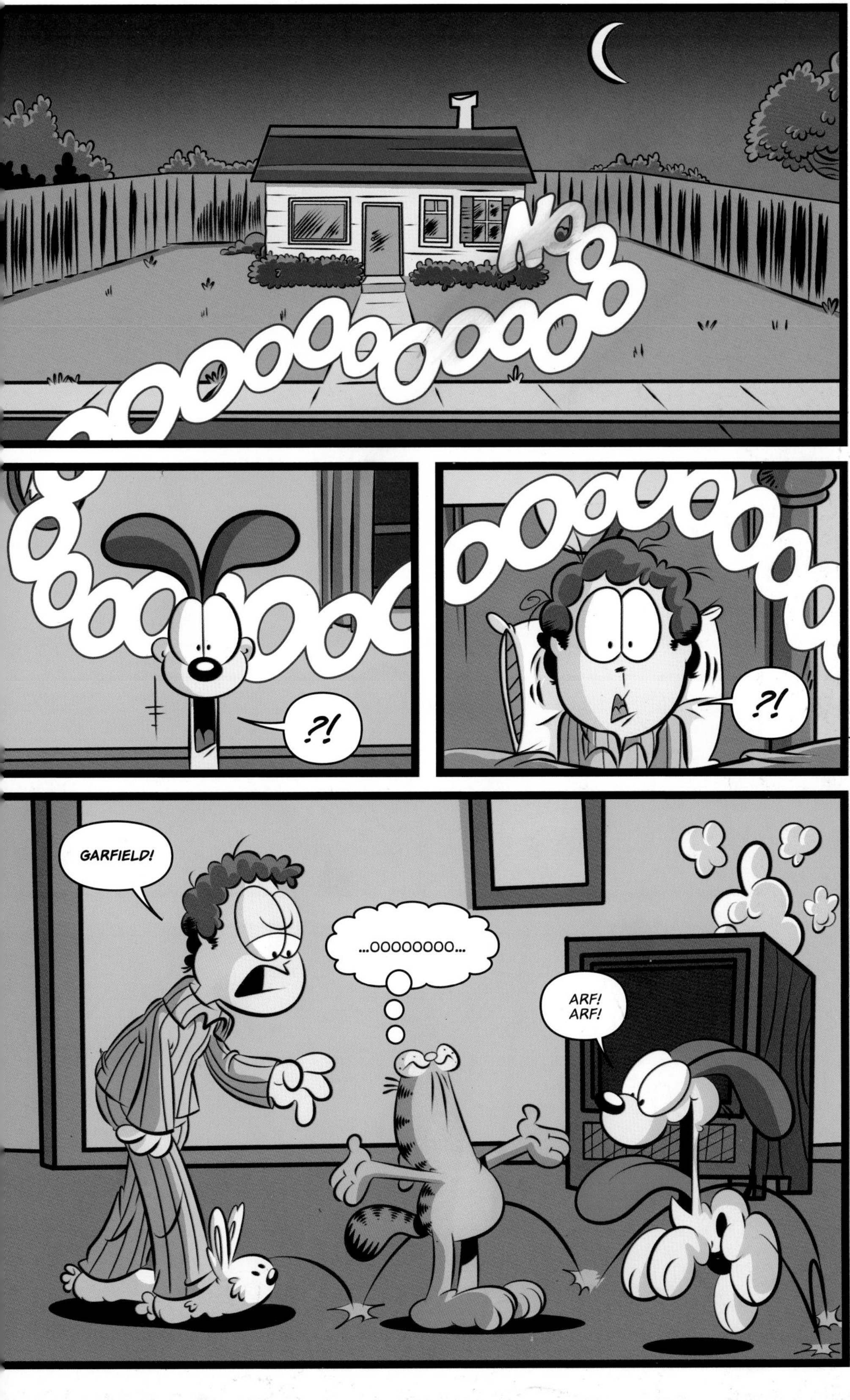
NOOOOOOOOOOOOOOOO
?!
?!
GARFIELD!
...OOOOOOOO...
ARF! ARF!

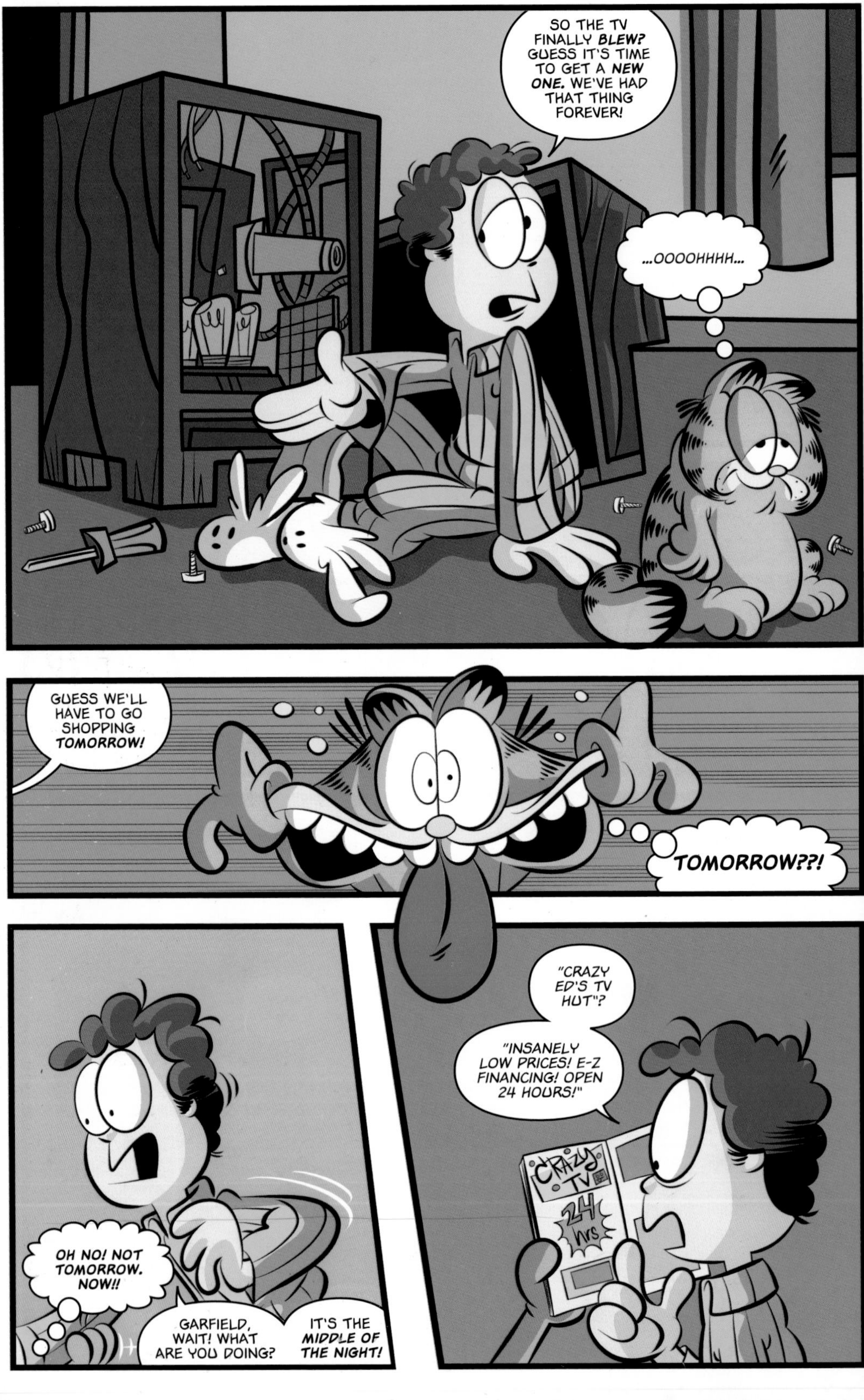
SO THE TV FINALLY BLEW? GUESS IT'S TIME TO GET A NEW ONE. WE'VE HAD THAT THING FOREVER!
...OOOOHHHH...
GUESS WE'LL HAVE TO GO SHOPPING TOMORROW!
TOMORROW??!
OH NO! NOT TOMORROW. NOW!!
GARFIELD, WAIT! WHAT ARE YOU DOING?
IT'S THE MIDDLE OF THE NIGHT!
"CRAZY ED'S TV HUT"?
"INSANELY LOW PRICES! E-Z FINANCING! OPEN 24 HOURS!"
CRAZY TV
24 hrs.

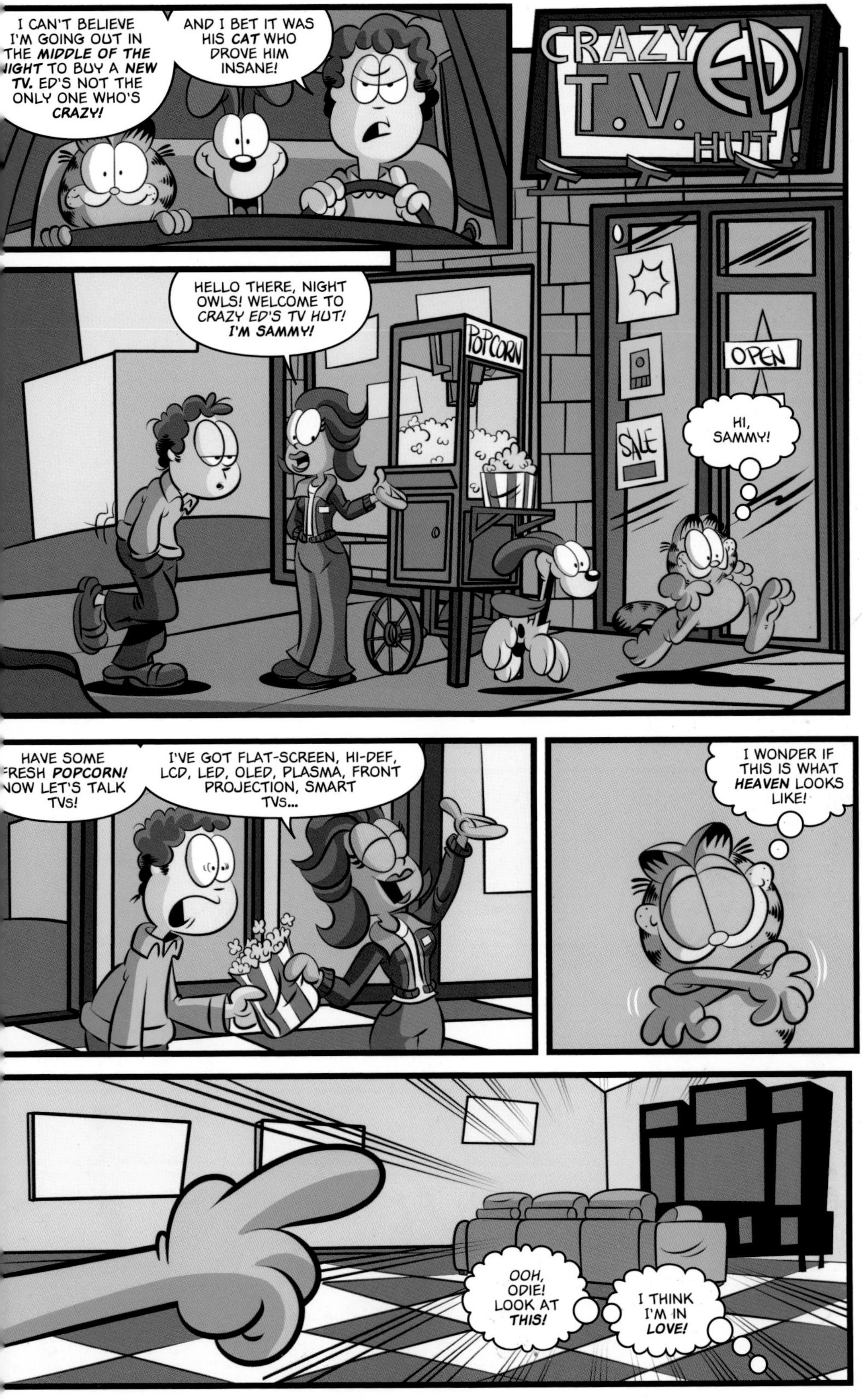
I CAN'T BELIEVE I'M GOING OUT IN THE MIDDLE OF THE NIGHT TO BUY A NEW TV. ED'S NOT THE ONLY ONE WHO'S CRAZY!
AND I BET IT WAS HIS CAT WHO DROVE HIM INSANE!
CRAZY ED T.V. HUT!
HELLO THERE, NIGHT OWLS! WELCOME TO CRAZY ED'S TV HUT! I'M SAMMY!
POPCORN
OPEN
SALE
HI, SAMMY!
HAVE SOME FRESH POPCORN! NOW LET'S TALK TVs!
I'VE GOT FLAT-SCREEN, HI-DEF, LCD, LED, OLED, PLASMA, FRONT PROJECTION, SMART TVs...
I WONDER IF THIS IS WHAT HEAVEN LOOKS LIKE!
OOH, ODIE! LOOK AT THIS!
I THINK I'M IN LOVE!

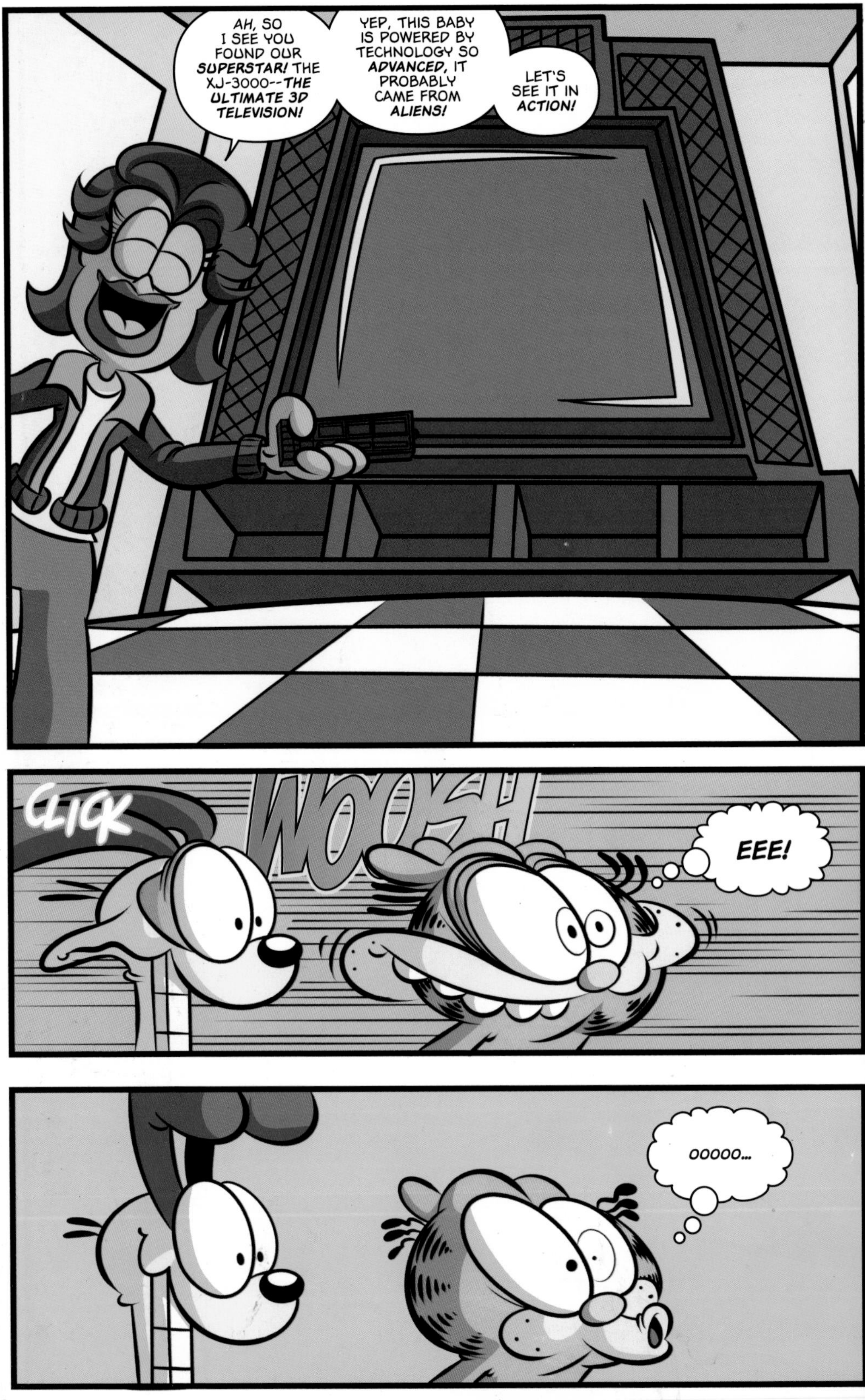
AH, SO I SEE YOU FOUND OUR SUPERSTAR! THE XJ-3000--THE ULTIMATE 3D TELEVISION!
YEP, THIS BABY IS POWERED BY TECHNOLOGY SO ADVANCED, IT PROBABLY CAME FROM ALIENS!
LET'S SEE IT IN ACTION!
CLICK
WOOSH
EEE!
OOOOO...

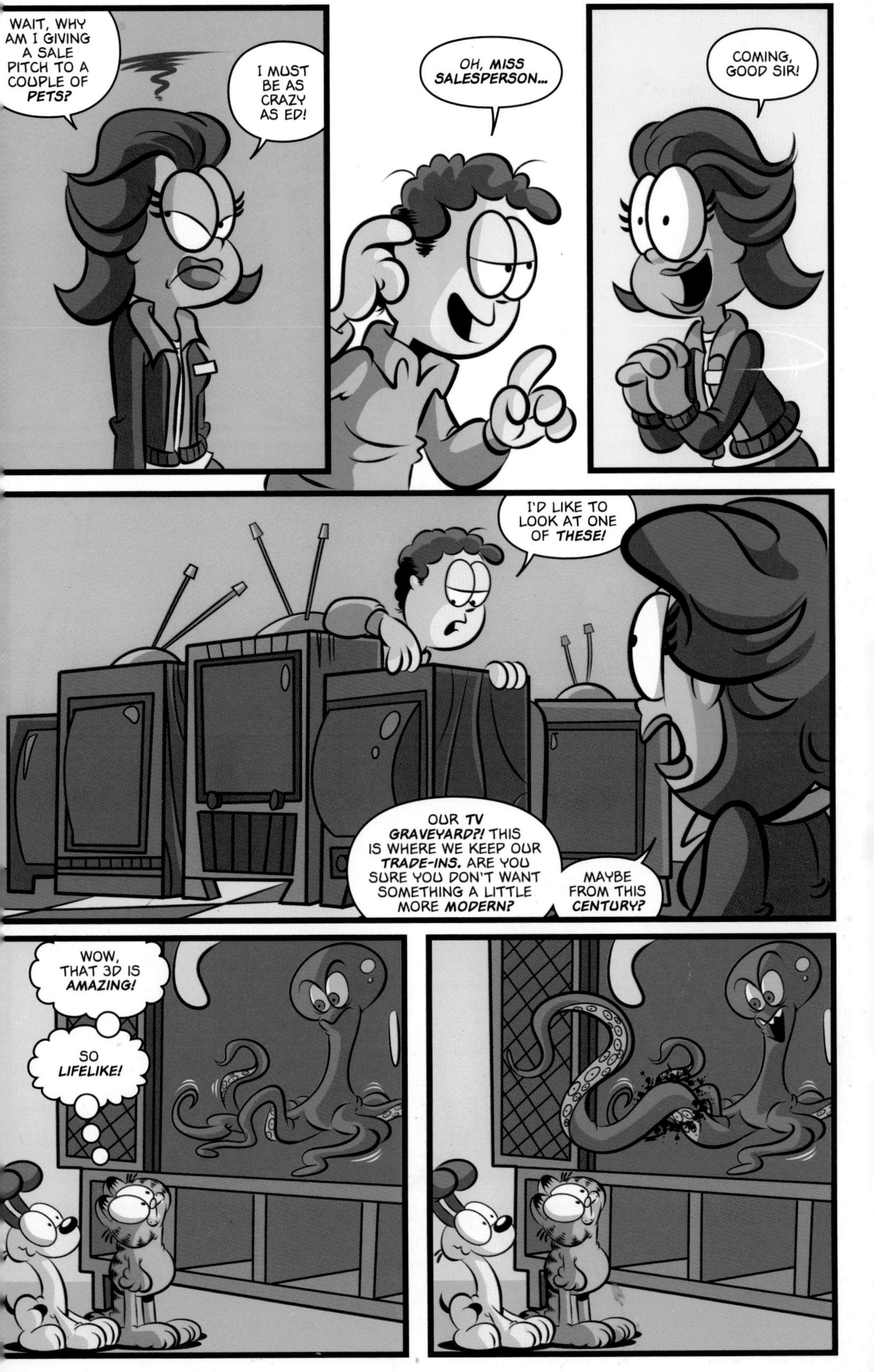
WAIT, WHY AM I GIVING A SALE PITCH TO A COUPLE OF PETS?
I MUST BE AS CRAZY AS ED!
OH, MISS SALESPERSON...
COMING, GOOD SIR!
I'D LIKE TO LOOK AT ONE OF THESE!
OUR TV GRAVEYARD?! THIS IS WHERE WE KEEP OUR TRADE-INS. ARE YOU SURE YOU DON'T WANT SOMETHING A LITTLE MORE MODERN?
MAYBE FROM THIS CENTURY?
WOW, THAT 3D IS AMAZING!
SO LIFELIKE!

HURKK!
TOO LIFELIKE!
URKK!
HEY, WHAT'S GOING ON??!
ZIP!
ZIP!

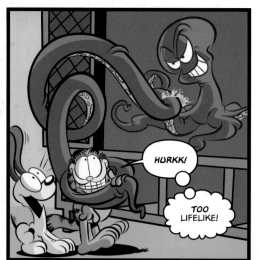

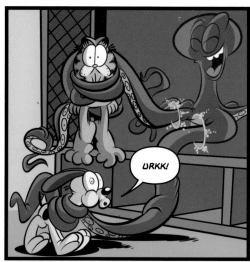

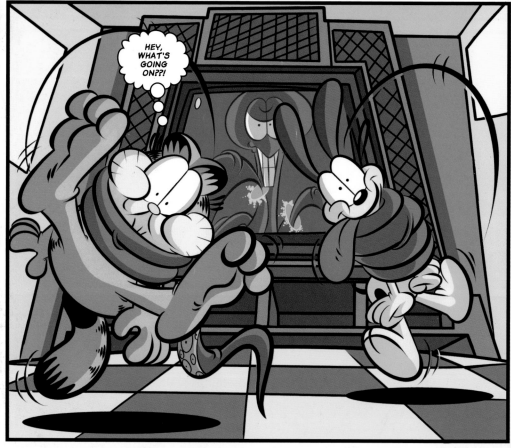

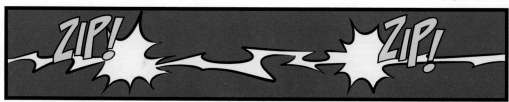

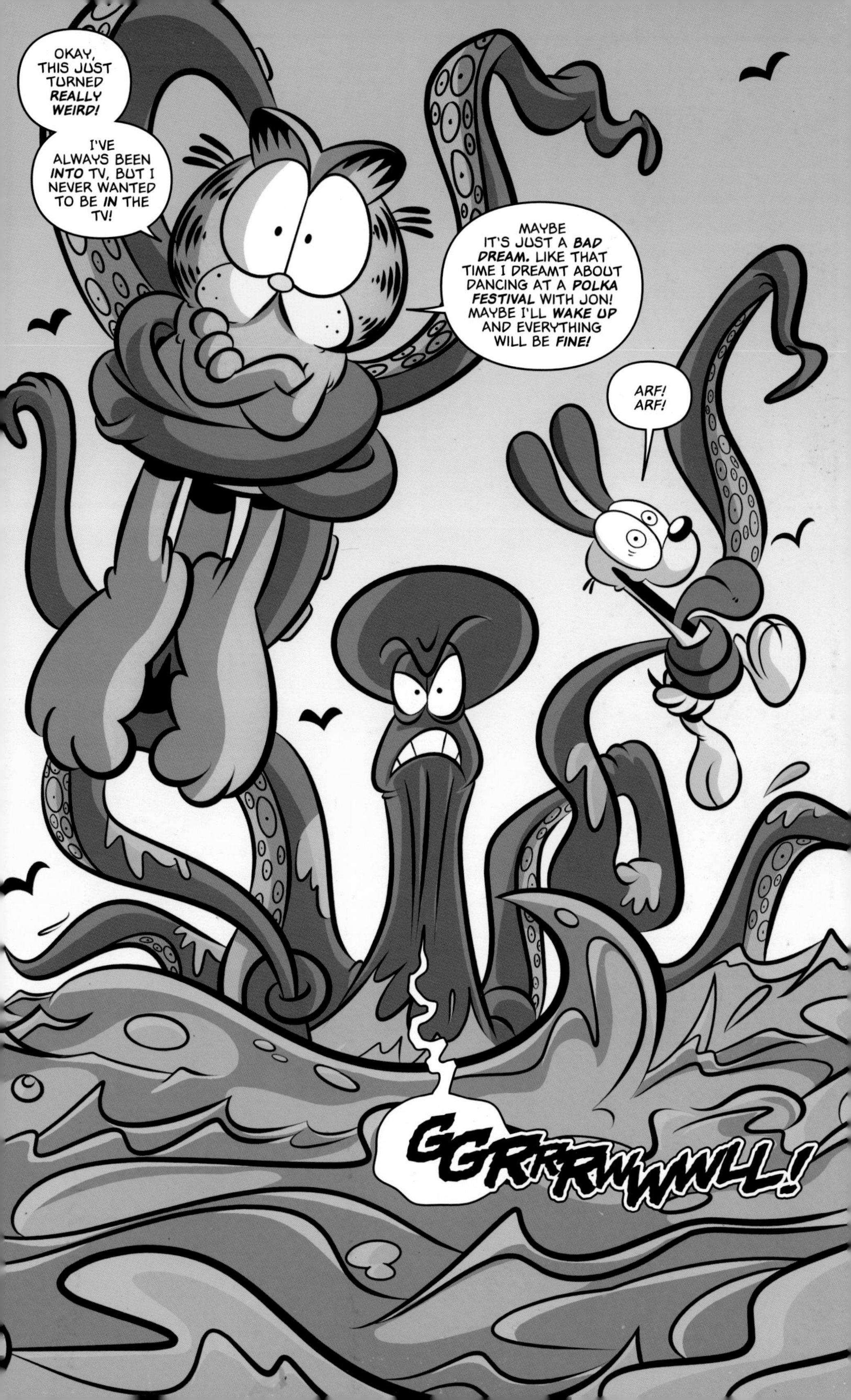
OKAY, THIS JUST TURNED REALLY WEIRD!
I'VE ALWAYS BEEN INTO TV, BUT I NEVER WANTED TO BE IN THE TV!
MAYBE IT'S JUST A BAD DREAM. LIKE THAT TIME I DREAMT ABOUT DANCING AT A POLKA FESTIVAL WITH JON! MAYBE I'LL WAKE UP AND EVERYTHING WILL BE FINE!
ARF! ARF!
GGRRRWWWLL!

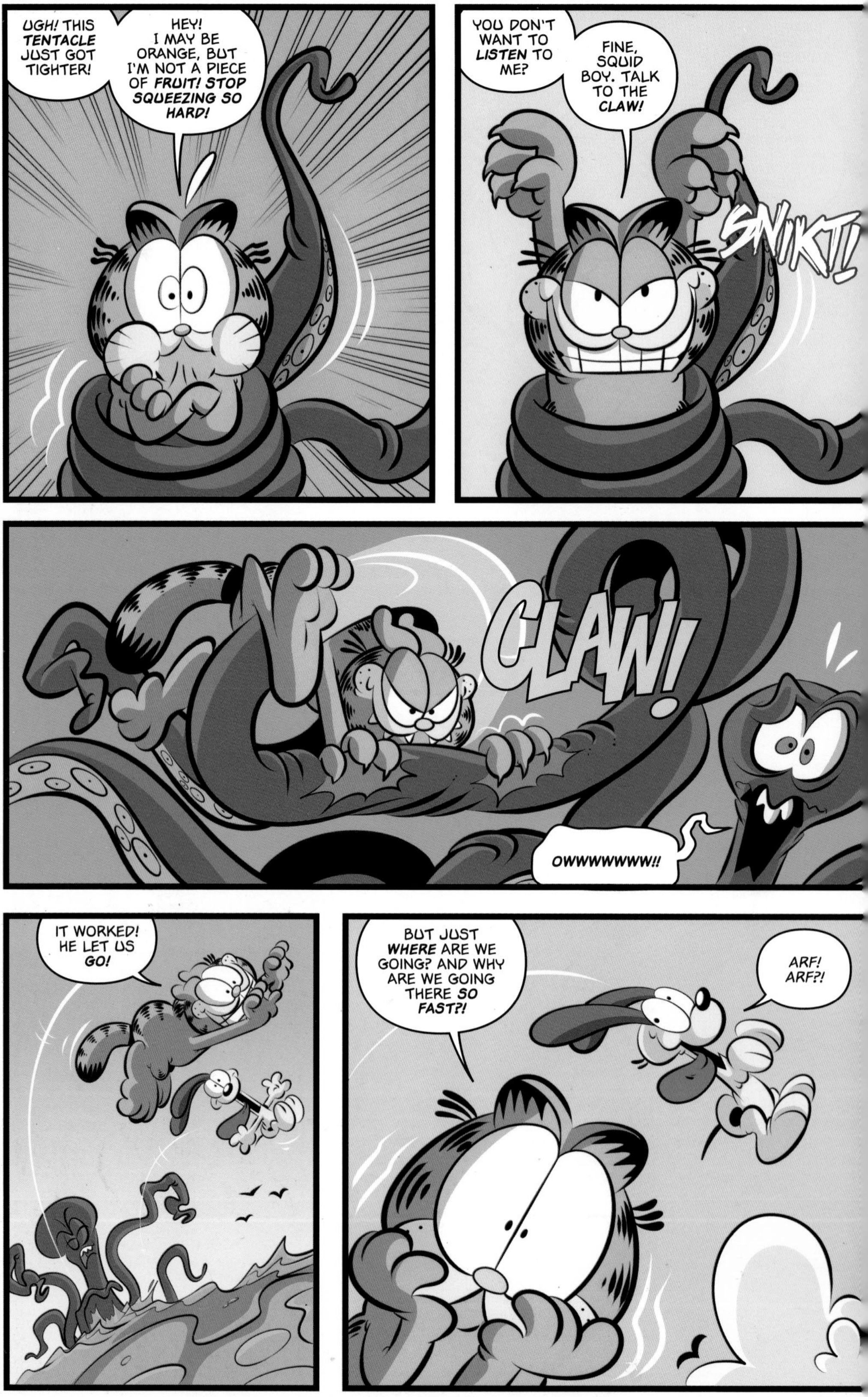
UGH! THIS TENTACLE JUST GOT TIGHTER!
HEY! I MAY BE ORANGE, BUT I'M NOT A PIECE OF FRUIT! STOP SQUEEZING SO HARD!
YOU DON'T WANT TO LISTEN TO ME?
FINE, SQUID BOY. TALK TO THE CLAW!
SNIKT!
CLAW!
OWWWWWWW!!
IT WORKED! HE LET US GO!
BUT JUST WHERE ARE WE GOING? AND WHY ARE WE GOING THERE SO FAST?!
ARF! ARF?!

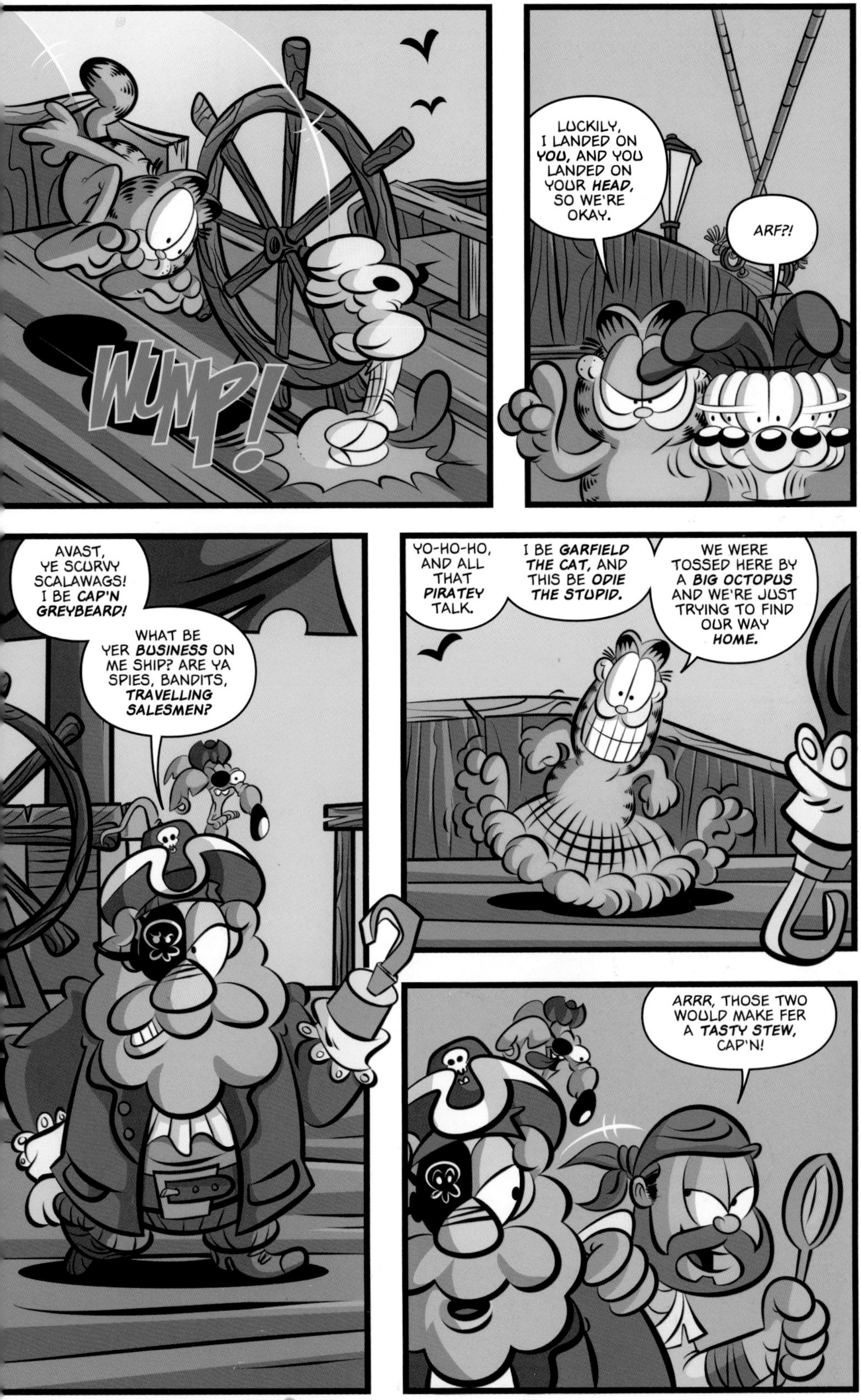
WUMP!
LUCKILY, I LANDED ON YOU, AND YOU LANDED ON YOUR HEAD, SO WE'RE OKAY.
ARF?!
AVAST, YE SCURVY SCALAWAGS! I BE CAP'N GREYBEARD!
WHAT BE YER BUSINESS ON ME SHIP? ARE YA SPIES, BANDITS, TRAVELLING SALESMEN?
YO-HO-HO, AND ALL THAT PIRATEY TALK.
I BE GARFIELD THE CAT, AND THIS BE ODIE THE STUPID.
WE WERE TOSSED HERE BY A BIG OCTOPUS AND WE'RE JUST TRYING TO FIND OUR WAY HOME.
ARRR, THOSE TWO WOULD MAKE FER A TASTY STEW, CAP'N!

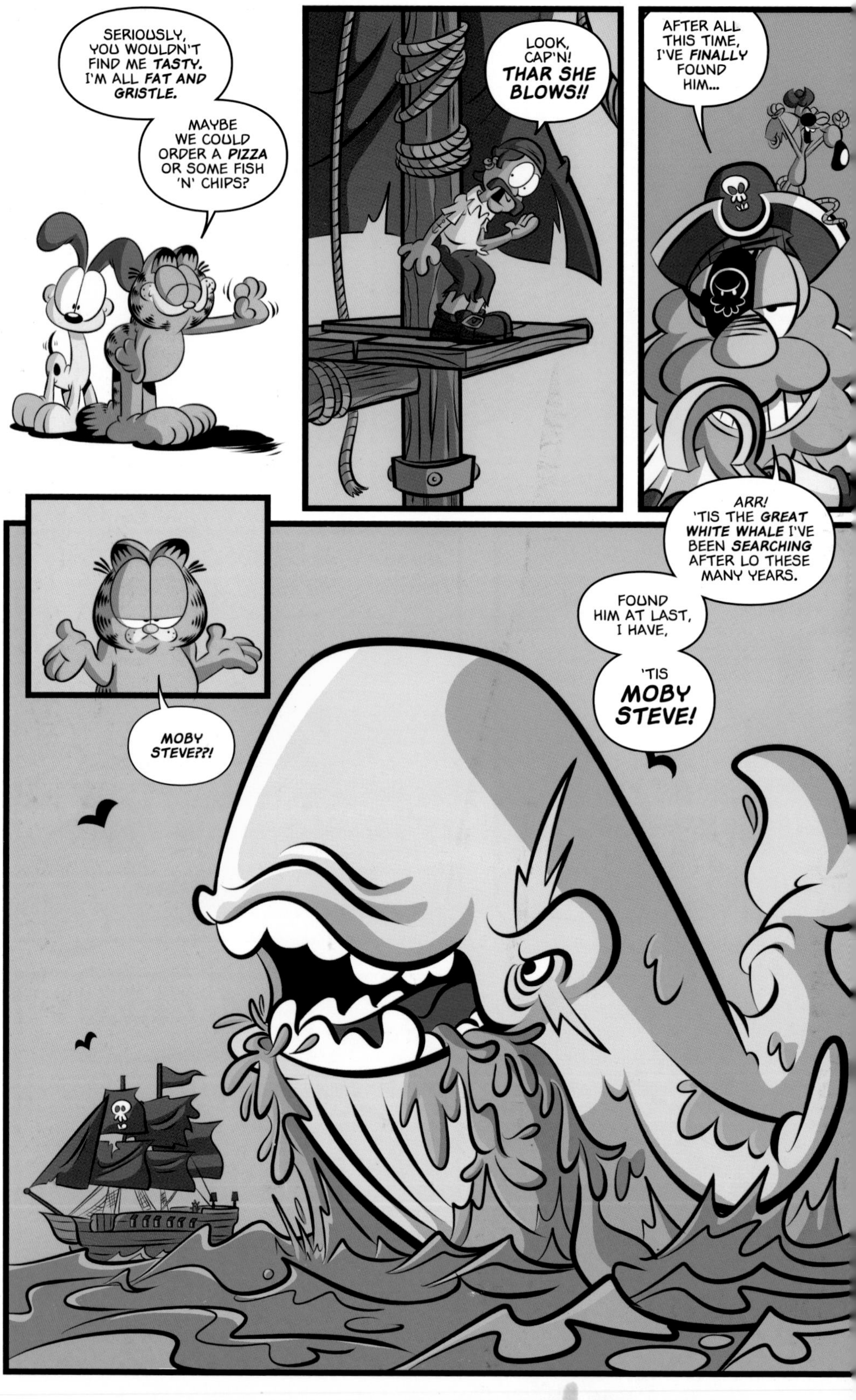

SERIOUSLY, YOU WOULDN'T FIND ME TASTY. I'M ALL FAT AND GRISTLE.
MAYBE WE COULD ORDER A PIZZA OR SOME FISH 'N' CHIPS?
LOOK, CAP'N! THAR SHE BLOWS!!
AFTER ALL THIS TIME, I'VE FINALLY FOUND HIM...
ARR! 'TIS THE GREAT WHITE WHALE I'VE BEEN SEARCHING AFTER LO THESE MANY YEARS.
FOUND HIM AT LAST, I HAVE,
'TIS MOBY STEVE!
MOBY STEVE??!

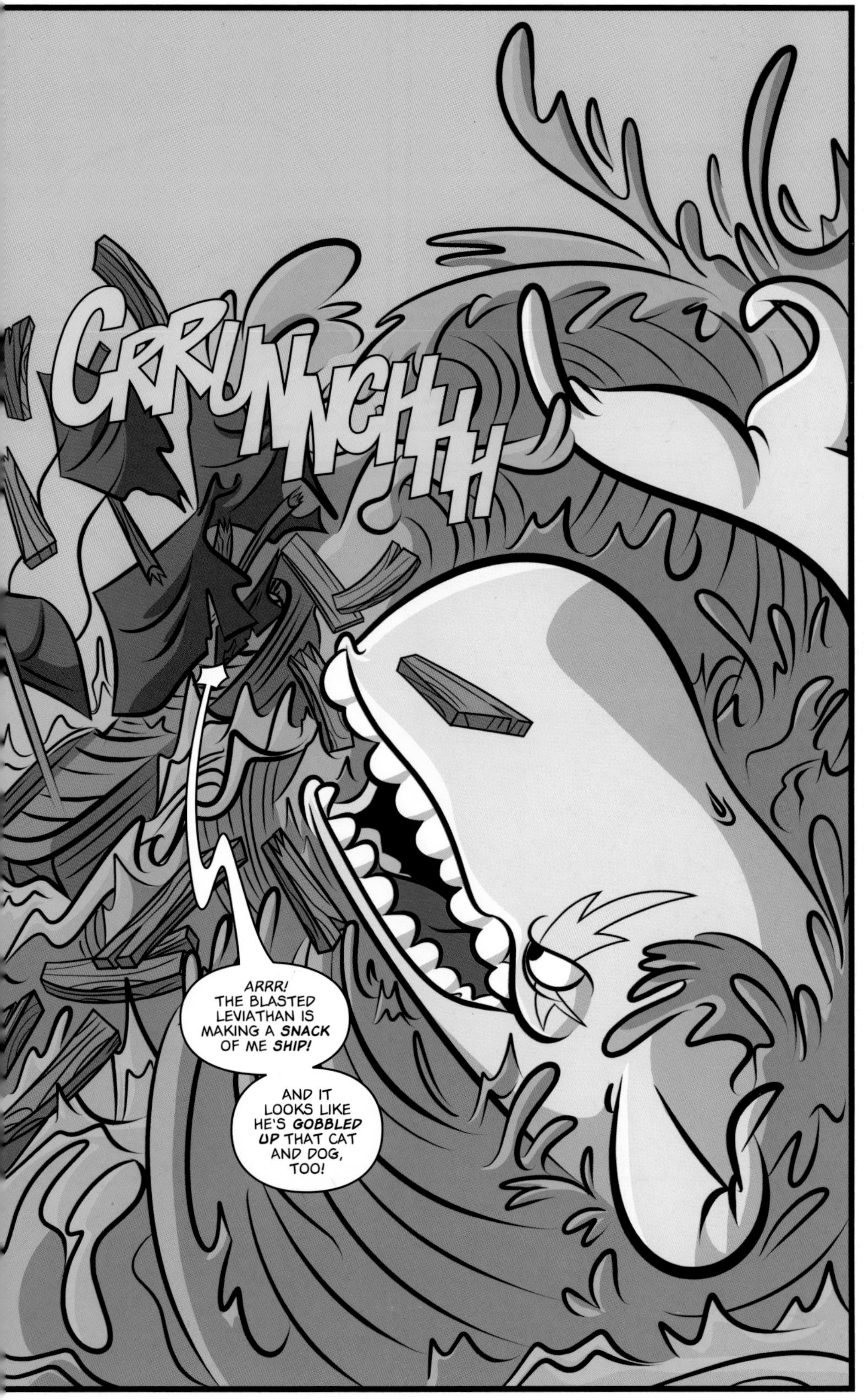
CRRUNNCHHH
ARRR! THE BLASTED LEVIATHAN IS MAKING A SNACK OF ME SHIP!
AND IT LOOKS LIKE HE'S GOBBLED UP THAT CAT AND DOG, TOO!

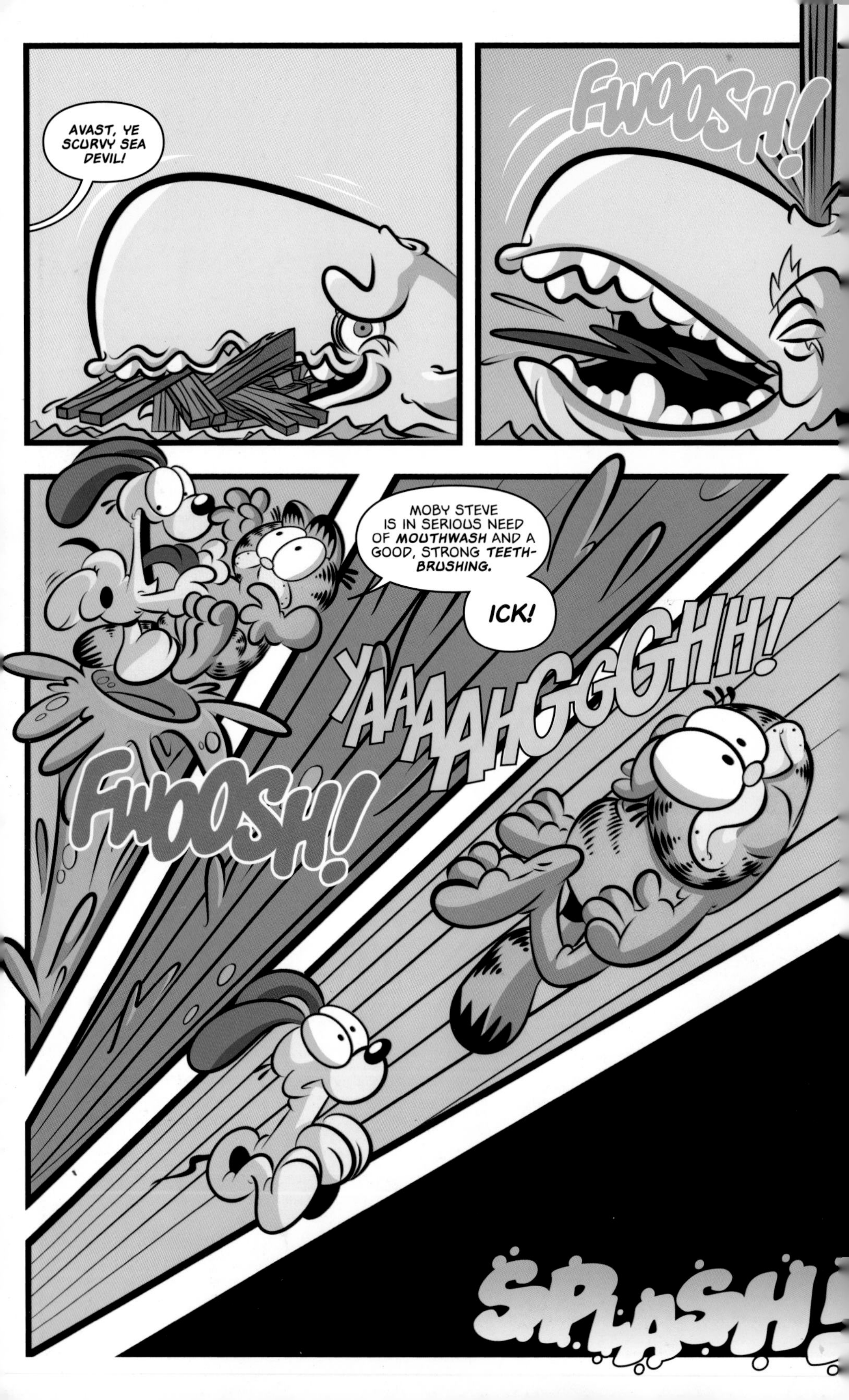
AVAST, YE SCURVY SEA DEVIL!
FWOOSH!
MOBY STEVE IS IN SERIOUS NEED OF MOUTHWASH AND A GOOD, STRONG TEETH-BRUSHING.
ICK!
YAAAAHGGGHH!
FWOOSH!
SPLASH!

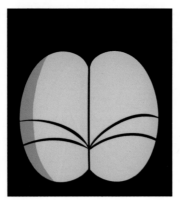

BY ECHLOR'S ELBOW, YOU'RE *ALIVE!*

WHAT? WHO? WHERE? WHY? HUH??!

EASY, NOW, *LITTLE ONE.*

WE'D BEST BE *GONE* BEFORE WE *AWAKEN* THE *ICE GIANTS!*

KAY, *HOLD ON!* ONE MINUTE, ODIE AND I ARE GETTING SHOT OUT OF A *WHALE'S BLOWHOLE,* AND THE NEXT MINUTE, I WAKE UP IN THE SNOW DRESSED LIKE SOME *COSPLAY* REJECT FROM A FANTASY CONVENTION!!

WHAT'S UP WITH THAT?

AND SPEAKING OF *ODIE,* WHERE IS THAT MUTT?

I KNOW NOT OF THIS *ODIE* YOU SPEAK. NOR OF THIS *COSPLAY,* BUT I AM MOST FAMILIAR WITH *WHALES* AND THEIR *BLOWHOLES.*

I AM *MILO OF HIBERNIA.* I AM ON A *QUEST FOR TREASURE* IN THESE MOUNTAINS. IT IS SAID THAT THE FABLED *GOLDEN GIRDLE* RESIDES SOMEWHERE IN AN *ICE CAVE...*

A *QUEST FOR TREASURE?* YOU MIGHT ALSO WANT TO GO ON A QUEST FOR A *BARBER,* SHAGGY.

I'M *STARVING!* DO WE HAVE ANYTHING LIKE *YAK JERKY,* OR MAYBE SOME *CHERRY SYRUP?* I COULD MAKE A GIANT *SNOW CONE!*

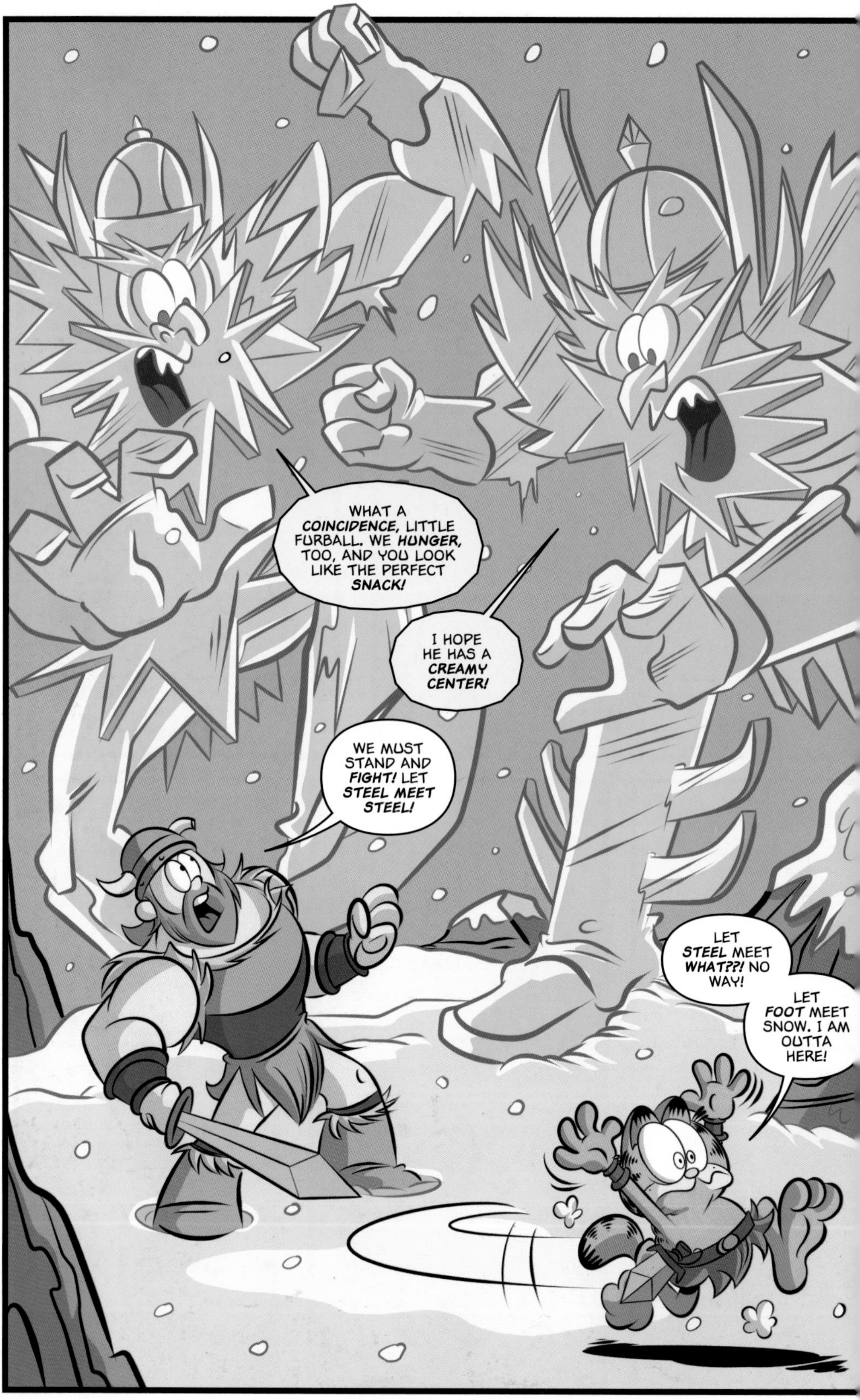
WHAT A COINCIDENCE, LITTLE FURBALL. WE HUNGER, TOO, AND YOU LOOK LIKE THE PERFECT SNACK!
I HOPE HE HAS A CREAMY CENTER!
WE MUST STAND AND FIGHT! LET STEEL MEET STEEL!
LET STEEL MEET WHAT??! NO WAY!
LET FOOT MEET SNOW. I AM OUTTA HERE!

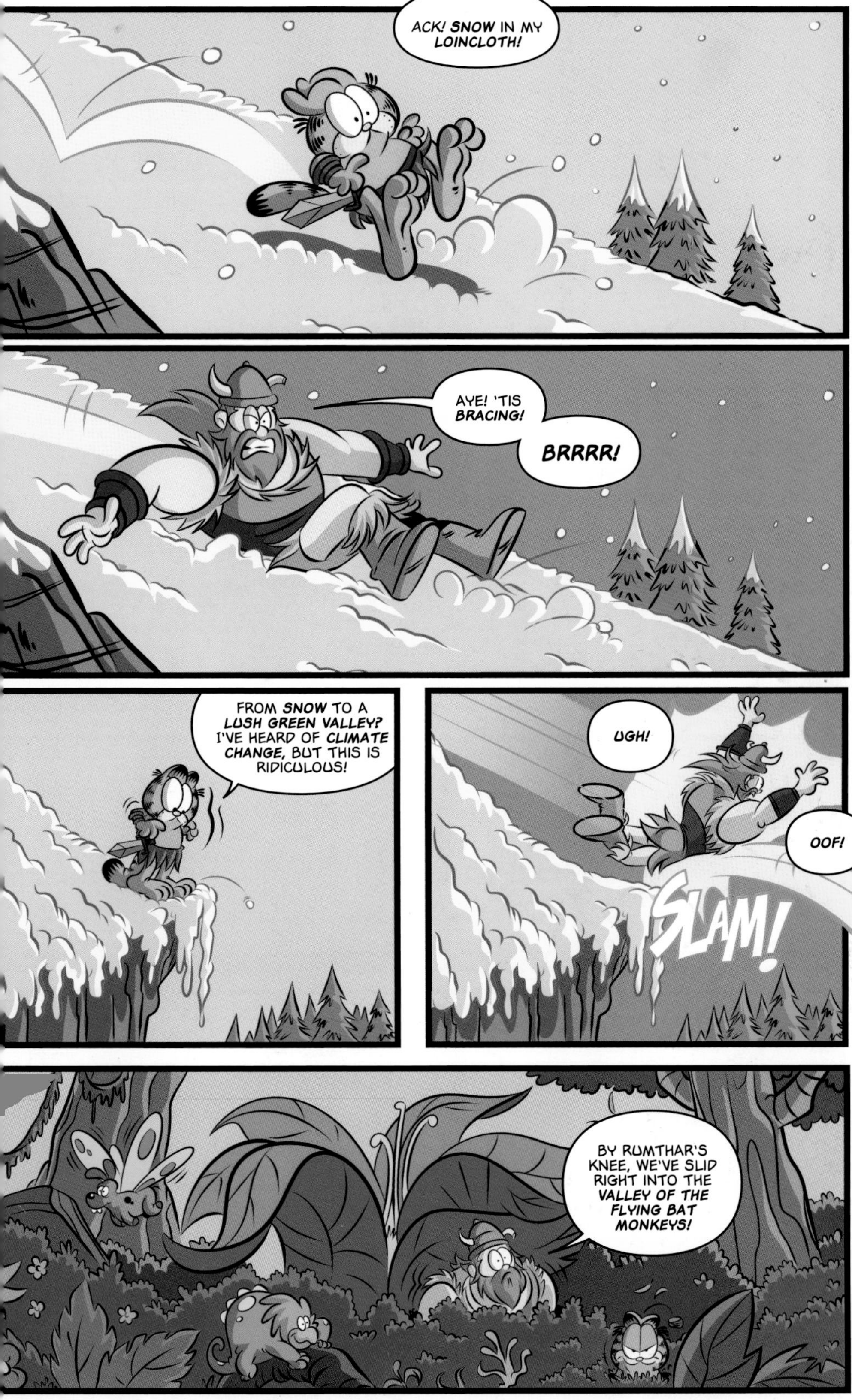
ACK! SNOW IN MY LOINCLOTH!
AYE! 'TIS BRACING!
BRRRR!
FROM SNOW TO A LUSH GREEN VALLEY? I'VE HEARD OF CLIMATE CHANGE, BUT THIS IS RIDICULOUS!
UGH!
OOF!
SLAM!
BY RUMTHAR'S KNEE, WE'VE SLID RIGHT INTO THE VALLEY OF THE FLYING BAT MONKEYS!

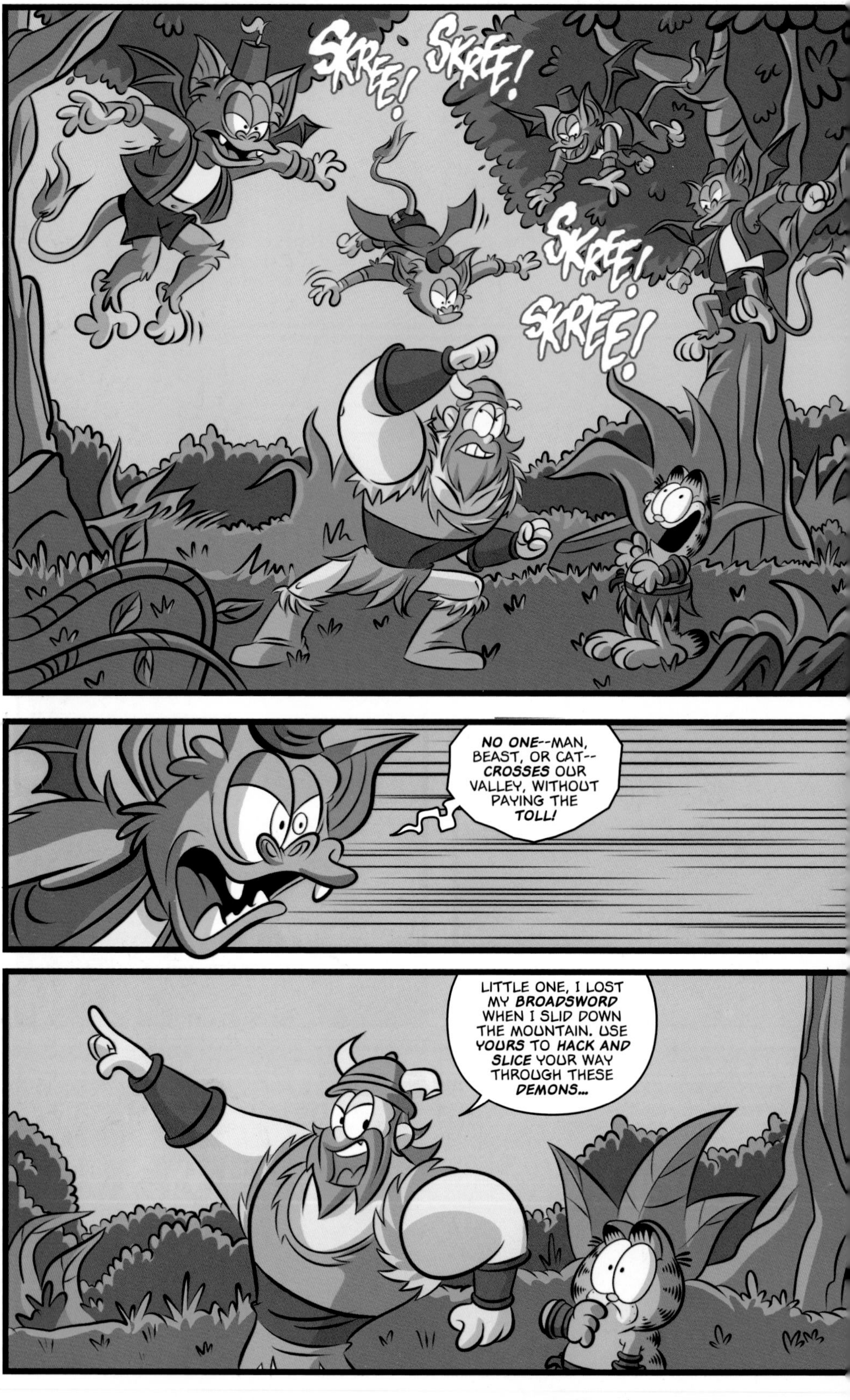
SKREE! SKREE!
SKREE!
SKREE!
NO ONE--MAN, BEAST, OR CAT--CROSSES OUR VALLEY, WITHOUT PAYING THE TOLL!
LITTLE ONE, I LOST MY BROADSWORD WHEN I SLID DOWN THE MOUNTAIN. USE YOURS TO HACK AND SLICE YOUR WAY THROUGH THESE DEMONS...

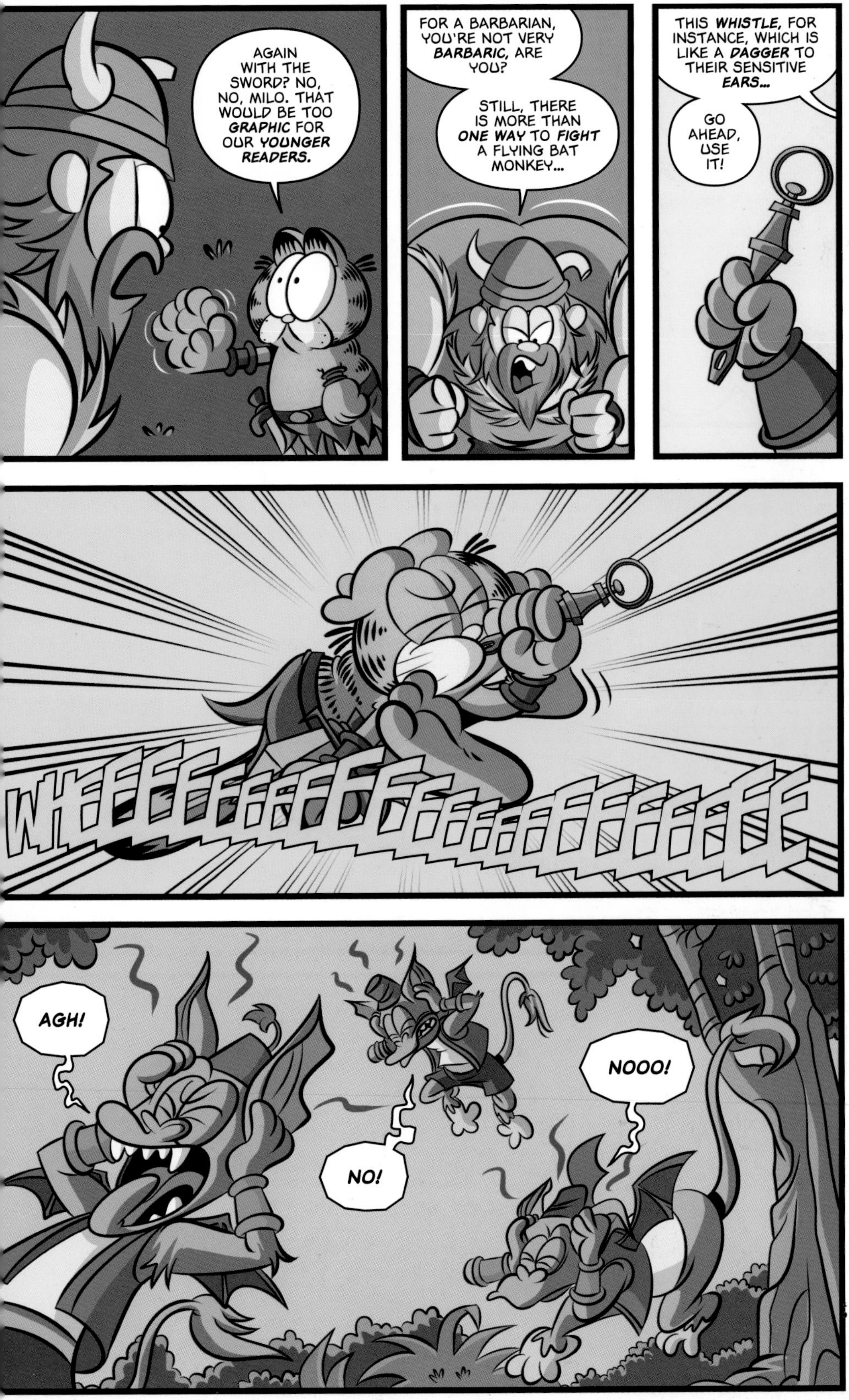
AGAIN WITH THE SWORD? NO, NO, MILO. THAT WOULD BE TOO GRAPHIC FOR OUR YOUNGER READERS.
FOR A BARBARIAN, YOU'RE NOT VERY BARBARIC, ARE YOU?
STILL, THERE IS MORE THAN ONE WAY TO FIGHT A FLYING BAT MONKEY...
THIS WHISTLE, FOR INSTANCE, WHICH IS LIKE A DAGGER TO THEIR SENSITIVE EARS...
GO AHEAD, USE IT!
WHEEEEEEEEEEEEEEEEEEEEEEEEEEEE
AGH!
NO!
NOOO!

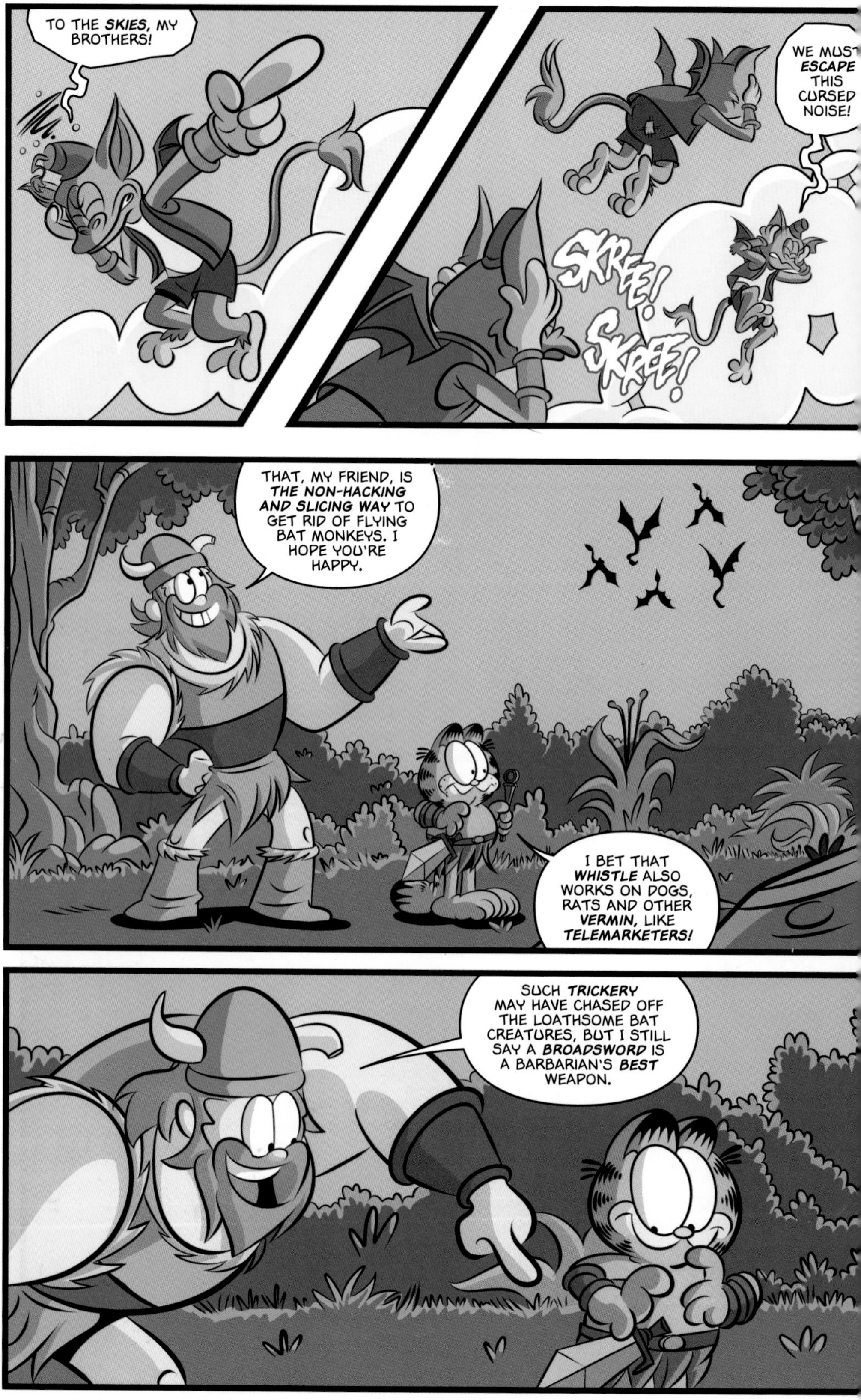
TO THE SKIES, MY BROTHERS!
WE MUST ESCAPE THIS CURSED NOISE!
SKREE! SKREE!
THAT, MY FRIEND, IS THE NON-HACKING AND SLICING WAY TO GET RID OF FLYING BAT MONKEYS. I HOPE YOU'RE HAPPY.
I BET THAT WHISTLE ALSO WORKS ON DOGS, RATS AND OTHER VERMIN, LIKE TELEMARKETERS!
SUCH TRICKERY MAY HAVE CHASED OFF THE LOATHSOME BAT CREATURES, BUT I STILL SAY A BROADSWORD IS A BARBARIAN'S BEST WEAPON.

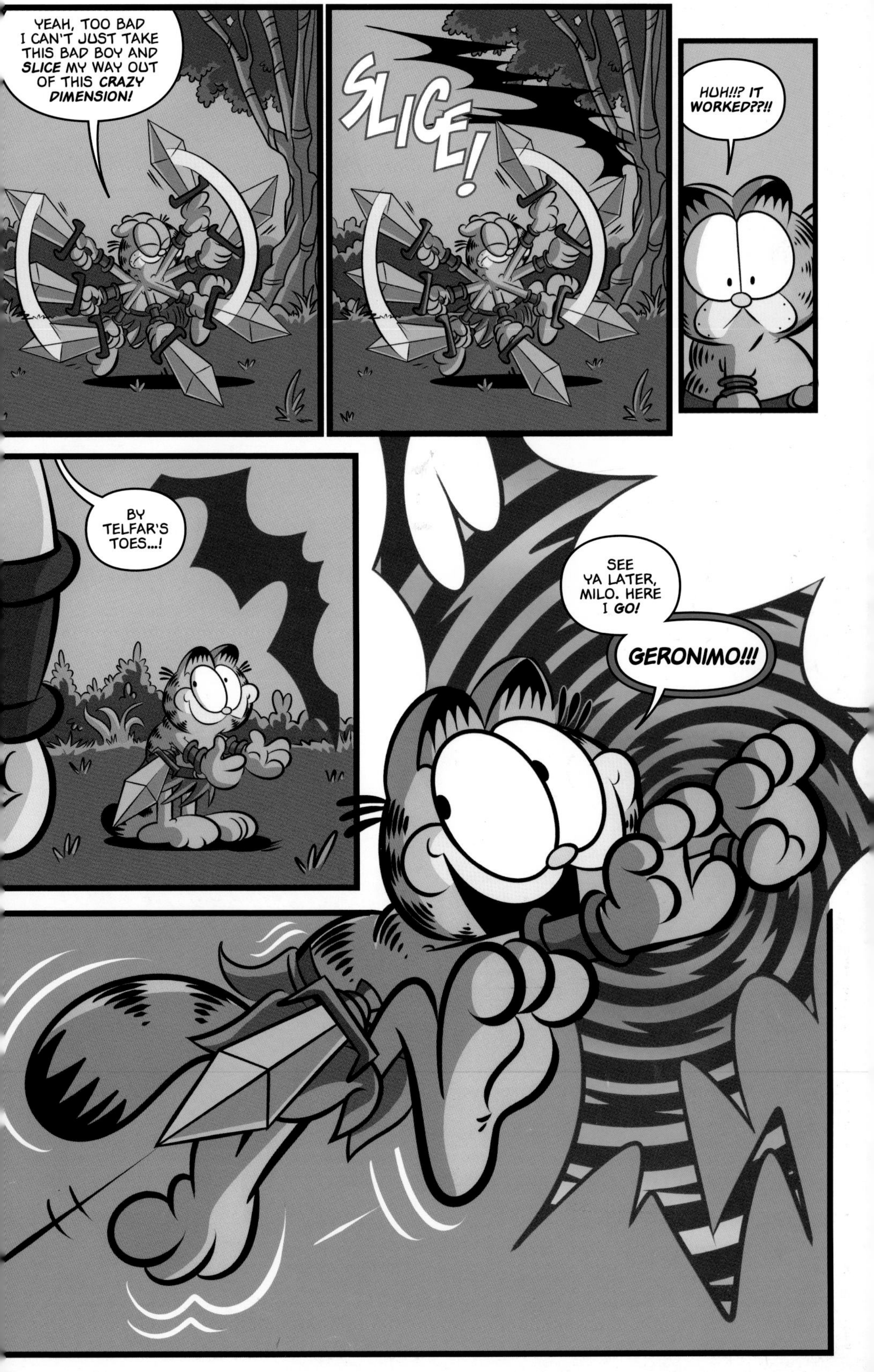
YEAH, TOO BAD I CAN'T JUST TAKE THIS BAD BOY AND SLICE MY WAY OUT OF THIS CRAZY DIMENSION!
SLICE!
HUH!!? IT WORKED??!!
BY TELFAR'S TOES...!
SEE YA LATER, MILO. HERE I GO!
GERONIMO!!!

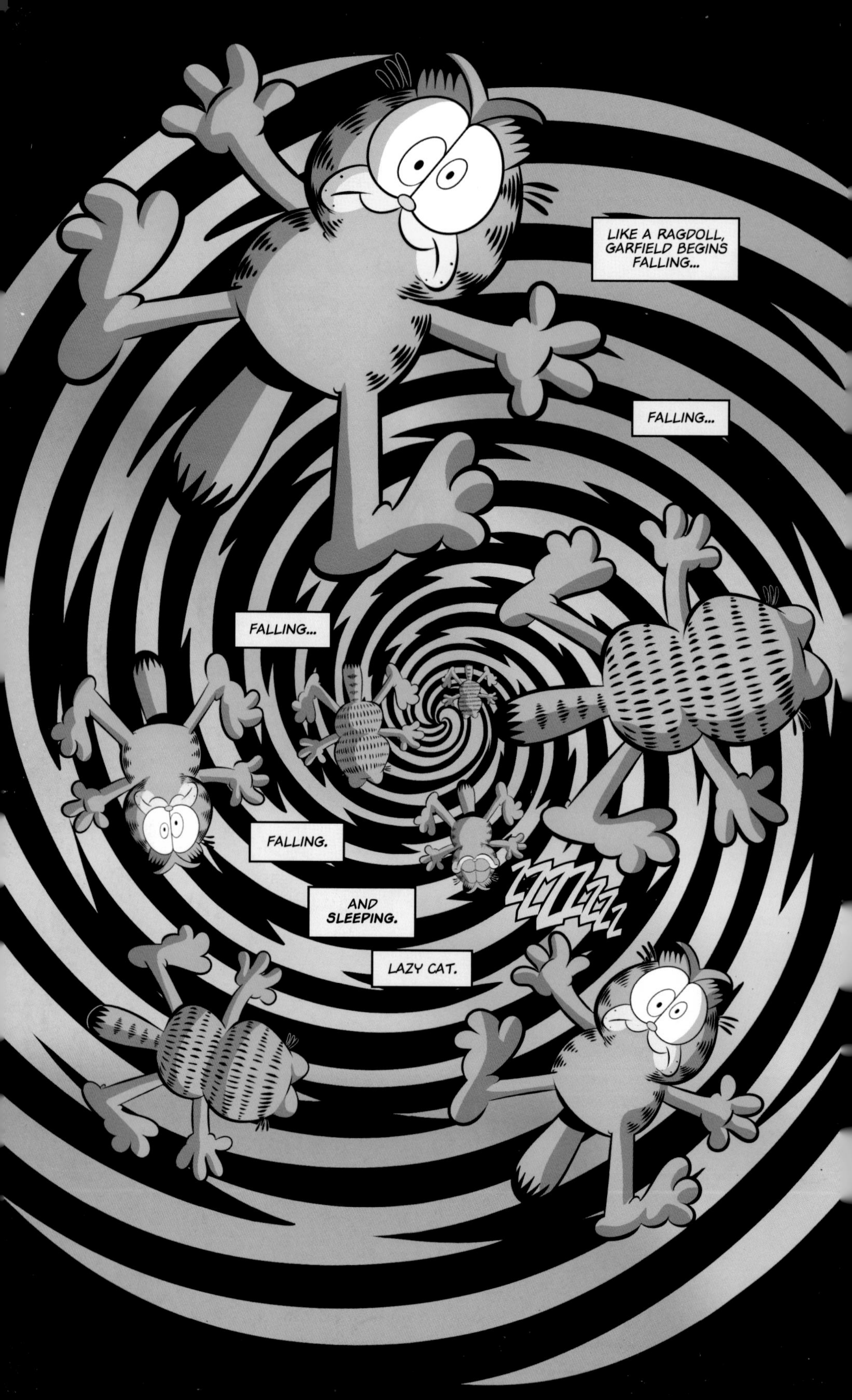
LIKE A RAGDOLL, GARFIELD BEGINS FALLING...
FALLING...
FALLING...
FALLING.
AND SLEEPING.
ZZZZZZZ
LAZY CAT.

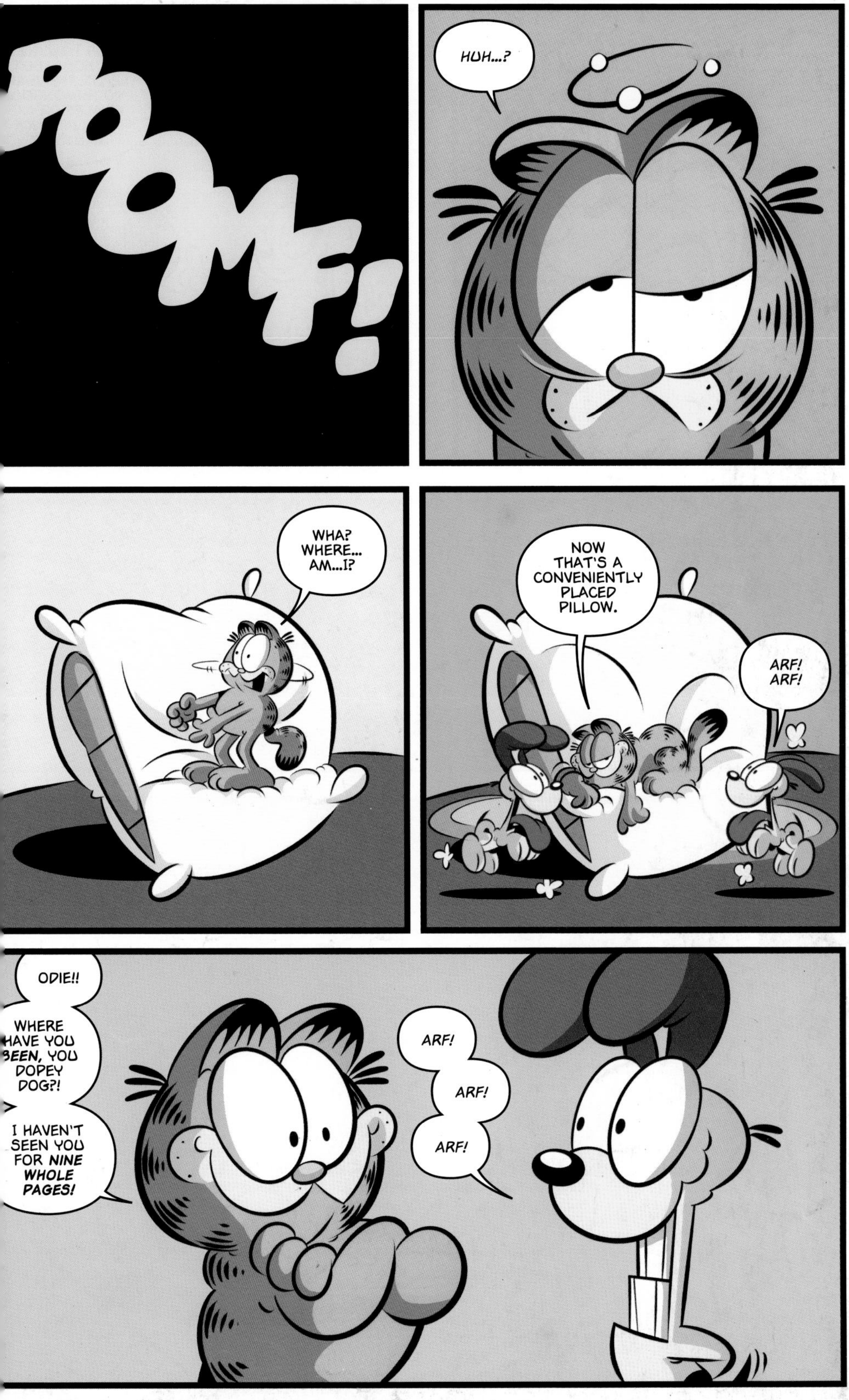
POOMF!
HUH...?
WHA? WHERE... AM...I?
NOW THAT'S A CONVENIENTLY PLACED PILLOW.
ARF! ARF!
ODIE!!
WHERE HAVE YOU BEEN, YOU DOPEY DOG?!
I HAVEN'T SEEN YOU FOR NINE WHOLE PAGES!
ARF!
ARF!
ARF!

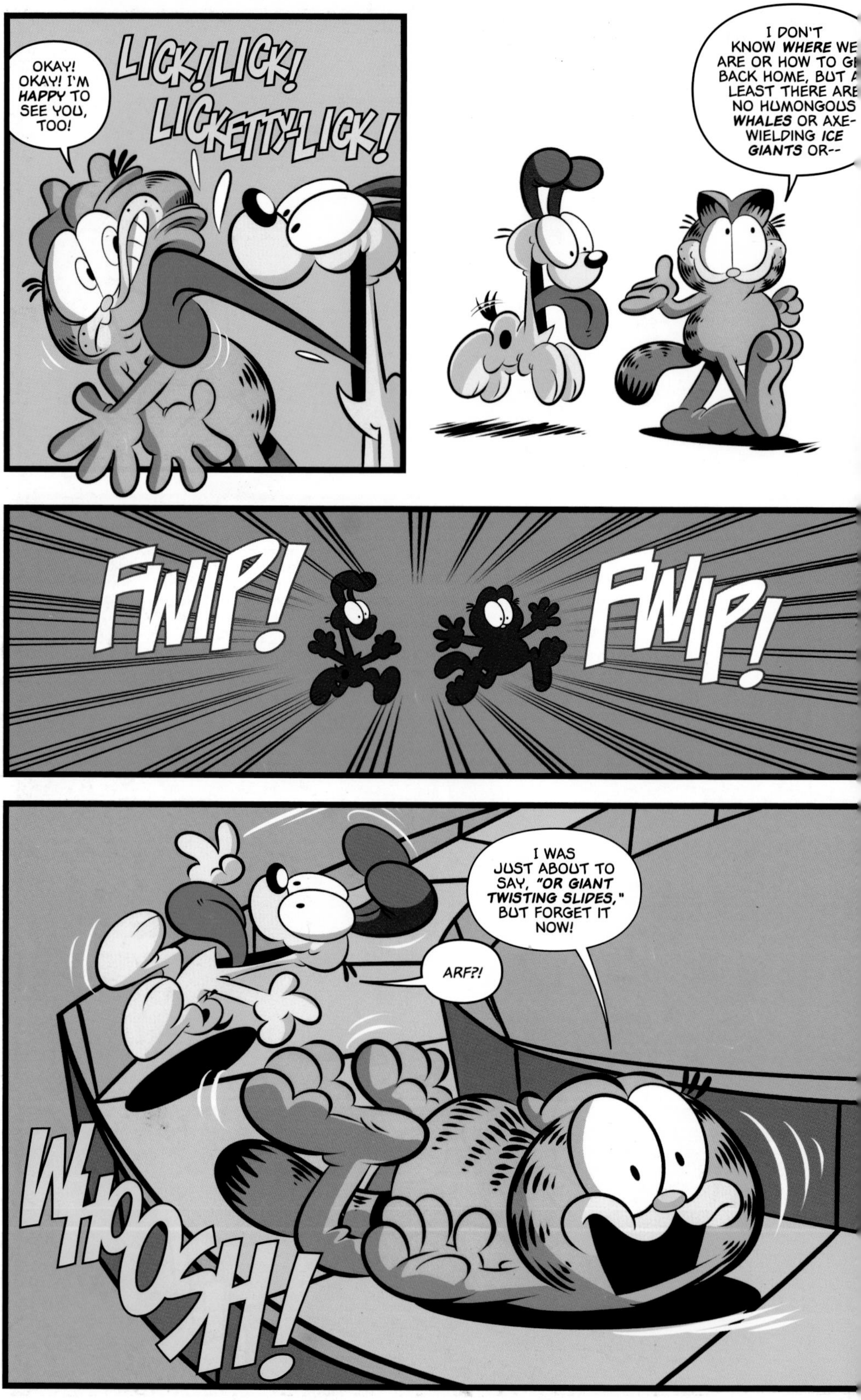
OKAY! OKAY! I'M HAPPY TO SEE YOU, TOO!
LICK! LICK! LICKETTY-LICK!
I DON'T KNOW WHERE WE ARE OR HOW TO GE BACK HOME, BUT A LEAST THERE ARE NO HUMONGOUS WHALES OR AXE-WIELDING ICE GIANTS OR--
FWIP!
FWIP!
I WAS JUST ABOUT TO SAY, "OR GIANT TWISTING SLIDES," BUT FORGET IT NOW!
ARF?!
WHOOSH!

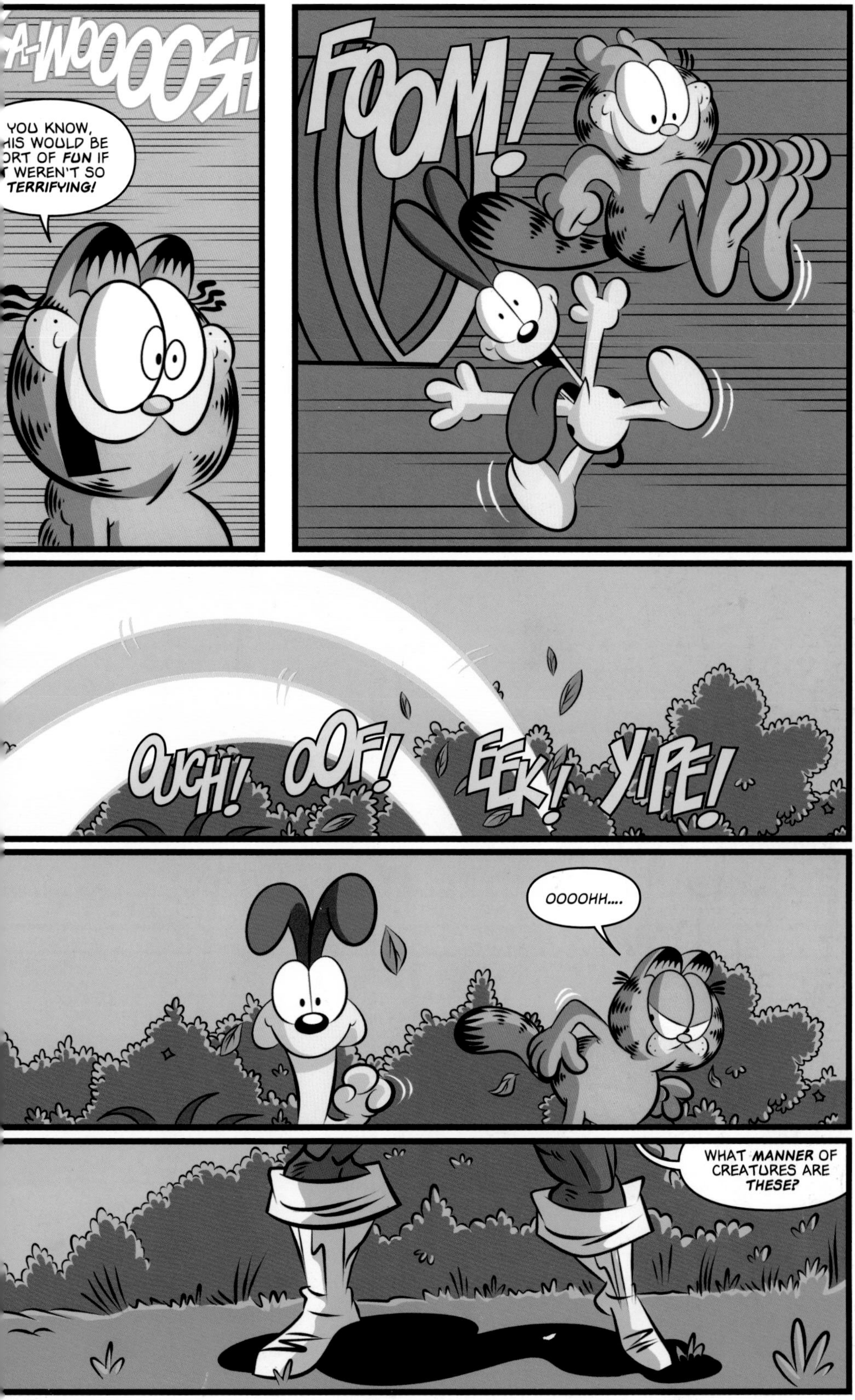

A-WOOOOSH
YOU KNOW, HIS WOULD BE ORT OF FUN IF WEREN'T SO TERRIFYING!
FOOM!
OUCH! OOF! EEK! YIPE!
OOOOHH....
WHAT MANNER OF CREATURES ARE THESE?

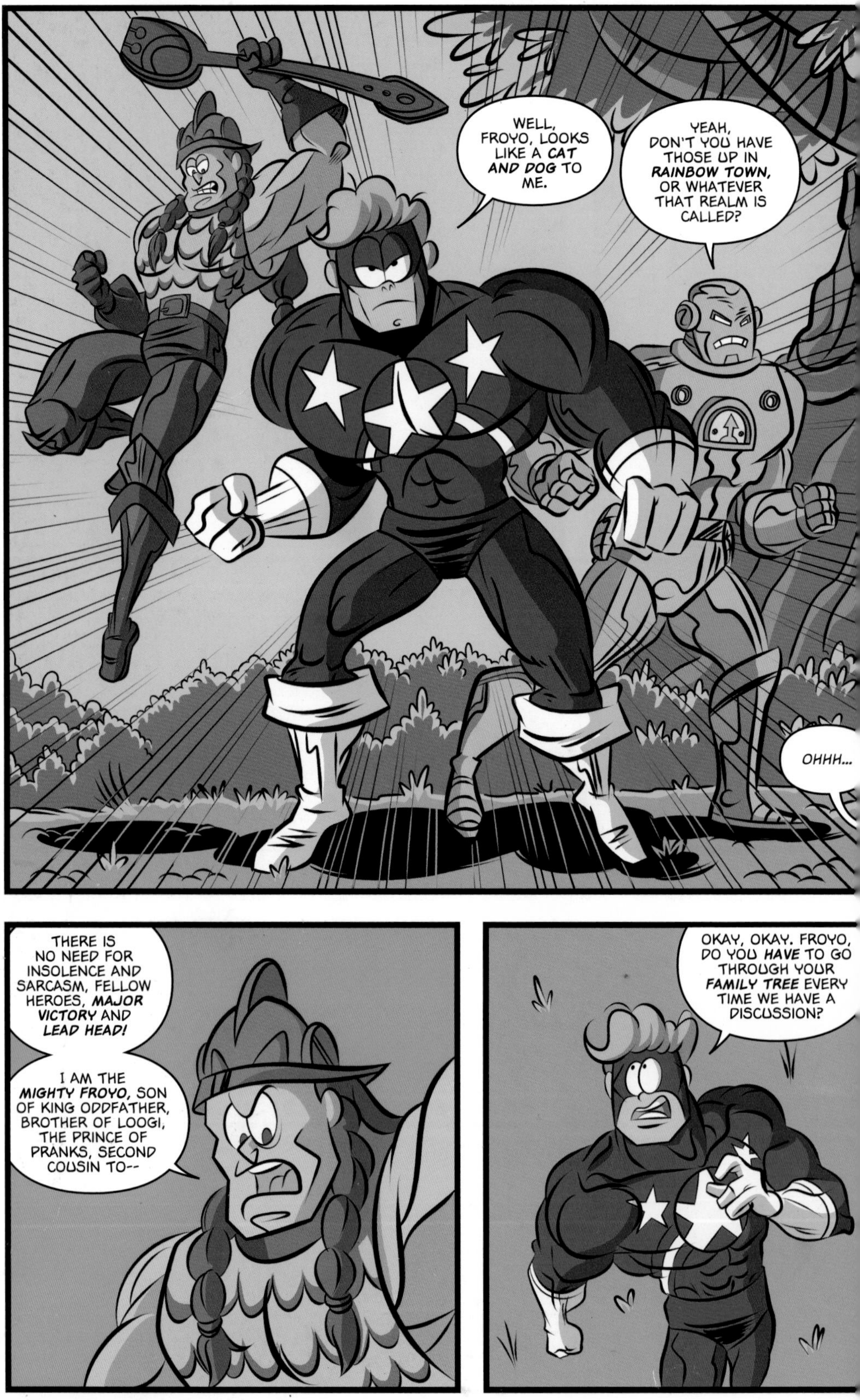

WELL, FROYO, LOOKS LIKE A CAT AND DOG TO ME.
YEAH, DON'T YOU HAVE THOSE UP IN RAINBOW TOWN, OR WHATEVER THAT REALM IS CALLED?
OHHH...
THERE IS NO NEED FOR INSOLENCE AND SARCASM, FELLOW HEROES, MAJOR VICTORY AND LEAD HEAD!
I AM THE MIGHTY FROYO, SON OF KING ODDFATHER, BROTHER OF LOOGI, THE PRINCE OF PRANKS, SECOND COUSIN TO--
OKAY, OKAY. FROYO, DO YOU HAVE TO GO THROUGH YOUR FAMILY TREE EVERY TIME WE HAVE A DISCUSSION?

UH, GUYS...YOU *MIGHT* WANT TO CHECK THIS OUT...

WHOA.

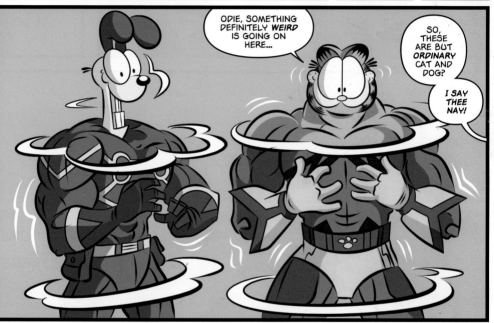

ODIE, SOMETHING DEFINITELY *WEIRD* IS GOING ON HERE...

SO, THESE ARE BUT *ORDINARY* CAT AND DOG?

I SAY THEE NAY!

AGAIN, I ASK...*WHAT MANNER OF CREATURES ARE YOU?*

SO ARE YOU A *MUTANT?*

WERE YOU *BITTEN* BY A *RADIOACTIVE CAT?*

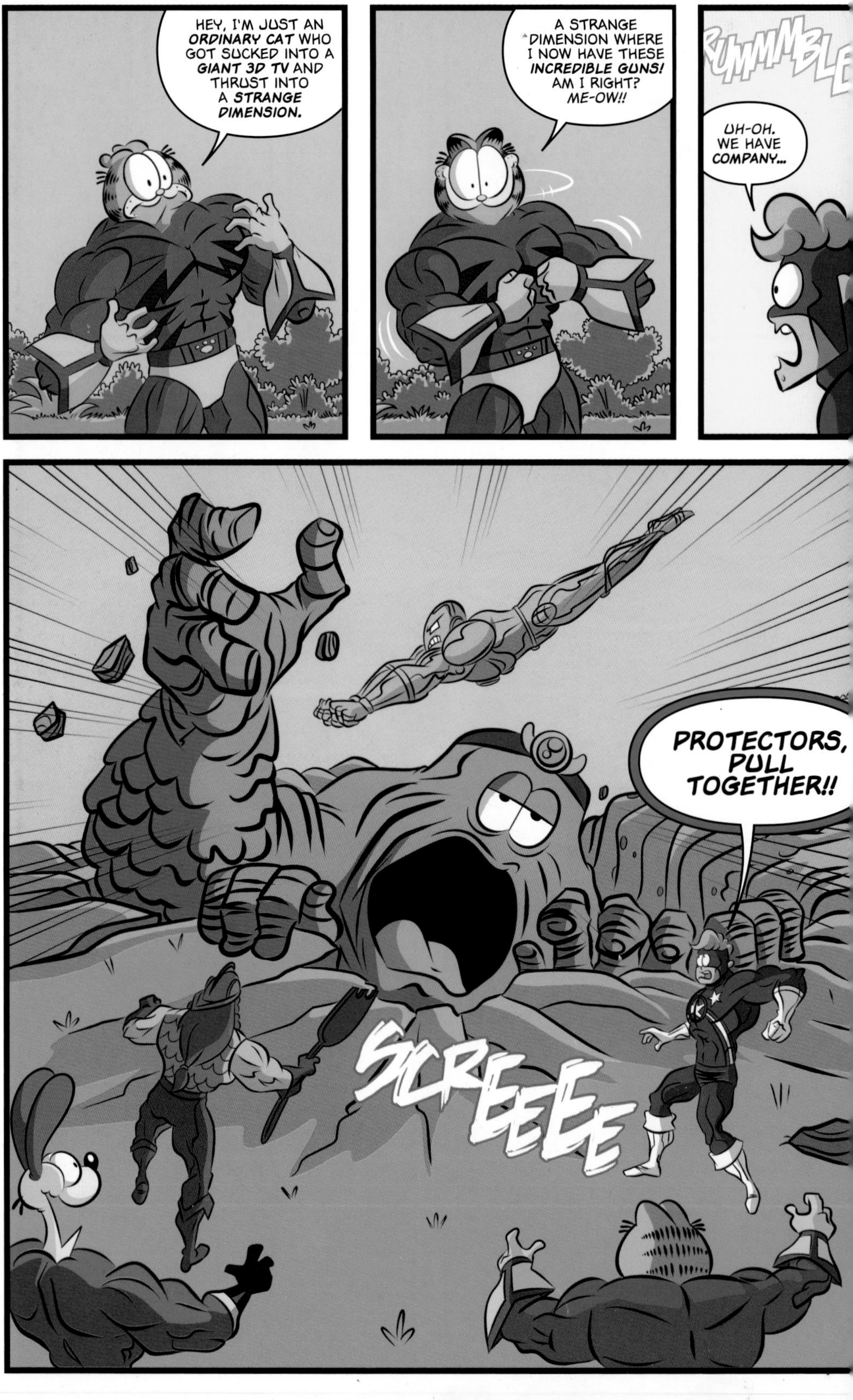
HEY, I'M JUST AN ORDINARY CAT WHO GOT SUCKED INTO A GIANT 3D TV AND THRUST INTO A STRANGE DIMENSION.
A STRANGE DIMENSION WHERE I NOW HAVE THESE INCREDIBLE GUNS! AM I RIGHT? ME-OW!!
RUMMMBLE
UH-OH. WE HAVE COMPANY...
PROTECTORS, PULL TOGETHER!!
SCREEEEE

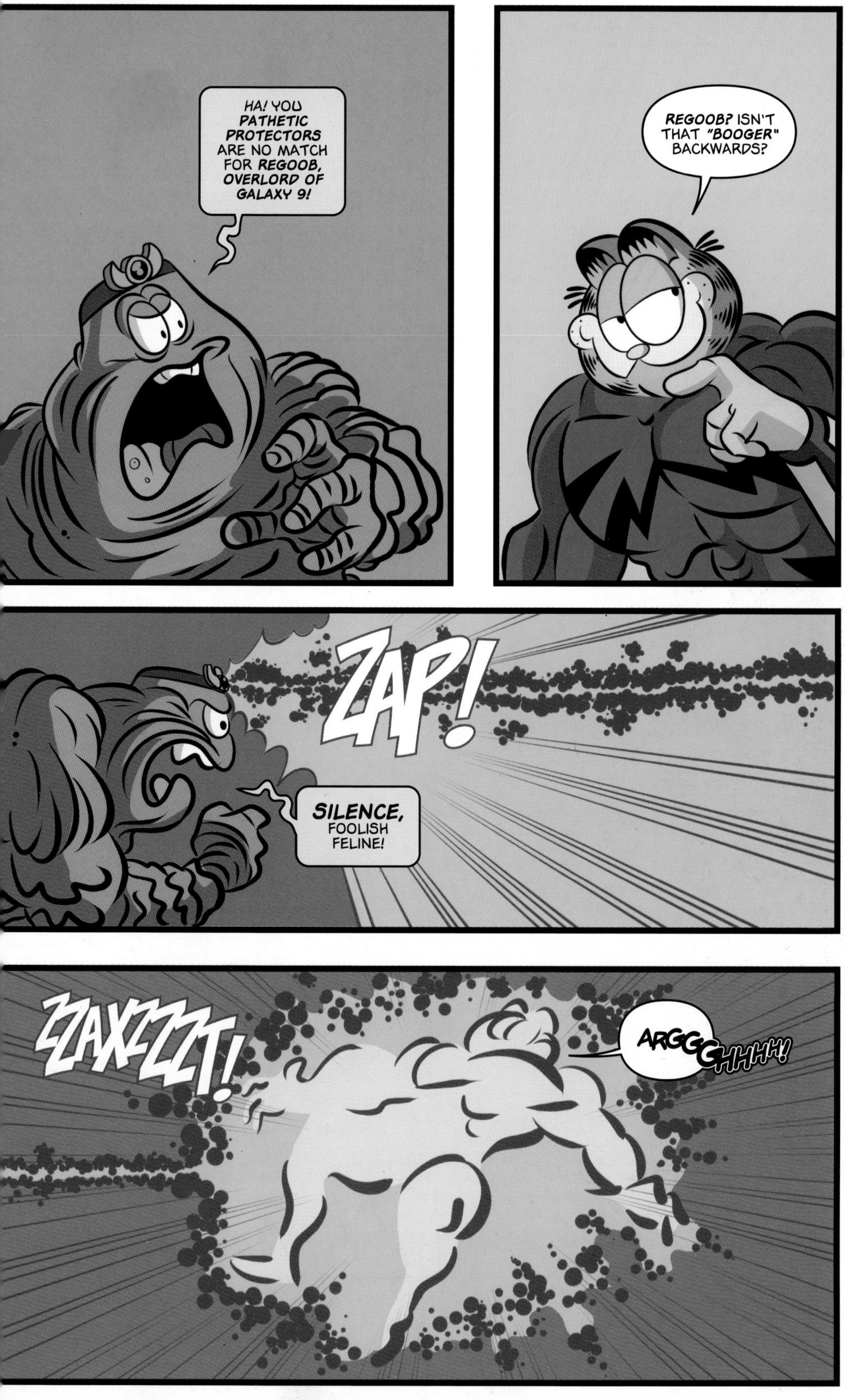
HA! YOU PATHETIC PROTECTORS ARE NO MATCH FOR REGOOB, OVERLORD OF GALAXY 9!
REGOOB? ISN'T THAT "BOOGER" BACKWARDS?
ZAP!
SILENCE, FOOLISH FELINE!
ZZAXZZZT!
ARGGGHHHH!

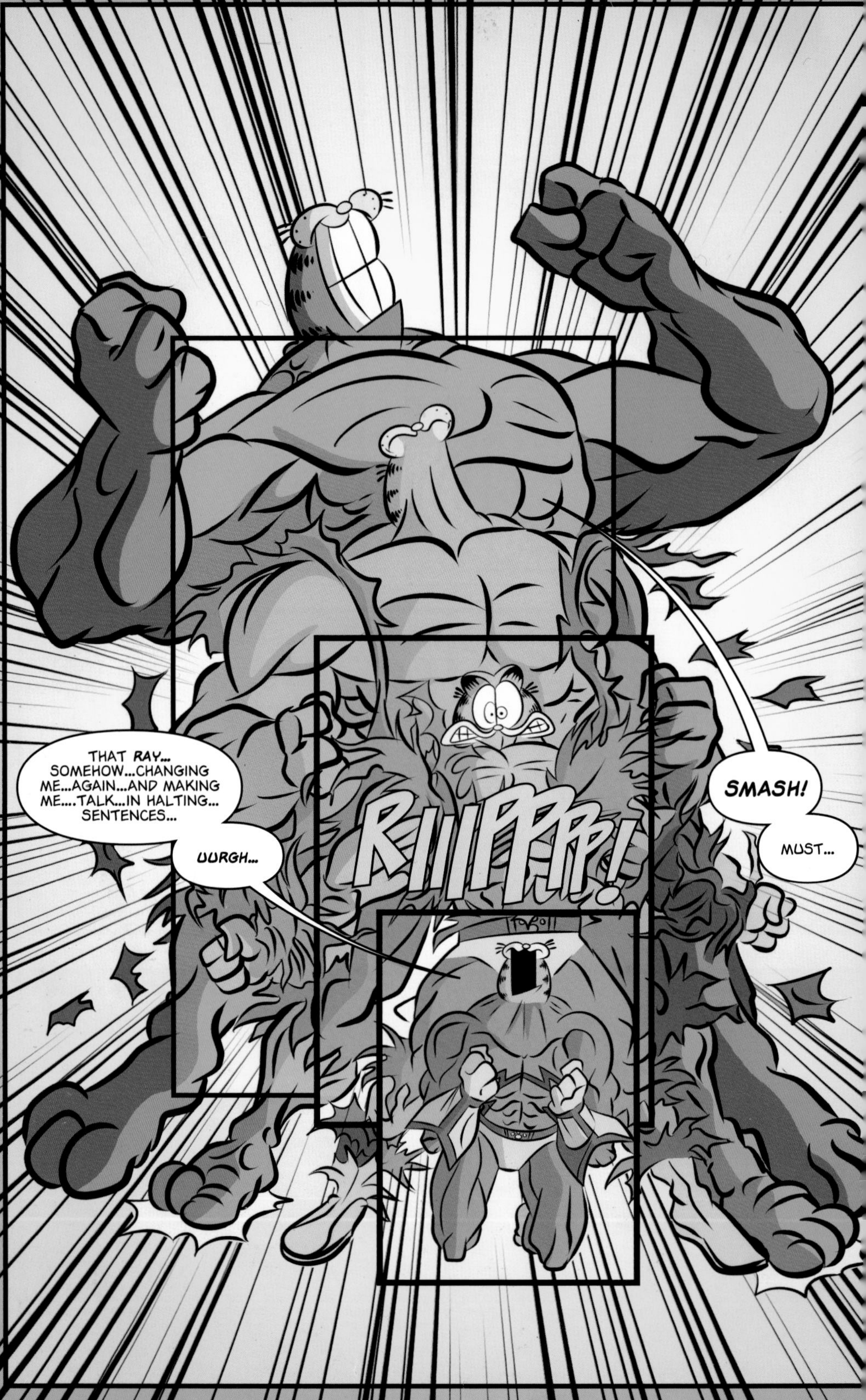
THAT RAY... SOMEHOW...CHANGING ME...AGAIN...AND MAKING ME....TALK...IN HALTING... SENTENCES...
UURGH...
RIIIPPPP!
SMASH!
MUST...

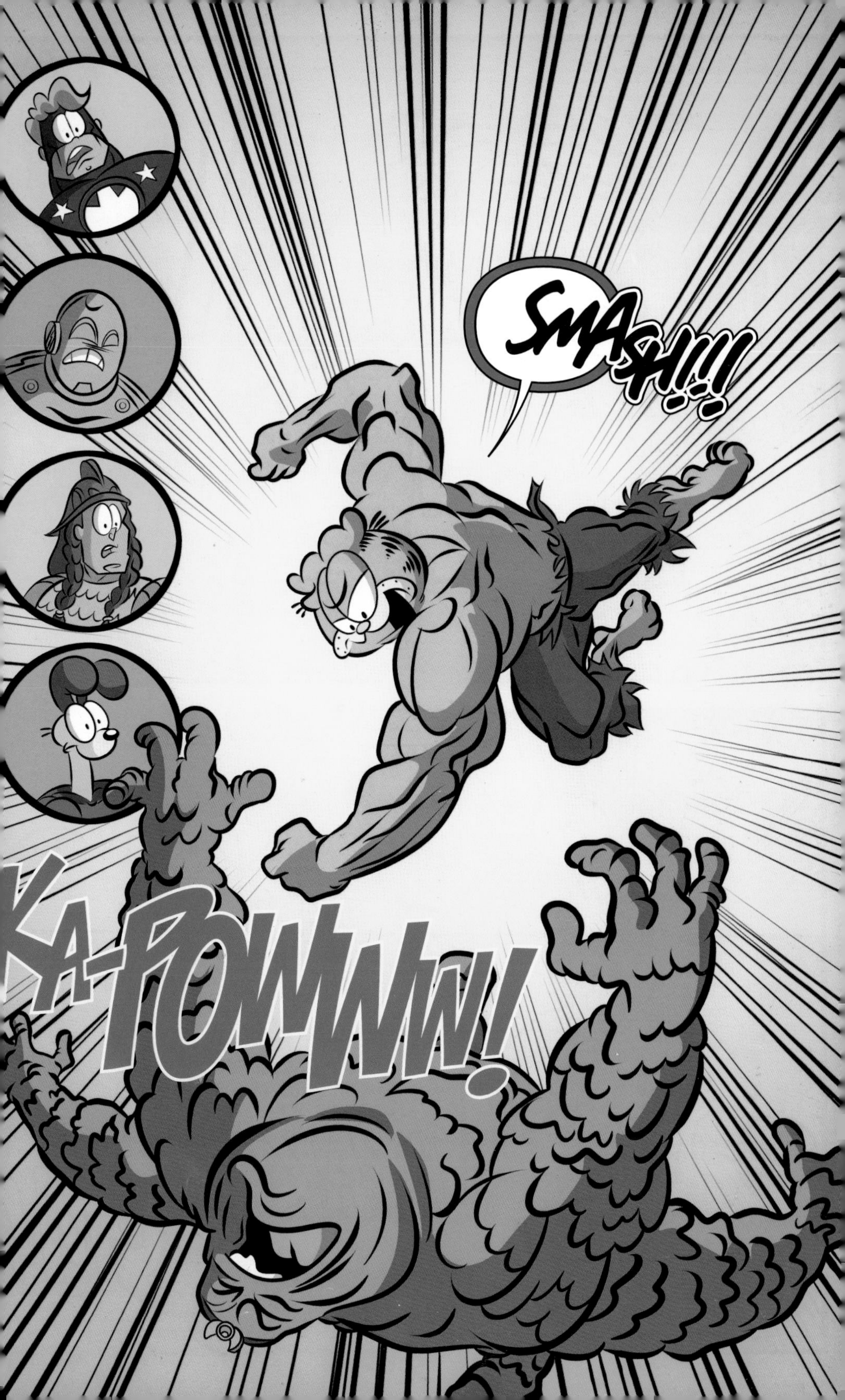
SMASH!!!
KA-POWWW!

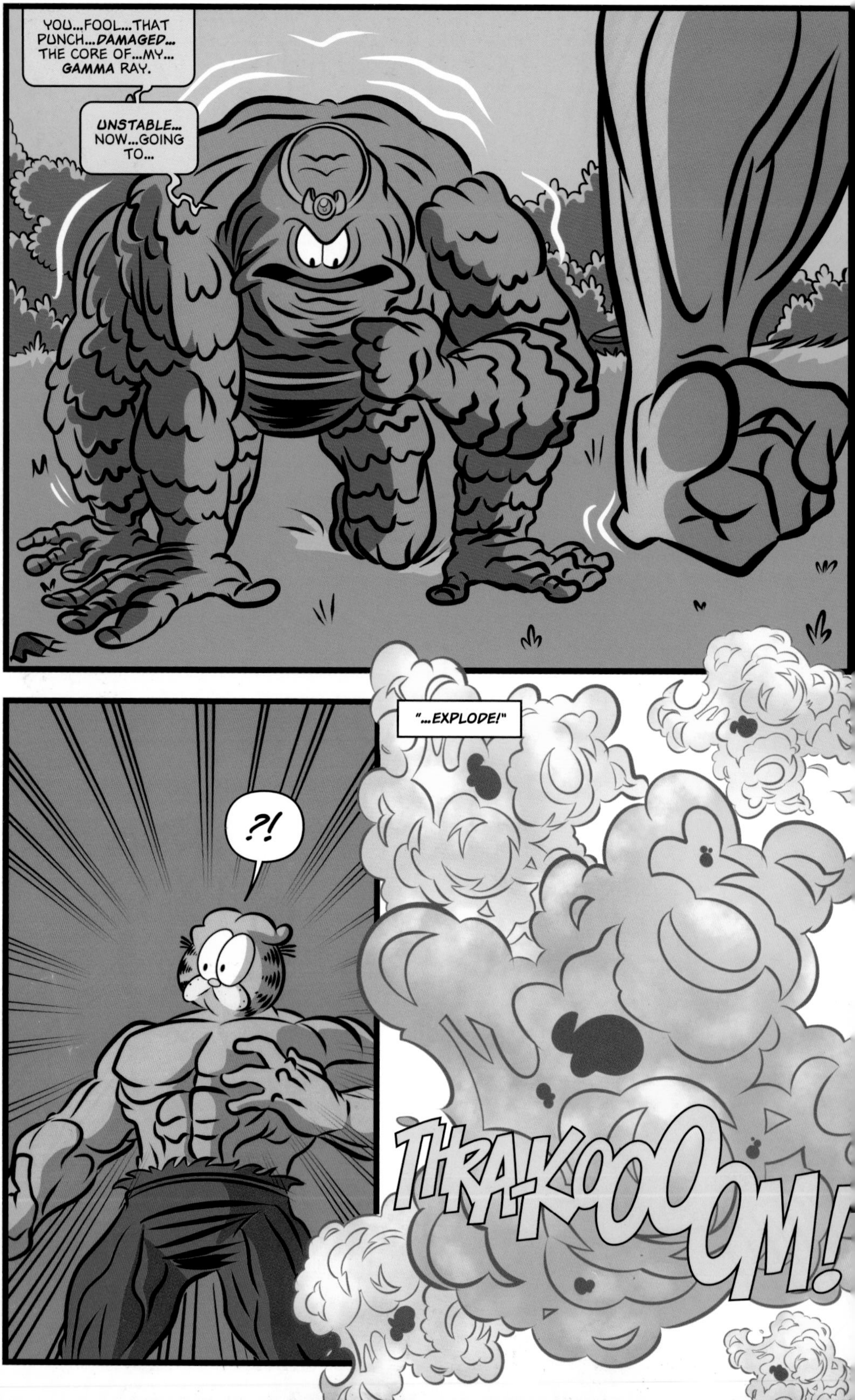
YOU...FOOL...THAT PUNCH...DAMAGED... THE CORE OF...MY... GAMMA RAY.
UNSTABLE... NOW...GOING TO...
?!
"...EXPLODE!"
THRA-KOOOOOM!

ODIE?

ODIE? YOU *HERE?*

ARF!

ARF!

CLICK!

LET THERE BE *LIGHT!*

LET THERE ALSO BE *PIZZA.* I'M *STARVING!*

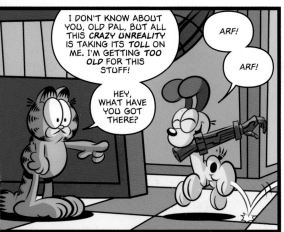

I DON'T KNOW ABOUT YOU, OLD PAL, BUT ALL THIS *CRAZY UNREALITY* IS TAKING ITS *TOLL* ON ME. I'M GETTING *TOO OLD* FOR THIS STUFF!

HEY, WHAT HAVE YOU GOT THERE?

ARF!

ARF!

I GUESS THAT *BIG EXPLOSION* PUSHED US INTO THIS *DIMENSION,* WHEREVER OR WHATEVER IT IS...

THIS LOOKS LIKE SOME SORT OF *ROBOT HAND* OR--

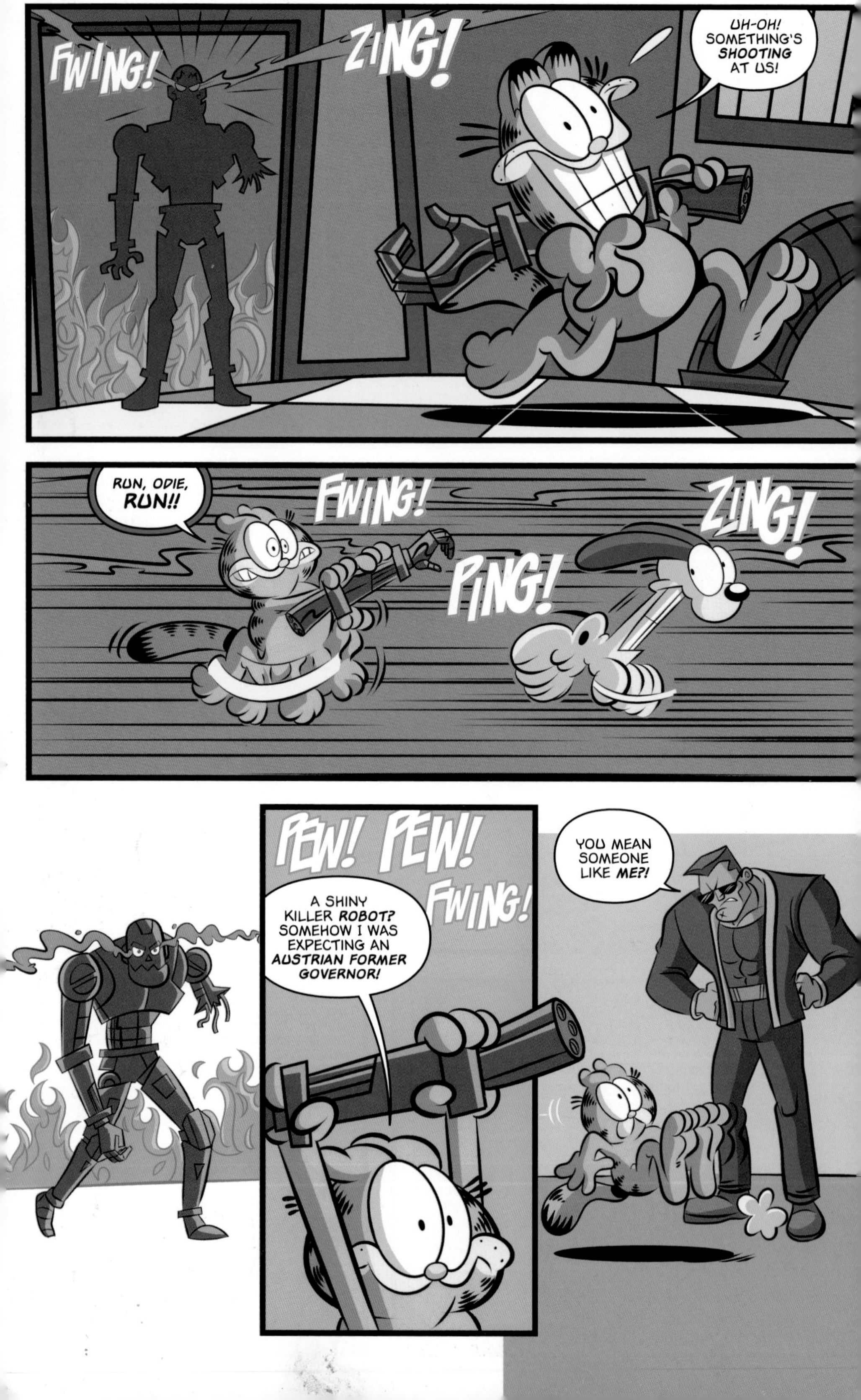
FWING!
ZING!
UH-OH! SOMETHING'S SHOOTING AT US!
RUN, ODIE, RUN!!
FWING!
ZING!
PING!
PEW! PEW!
FWING!
A SHINY KILLER ROBOT? SOMEHOW I WAS EXPECTING AN AUSTRIAN FORMER GOVERNOR!
YOU MEAN SOMEONE LIKE ME?!

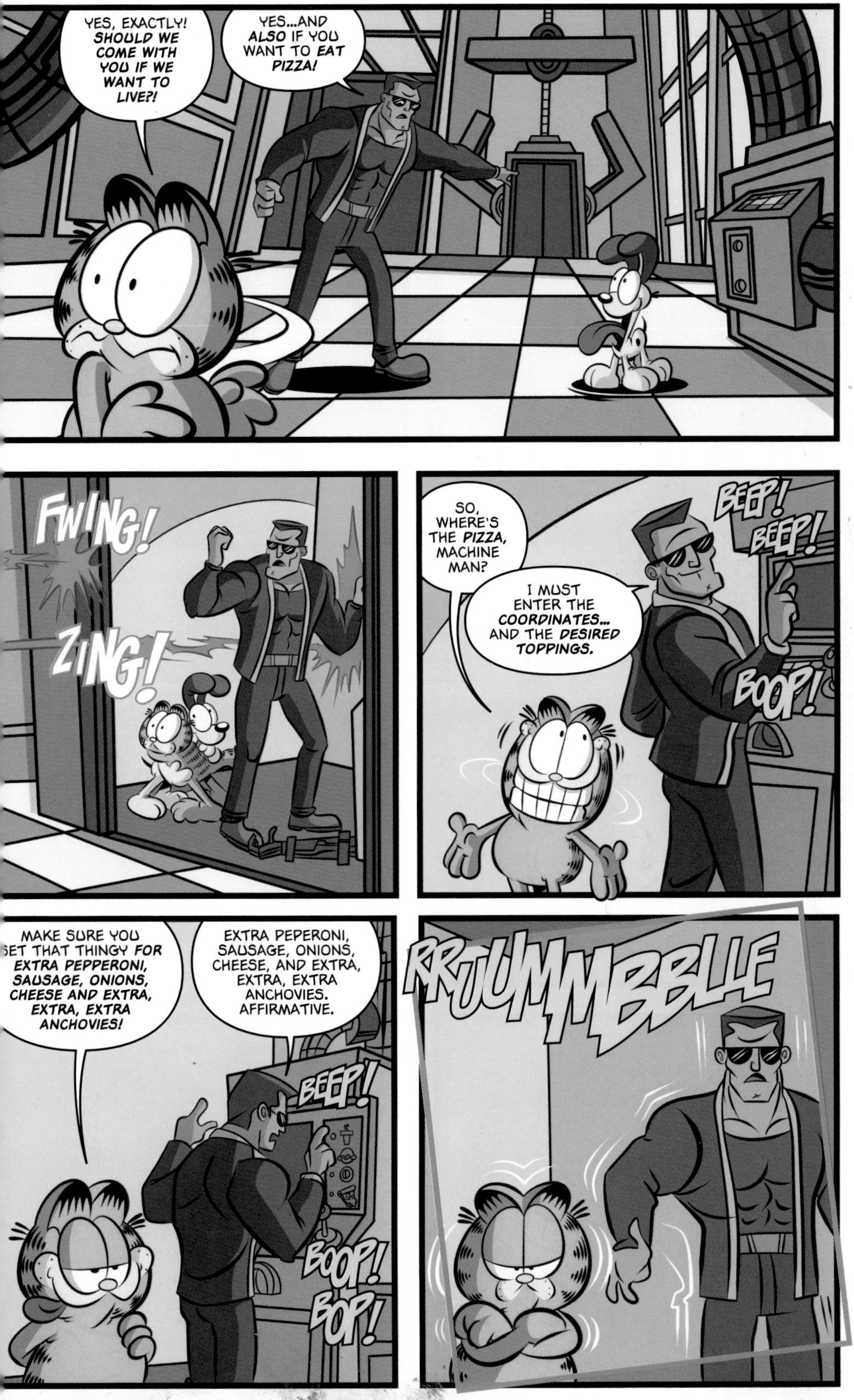

YES, EXACTLY! SHOULD WE COME WITH YOU IF WE WANT TO LIVE?!
YES...AND ALSO IF YOU WANT TO EAT PIZZA!
FWING!
ZING!
SO, WHERE'S THE PIZZA, MACHINE MAN?
I MUST ENTER THE COORDINATES... AND THE DESIRED TOPPINGS.
BEEP! BEEP!
BOOP!
MAKE SURE YOU SET THAT THINGY FOR EXTRA PEPPERONI, SAUSAGE, ONIONS, CHEESE AND EXTRA, EXTRA, EXTRA ANCHOVIES!
EXTRA PEPERONI, SAUSAGE, ONIONS, CHEESE, AND EXTRA, EXTRA, EXTRA ANCHOVIES. AFFIRMATIVE.
BEEP!
BOOP! BOP!
RRUUMMBBLLE

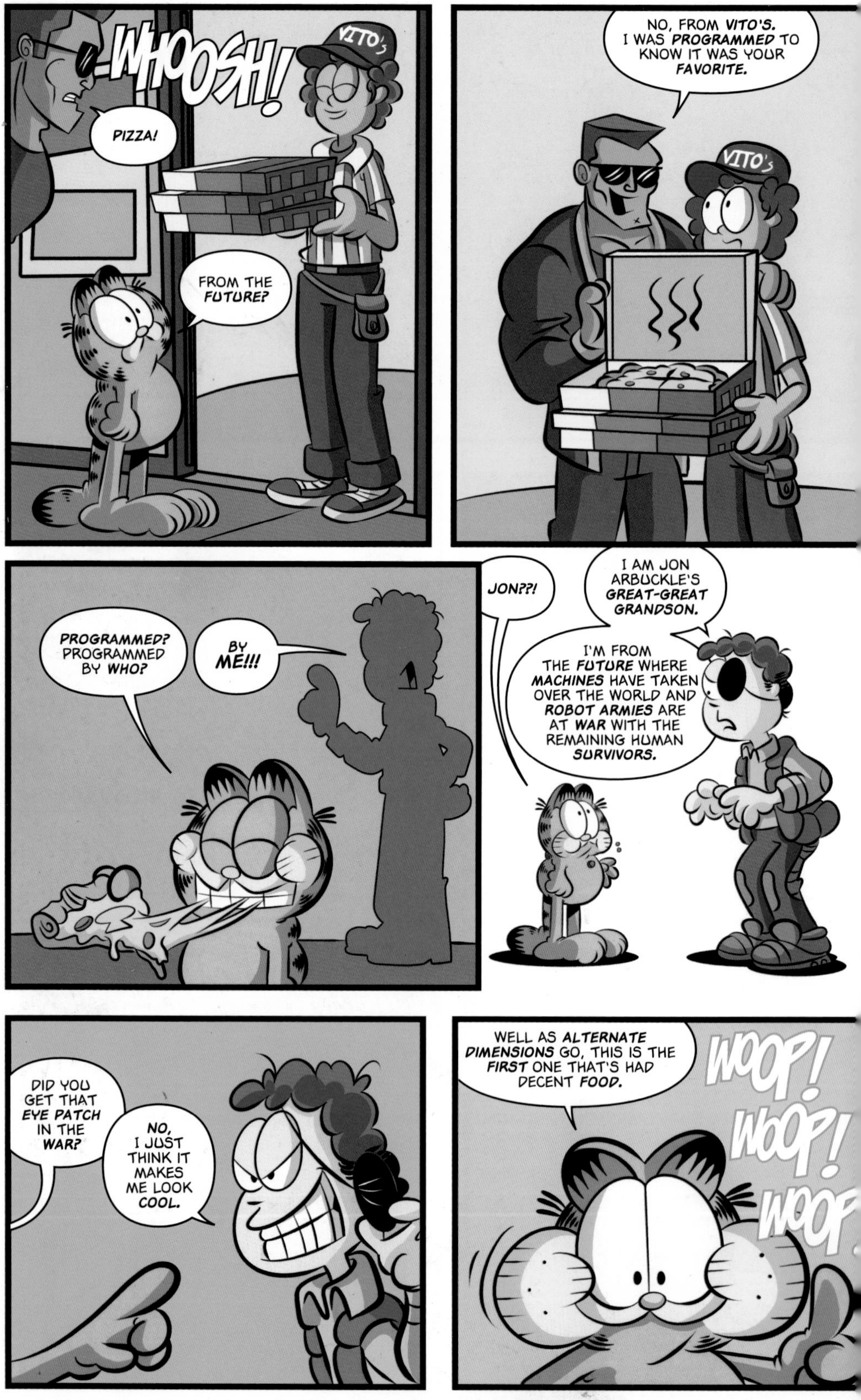

WHOOSH!
PIZZA!
FROM THE FUTURE?
NO, FROM VITO'S. I WAS PROGRAMMED TO KNOW IT WAS YOUR FAVORITE.
PROGRAMMED? PROGRAMMED BY WHO?
BY ME!!!
JON??!
I AM JON ARBUCKLE'S GREAT-GREAT GRANDSON.
I'M FROM THE FUTURE WHERE MACHINES HAVE TAKEN OVER THE WORLD AND ROBOT ARMIES ARE AT WAR WITH THE REMAINING HUMAN SURVIVORS.
DID YOU GET THAT EYE PATCH IN THE WAR?
NO, I JUST THINK IT MAKES ME LOOK COOL.
WELL AS ALTERNATE DIMENSIONS GO, THIS IS THE FIRST ONE THAT'S HAD DECENT FOOD.
WOOP! WOOP! WOOP

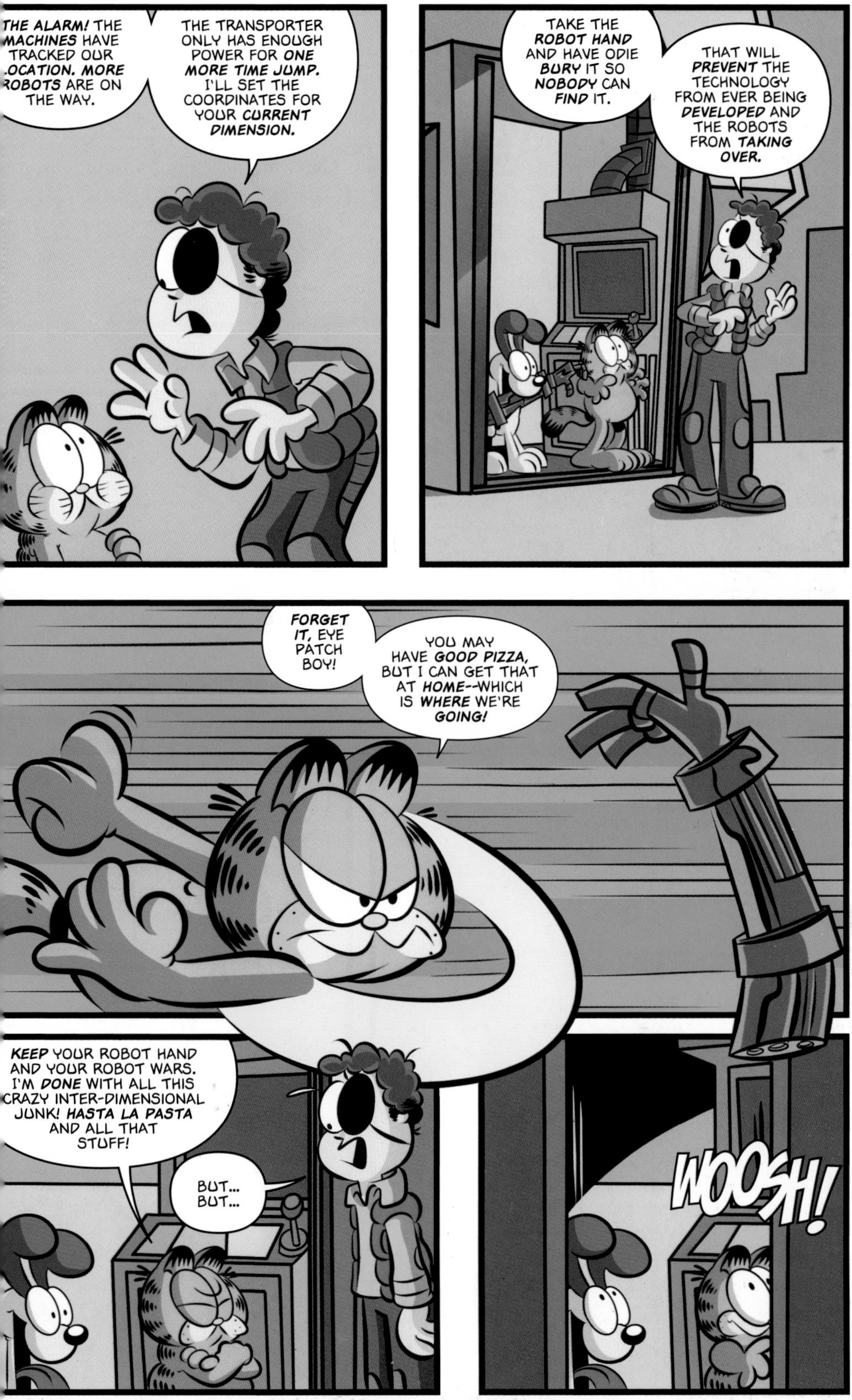

THE ALARM! THE MACHINES HAVE TRACKED OUR LOCATION. MORE ROBOTS ARE ON THE WAY.
THE TRANSPORTER ONLY HAS ENOUGH POWER FOR ONE MORE TIME JUMP. I'LL SET THE COORDINATES FOR YOUR CURRENT DIMENSION.
TAKE THE ROBOT HAND AND HAVE ODIE BURY IT SO NOBODY CAN FIND IT.
THAT WILL PREVENT THE TECHNOLOGY FROM EVER BEING DEVELOPED AND THE ROBOTS FROM TAKING OVER.
FORGET IT, EYE PATCH BOY!
YOU MAY HAVE GOOD PIZZA, BUT I CAN GET THAT AT HOME--WHICH IS WHERE WE'RE GOING!
KEEP YOUR ROBOT HAND AND YOUR ROBOT WARS. I'M DONE WITH ALL THIS CRAZY INTER-DIMENSIONAL JUNK! HASTA LA PASTA AND ALL THAT STUFF!
BUT... BUT...
WOOSH!

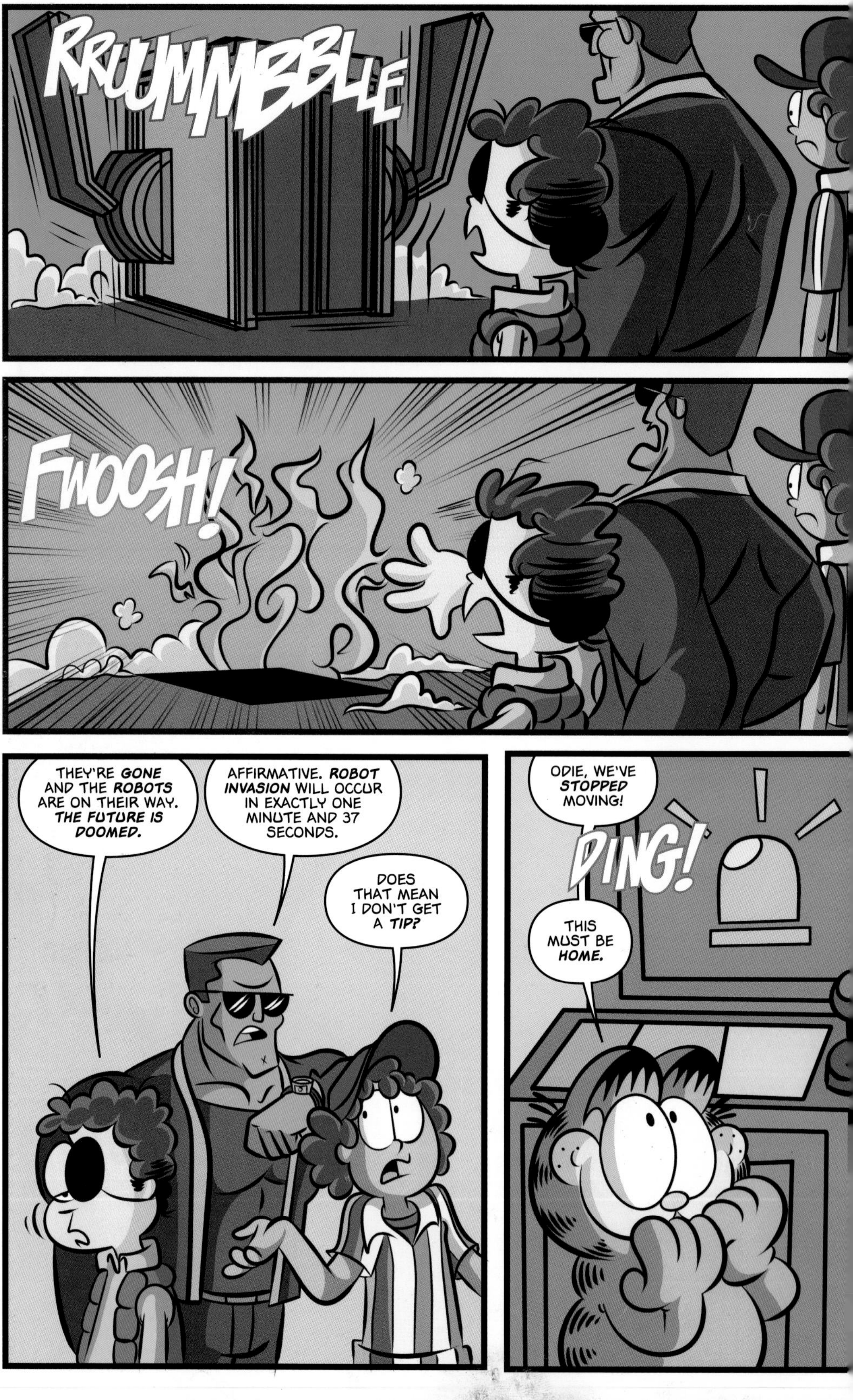
RRUUMMBBLLE
FWOOSH!
THEY'RE GONE AND THE ROBOTS ARE ON THEIR WAY. THE FUTURE IS DOOMED.
AFFIRMATIVE. ROBOT INVASION WILL OCCUR IN EXACTLY ONE MINUTE AND 37 SECONDS.
DOES THAT MEAN I DON'T GET A TIP?
ODIE, WE'VE STOPPED MOVING!
DING!
THIS MUST BE HOME.

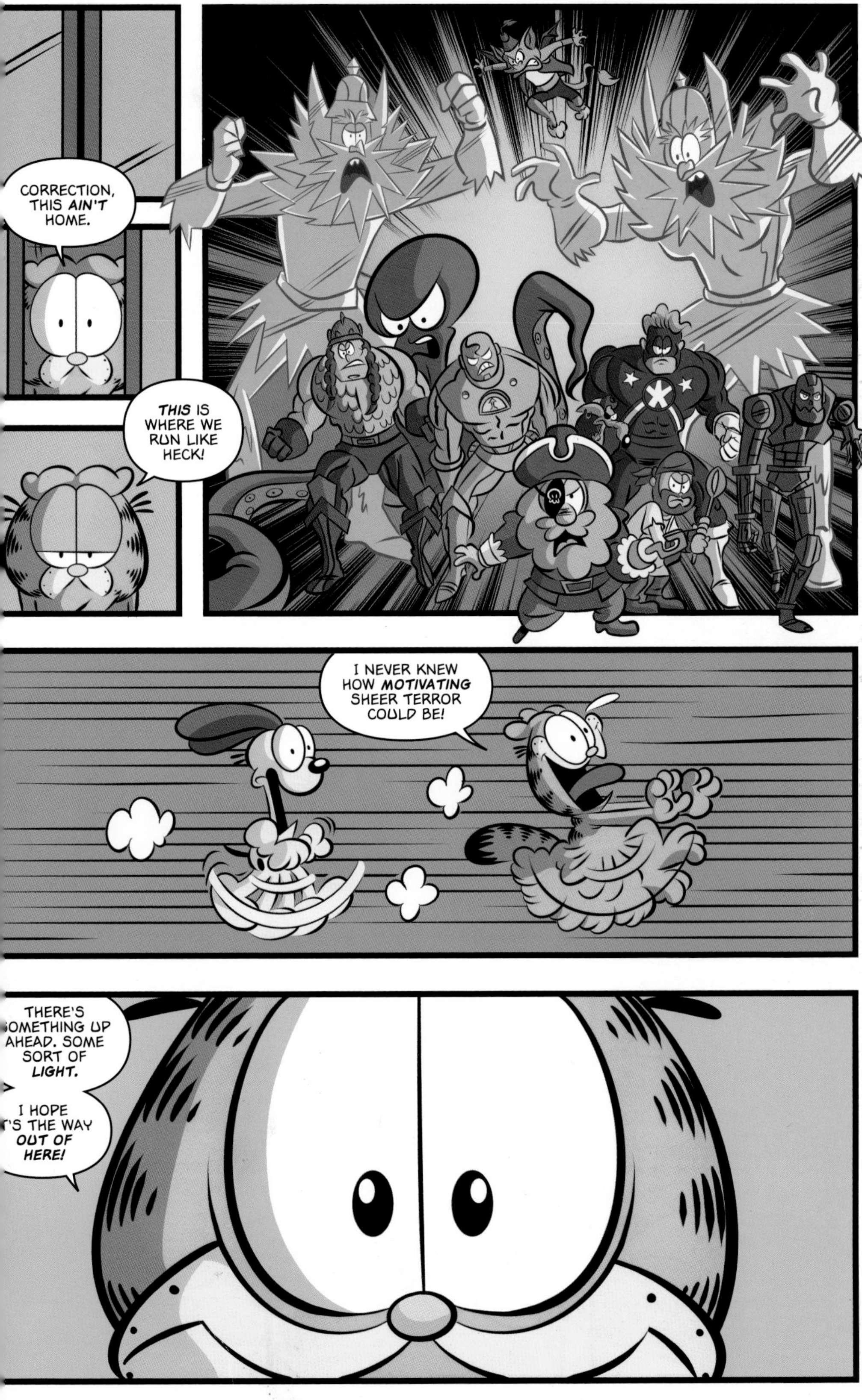
CORRECTION, THIS AIN'T HOME.
THIS IS WHERE WE RUN LIKE HECK!
I NEVER KNEW HOW MOTIVATING SHEER TERROR COULD BE!
THERE'S SOMETHING UP AHEAD. SOME SORT OF LIGHT.
I HOPE IT'S THE WAY OUT OF HERE!

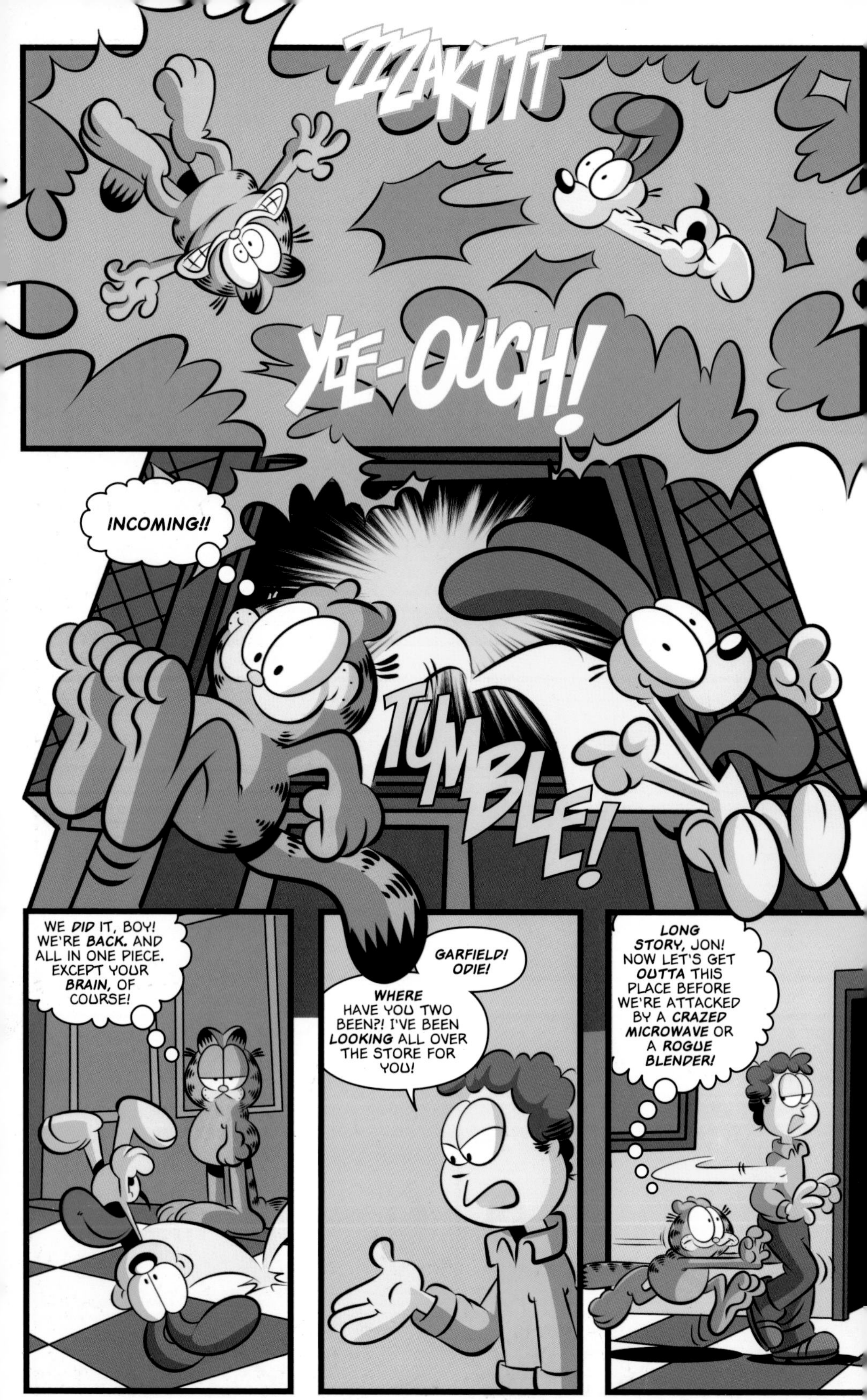
ZZZAKTTT
YEE-OUCH!
INCOMING!!
TUMBLE!
WE DID IT, BOY! WE'RE BACK. AND ALL IN ONE PIECE. EXCEPT YOUR BRAIN, OF COURSE!
GARFIELD! ODIE!
WHERE HAVE YOU TWO BEEN?! I'VE BEEN LOOKING ALL OVER THE STORE FOR YOU!
LONG STORY, JON! NOW LET'S GET OUTTA THIS PLACE BEFORE WE'RE ATTACKED BY A CRAZED MICROWAVE OR A ROGUE BLENDER!

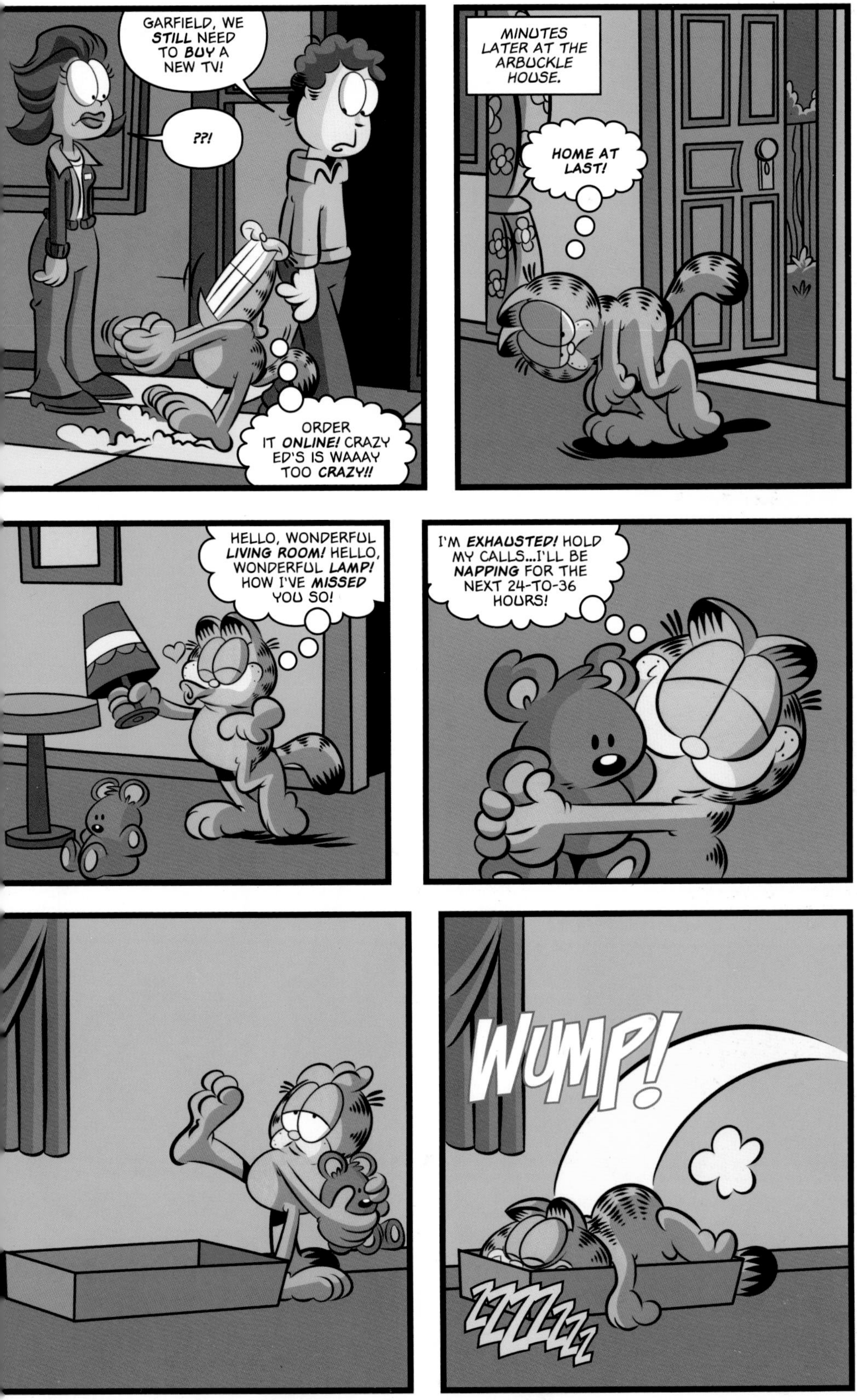
GARFIELD, WE STILL NEED TO BUY A NEW TV!
??!
ORDER IT ONLINE! CRAZY ED'S IS WAAAY TOO CRAZY!!
MINUTES LATER AT THE ARBUCKLE HOUSE.
HOME AT LAST!
HELLO, WONDERFUL LIVING ROOM! HELLO, WONDERFUL LAMP! HOW I'VE MISSED YOU SO!
I'M EXHAUSTED! HOLD MY CALLS...I'LL BE NAPPING FOR THE NEXT 24-TO-36 HOURS!
WUMP!
ZZZZZzzz

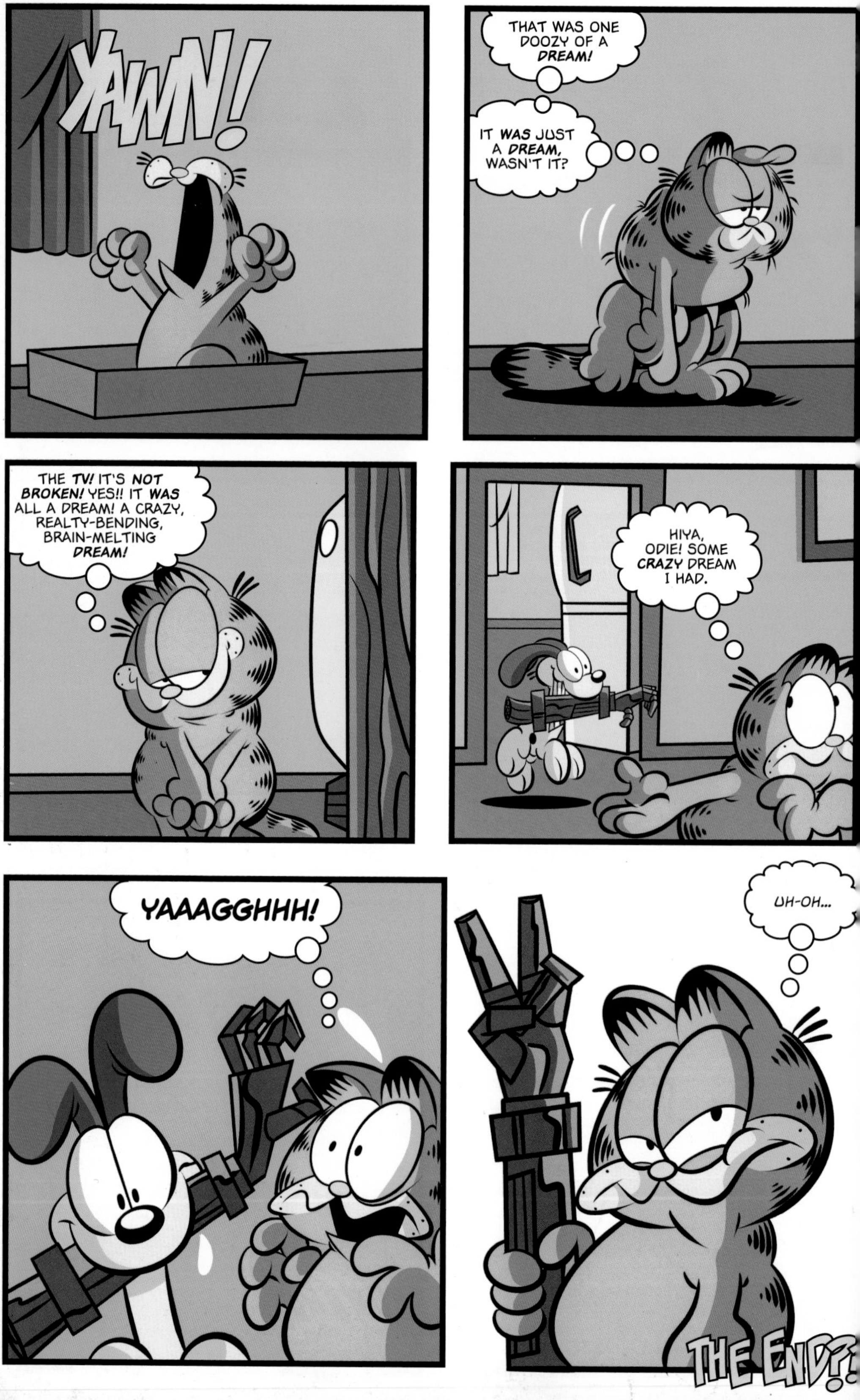
YAWN!
THAT WAS ONE DOOZY OF A DREAM!
IT WAS JUST A DREAM, WASN'T IT?
THE TV! IT'S NOT BROKEN! YES!! IT WAS ALL A DREAM! A CRAZY, REALTY-BENDING, BRAIN-MELTING DREAM!
HIYA, ODIE! SOME CRAZY DREAM I HAD.
YAAAGGHHH!
UH-OH...
THE END?!

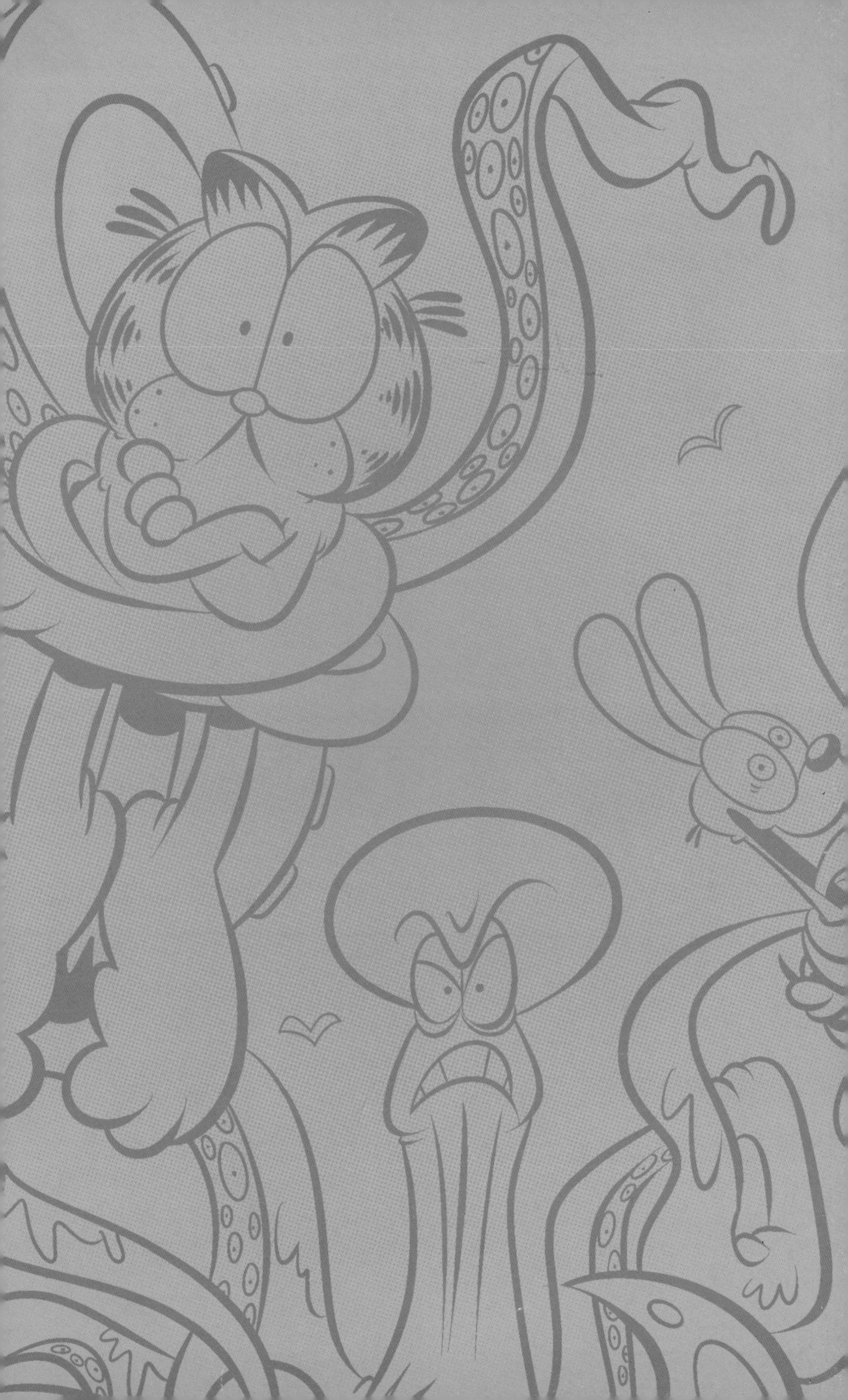

"THE CAT BURGLARS"

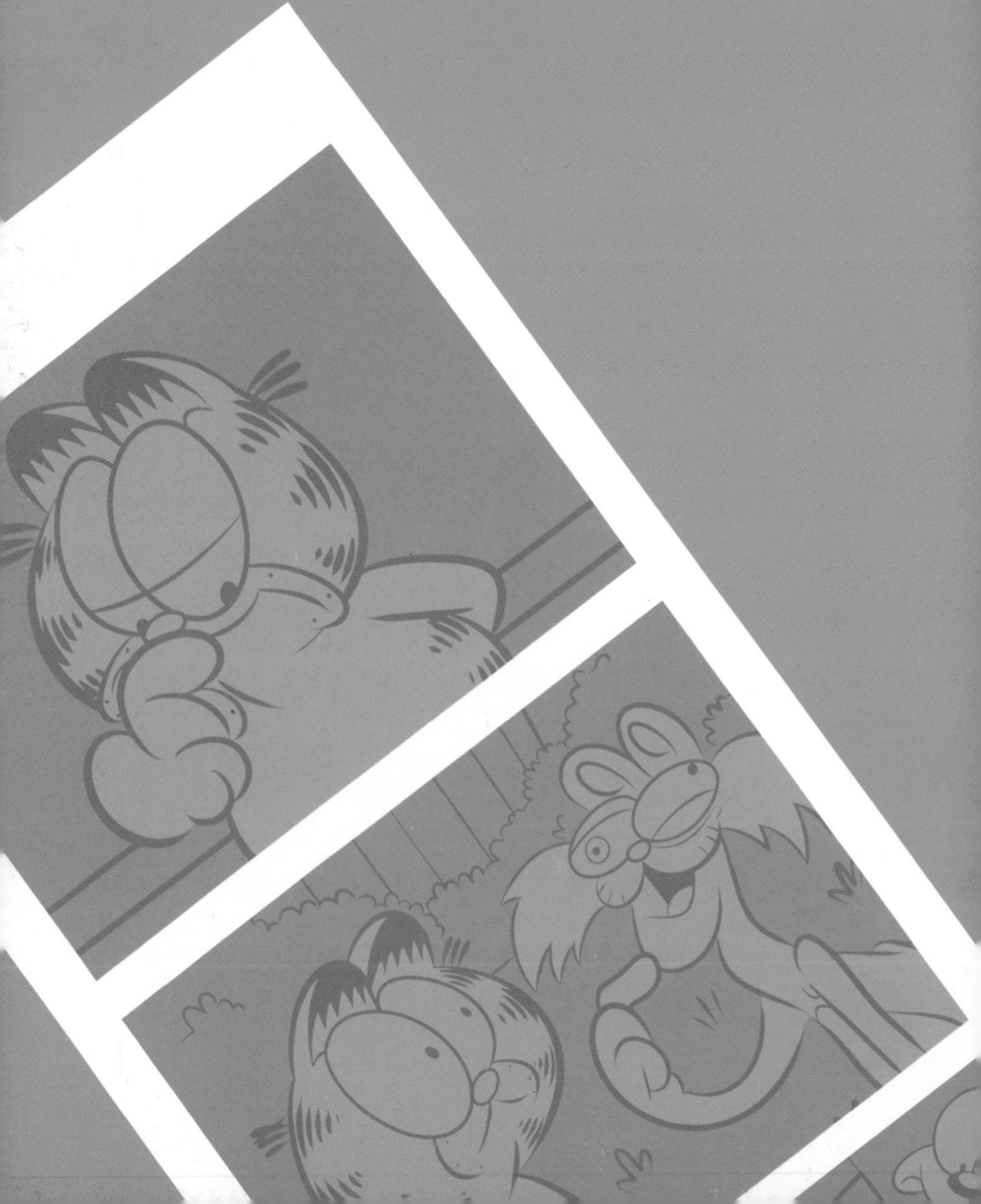

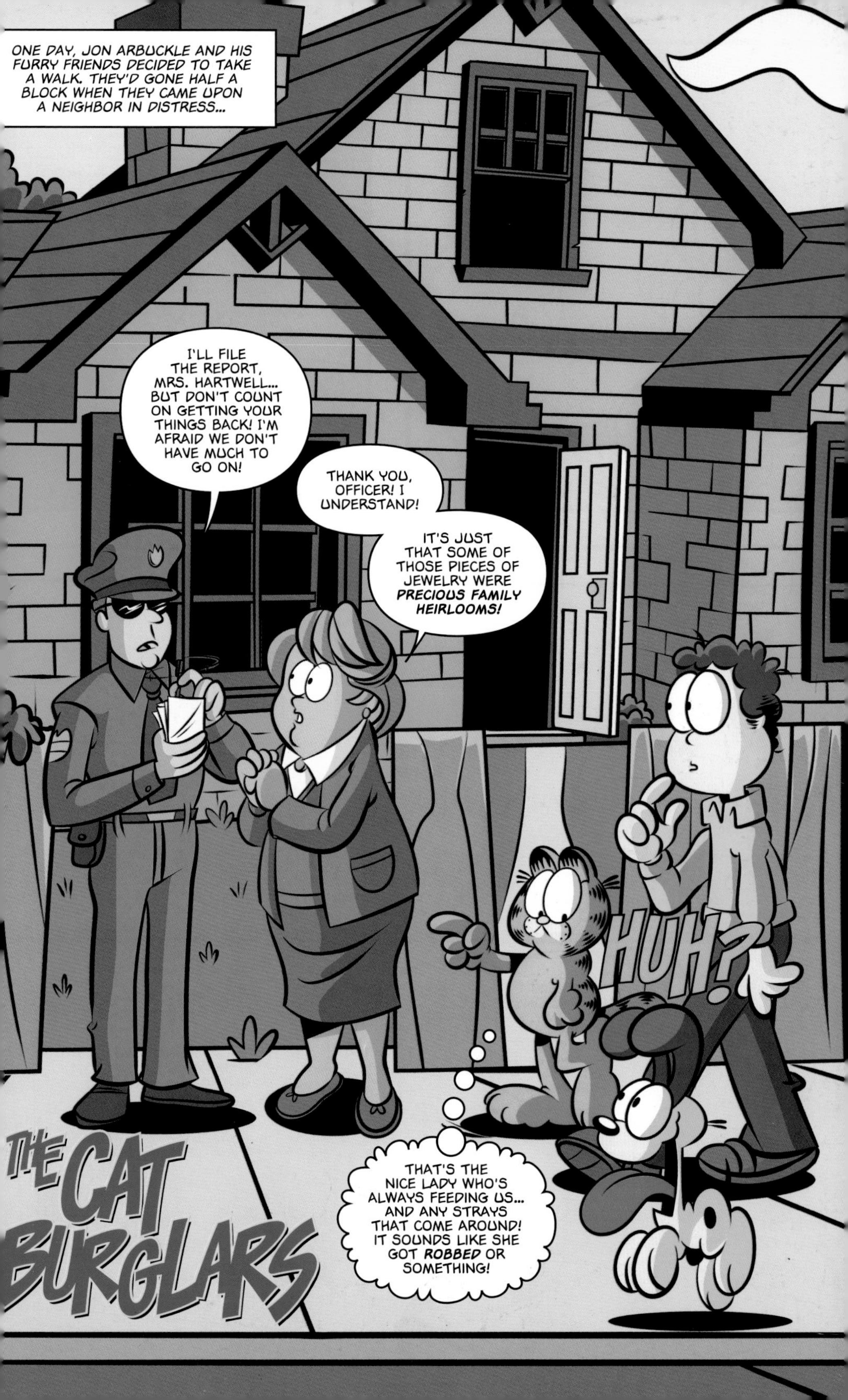
ONE DAY, JON ARBUCKLE AND HIS FURRY FRIENDS DECIDED TO TAKE A WALK. THEY'D GONE HALF A BLOCK WHEN THEY CAME UPON A NEIGHBOR IN DISTRESS...
I'LL FILE THE REPORT, MRS. HARTWELL... BUT DON'T COUNT ON GETTING YOUR THINGS BACK! I'M AFRAID WE DON'T HAVE MUCH TO GO ON!
THANK YOU, OFFICER! I UNDERSTAND!
IT'S JUST THAT SOME OF THOSE PIECES OF JEWELRY WERE *PRECIOUS FAMILY HEIRLOOMS!*
HUH?
THE CAT BURGLARS
THAT'S THE NICE LADY WHO'S ALWAYS FEEDING US... AND ANY STRAYS THAT COME AROUND! IT SOUNDS LIKE SHE GOT *ROBBED* OR SOMETHING!

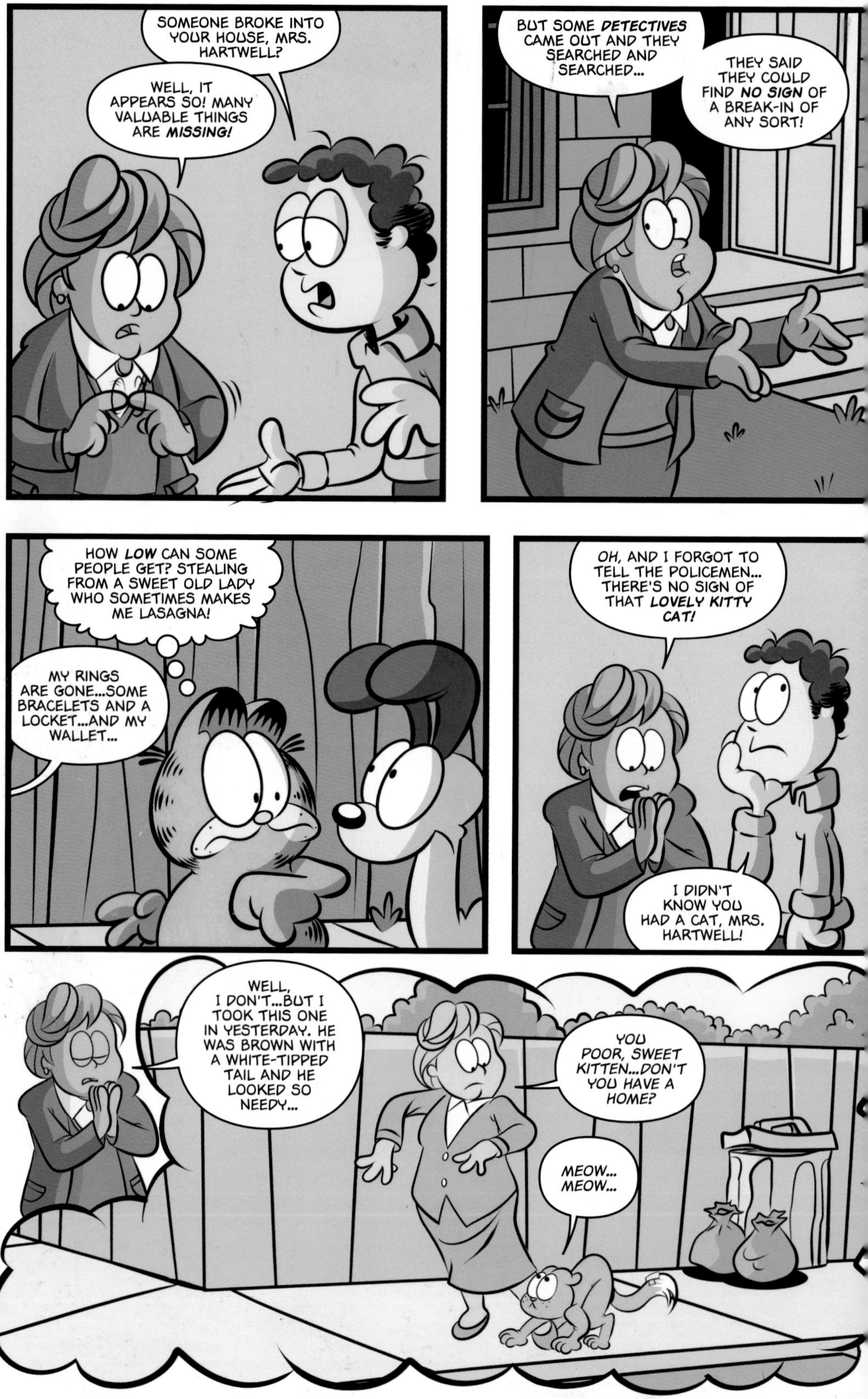
SOMEONE BROKE INTO YOUR HOUSE, MRS. HARTWELL?
WELL, IT APPEARS SO! MANY VALUABLE THINGS ARE *MISSING!*
BUT SOME *DETECTIVES* CAME OUT AND THEY SEARCHED AND SEARCHED...
THEY SAID THEY COULD FIND **NO SIGN** OF A BREAK-IN OF ANY SORT!
HOW **LOW** CAN SOME PEOPLE GET? STEALING FROM A SWEET OLD LADY WHO SOMETIMES MAKES ME LASAGNA!
MY RINGS ARE GONE...SOME BRACELETS AND A LOCKET...AND MY WALLET...
OH, AND I FORGOT TO TELL THE POLICEMEN... THERE'S NO SIGN OF THAT *LOVELY KITTY CAT!*
I DIDN'T KNOW YOU HAD A CAT, MRS. HARTWELL!
WELL, I DON'T...BUT I TOOK THIS ONE IN YESTERDAY. HE WAS BROWN WITH A WHITE-TIPPED TAIL AND HE LOOKED SO NEEDY...
YOU POOR, SWEET KITTEN...DON'T YOU HAVE A HOME?
MEOW... MEOW...

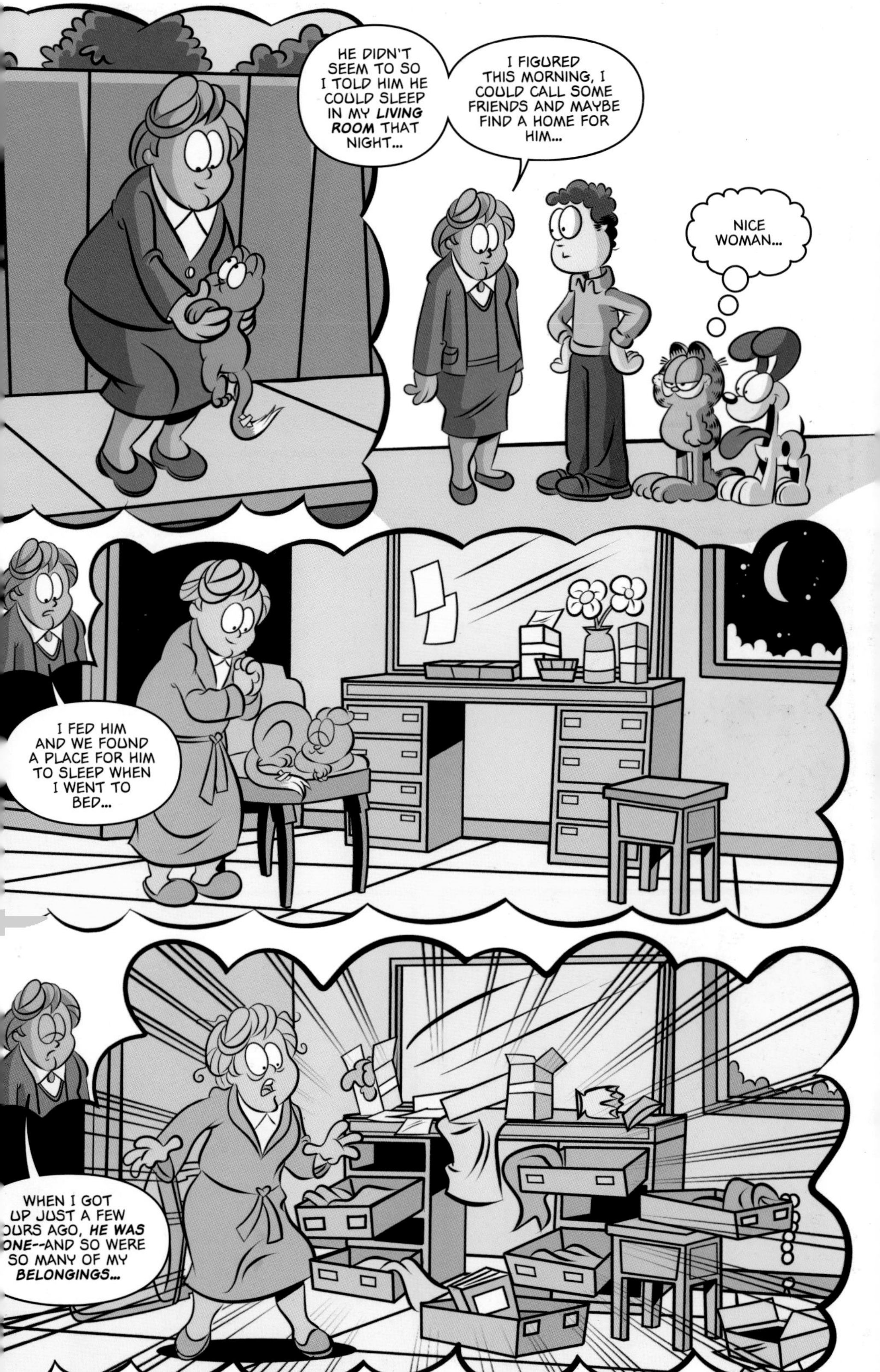

HE DIDN'T SEEM TO SO I TOLD HIM HE COULD SLEEP IN MY *LIVING ROOM* THAT NIGHT...
I FIGURED THIS MORNING, I COULD CALL SOME FRIENDS AND MAYBE FIND A HOME FOR HIM...
NICE WOMAN...
I FED HIM AND WE FOUND A PLACE FOR HIM TO SLEEP WHEN I WENT TO BED...
WHEN I GOT UP JUST A FEW OURS AGO, *HE WAS ONE*--AND SO WERE SO MANY OF MY *BELONGINGS*...

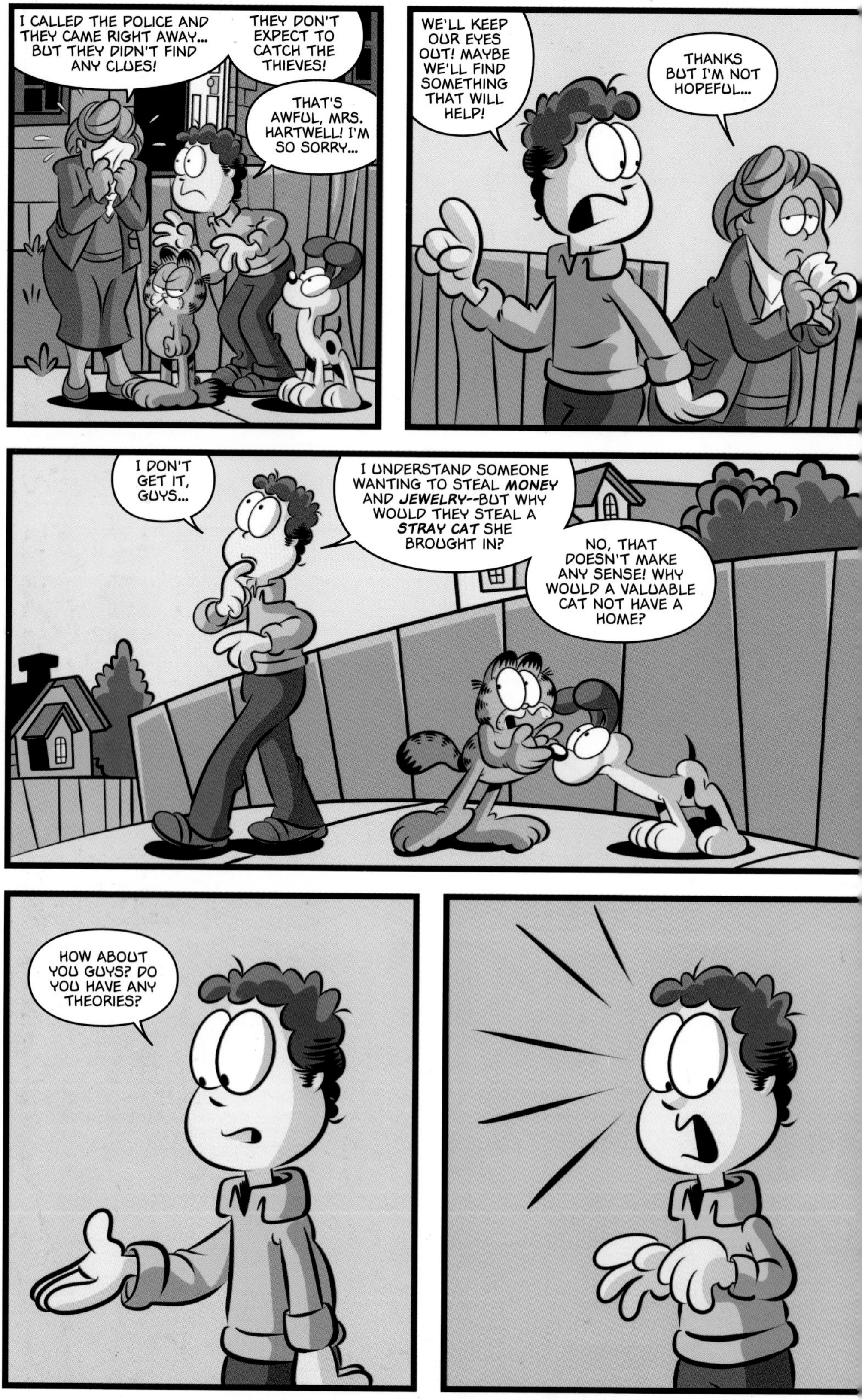
I CALLED THE POLICE AND THEY CAME RIGHT AWAY... BUT THEY DIDN'T FIND ANY CLUES!
THEY DON'T EXPECT TO CATCH THE THIEVES!
THAT'S AWFUL, MRS. HARTWELL! I'M SO SORRY...
WE'LL KEEP OUR EYES OUT! MAYBE WE'LL FIND SOMETHING THAT WILL HELP!
THANKS BUT I'M NOT HOPEFUL...
I DON'T GET IT, GUYS...
I UNDERSTAND SOMEONE WANTING TO STEAL MONEY AND JEWELRY--BUT WHY WOULD THEY STEAL A STRAY CAT SHE BROUGHT IN?
NO, THAT DOESN'T MAKE ANY SENSE! WHY WOULD A VALUABLE CAT NOT HAVE A HOME?
HOW ABOUT YOU GUYS? DO YOU HAVE ANY THEORIES?

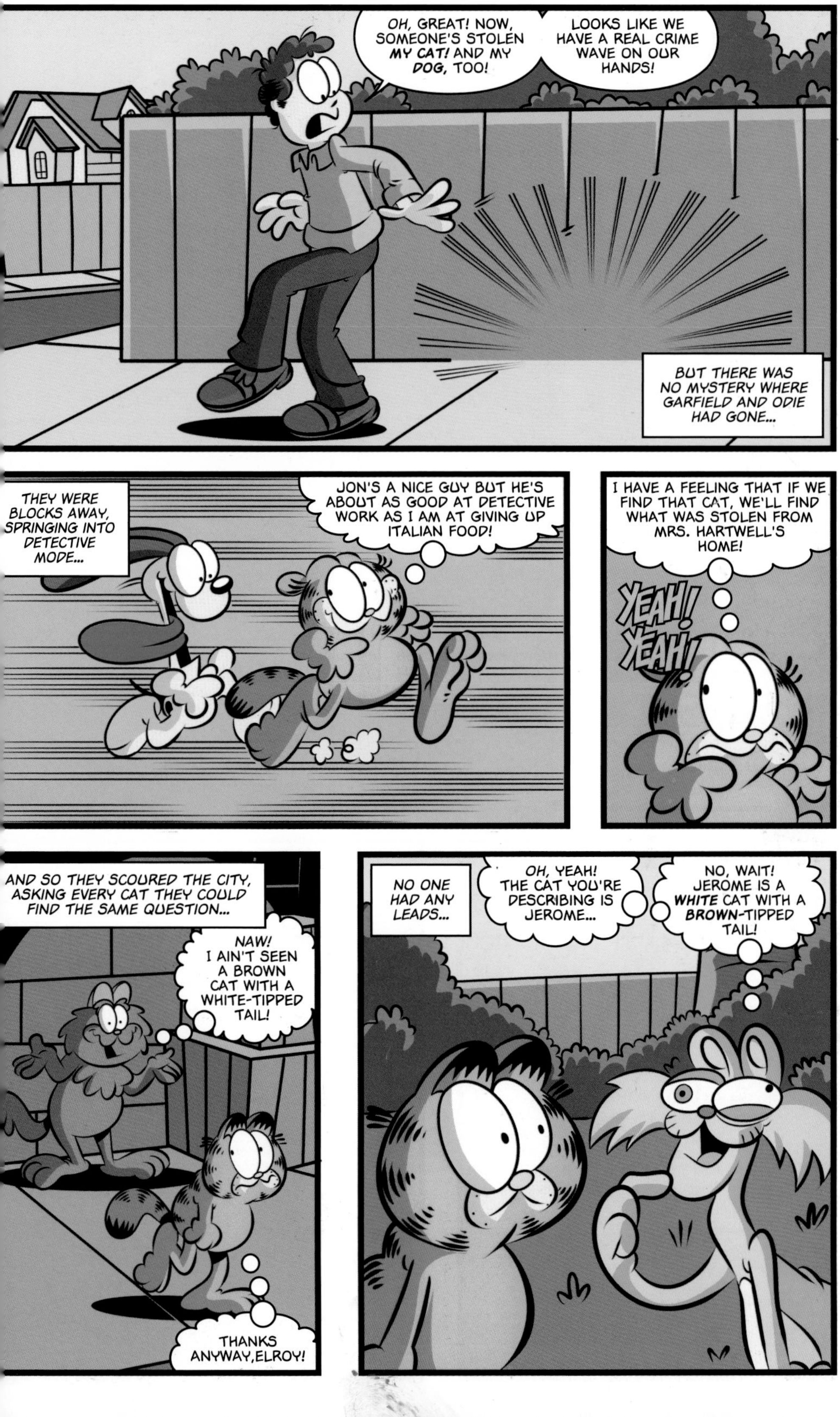
OH, GREAT! NOW, SOMEONE'S STOLEN MY CAT! AND MY DOG, TOO!
LOOKS LIKE WE HAVE A REAL CRIME WAVE ON OUR HANDS!
BUT THERE WAS NO MYSTERY WHERE GARFIELD AND ODIE HAD GONE...
THEY WERE BLOCKS AWAY, SPRINGING INTO DETECTIVE MODE...
JON'S A NICE GUY BUT HE'S ABOUT AS GOOD AT DETECTIVE WORK AS I AM AT GIVING UP ITALIAN FOOD!
I HAVE A FEELING THAT IF WE FIND THAT CAT, WE'LL FIND WHAT WAS STOLEN FROM MRS. HARTWELL'S HOME!
YEAH! YEAH!
AND SO THEY SCOURED THE CITY, ASKING EVERY CAT THEY COULD FIND THE SAME QUESTION...
NAW! I AIN'T SEEN A BROWN CAT WITH A WHITE-TIPPED TAIL!
THANKS ANYWAY, ELROY!
NO ONE HAD ANY LEADS...
OH, YEAH! THE CAT YOU'RE DESCRIBING IS JEROME...
NO, WAIT! JEROME IS A WHITE CAT WITH A BROWN-TIPPED TAIL!

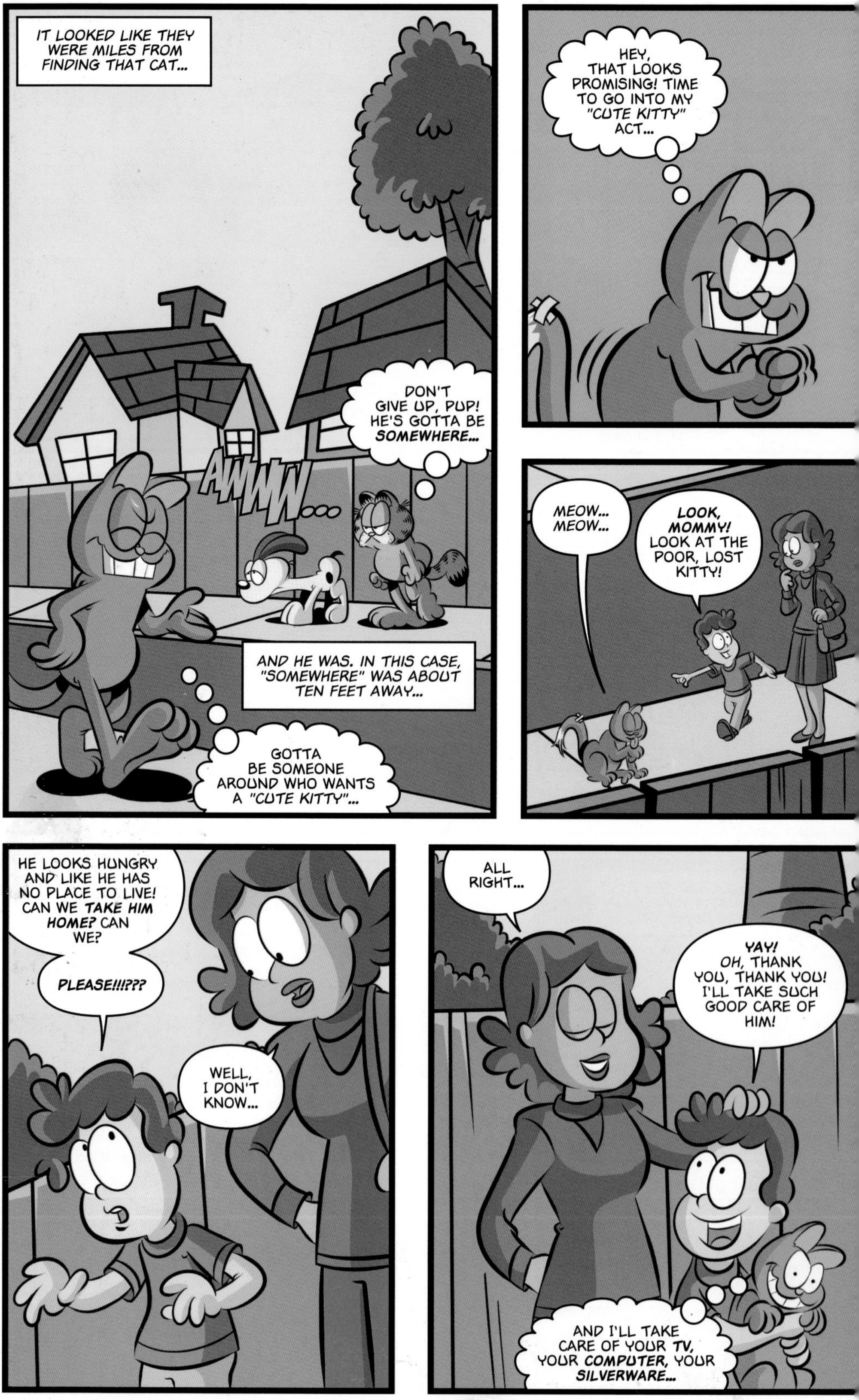
IT LOOKED LIKE THEY WERE MILES FROM FINDING THAT CAT...
DON'T GIVE UP, PUP! HE'S GOTTA BE SOMEWHERE...
AWWW...
AND HE WAS. IN THIS CASE, "SOMEWHERE" WAS ABOUT TEN FEET AWAY...
GOTTA BE SOMEONE AROUND WHO WANTS A "CUTE KITTY"...
HEY, THAT LOOKS PROMISING! TIME TO GO INTO MY "CUTE KITTY" ACT...
MEOW... MEOW...
LOOK, MOMMY! LOOK AT THE POOR, LOST KITTY!
HE LOOKS HUNGRY AND LIKE HE HAS NO PLACE TO LIVE! CAN WE TAKE HIM HOME? CAN WE?
PLEASE!!!???
WELL, I DON'T KNOW...
ALL RIGHT...
YAY! OH, THANK YOU, THANK YOU! I'LL TAKE SUCH GOOD CARE OF HIM!
AND I'LL TAKE CARE OF YOUR TV, YOUR COMPUTER, YOUR SILVERWARE...

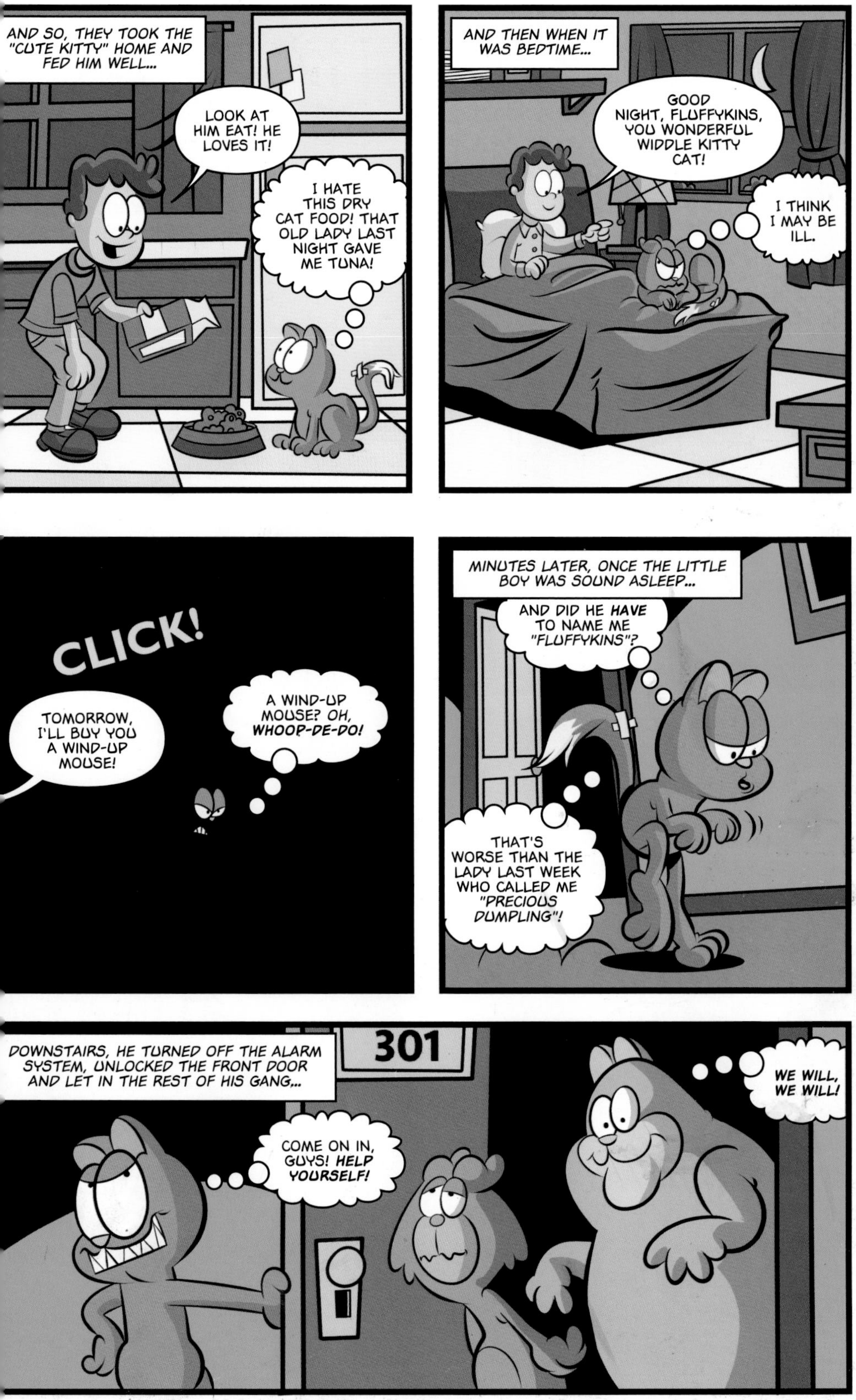
AND SO, THEY TOOK THE "CUTE KITTY" HOME AND FED HIM WELL...
LOOK AT HIM EAT! HE LOVES IT!
I HATE THIS DRY CAT FOOD! THAT OLD LADY LAST NIGHT GAVE ME TUNA!
AND THEN WHEN IT WAS BEDTIME...
GOOD NIGHT, FLUFFYKINS, YOU WONDERFUL WIDDLE KITTY CAT!
I THINK I MAY BE ILL.
CLICK!
TOMORROW, I'LL BUY YOU A WIND-UP MOUSE!
A WIND-UP MOUSE? OH, WHOOP-DE-DO!
MINUTES LATER, ONCE THE LITTLE BOY WAS SOUND ASLEEP...
AND DID HE HAVE TO NAME ME "FLUFFYKINS"?
THAT'S WORSE THAN THE LADY LAST WEEK WHO CALLED ME "PRECIOUS DUMPLING"!
DOWNSTAIRS, HE TURNED OFF THE ALARM SYSTEM, UNLOCKED THE FRONT DOOR AND LET IN THE REST OF HIS GANG...
301
COME ON IN, GUYS! HELP YOURSELF!
WE WILL, WE WILL!

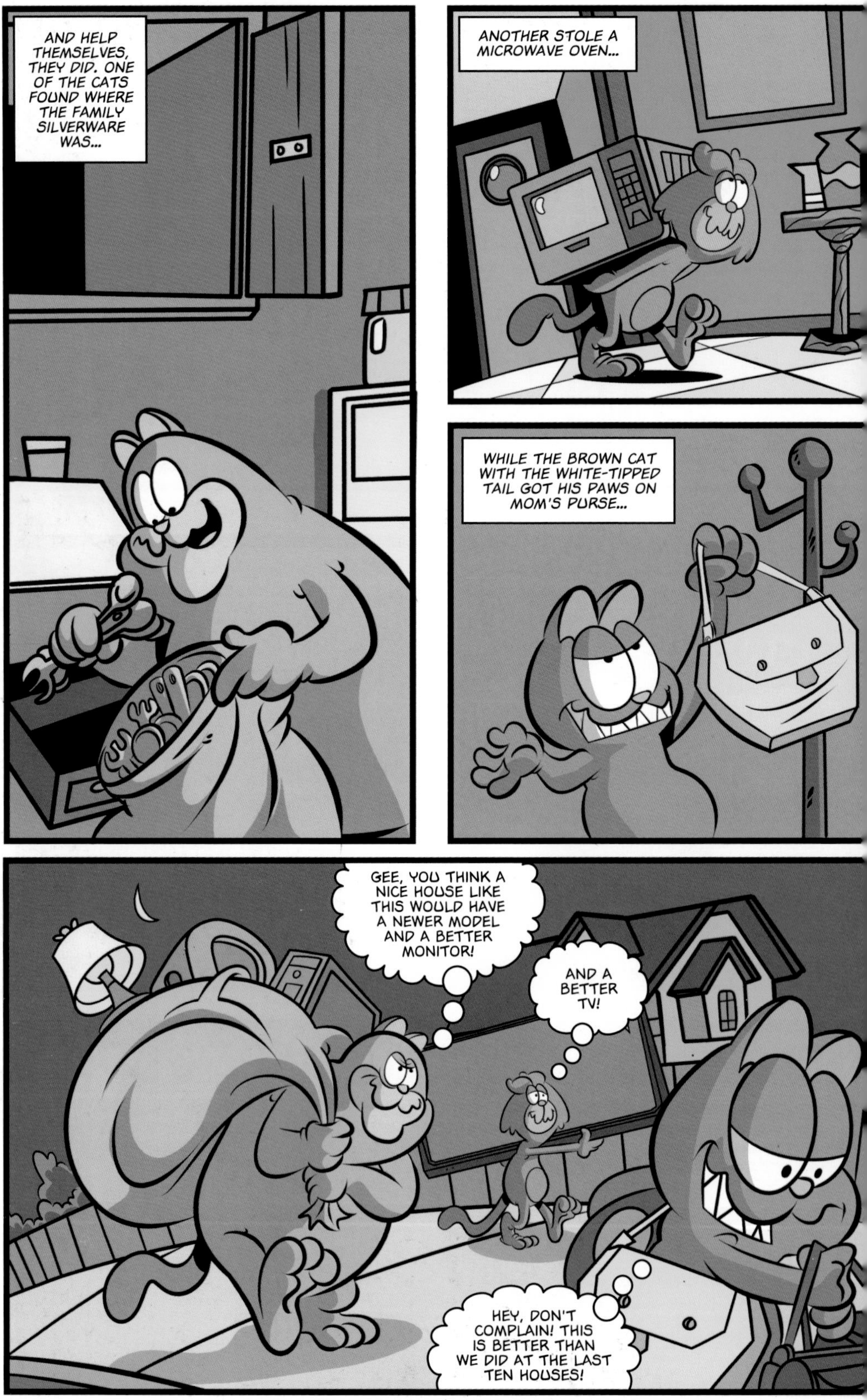
AND HELP THEMSELVES, THEY DID. ONE OF THE CATS FOUND WHERE THE FAMILY SILVERWARE WAS...
ANOTHER STOLE A MICROWAVE OVEN...
WHILE THE BROWN CAT WITH THE WHITE-TIPPED TAIL GOT HIS PAWS ON MOM'S PURSE...
GEE, YOU THINK A NICE HOUSE LIKE THIS WOULD HAVE A NEWER MODEL AND A BETTER MONITOR!
AND A BETTER TV!
HEY, DON'T COMPLAIN! THIS IS BETTER THAN WE DID AT THE LAST TEN HOUSES!

HALF THE NIGHT, THE CATS MADE REPEATED TRIPS TO AND FROM THE HOUSE...

DON'T PASS

...CARRYING FURNITURE, JEWELRY AND OTHER VALUABLE ITEMS TO THEIR HEADQUARTERS IN THE NOT-SO-NICE PART OF TOWN...

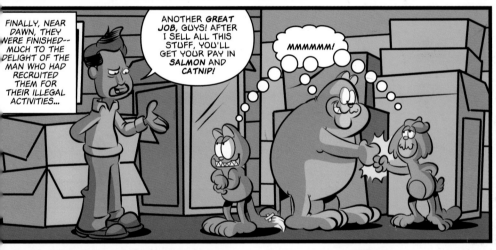

FINALLY, NEAR DAWN, THEY WERE FINISHED-- MUCH TO THE DELIGHT OF THE MAN WHO HAD RECRUITED THEM FOR THEIR ILLEGAL ACTIVITIES...

ANOTHER *GREAT JOB*, GUYS! AFTER I SELL ALL THIS STUFF, YOU'LL GET YOUR PAY IN *SALMON* AND *CATNIP!*

MMMMMM!

AFTER A FEW MORE JOBS, I THINK WE OUGHTA MOVE AND START WORKING THE NORTH END OF THE CITY!

BUT BEFORE WE ALL GO SLEEP FOR THE DAY, I WANT YOU GUYS TO PRACTICE YOUR "CUTE KITTY" LOOKS A LITTLE MORE! *LINE UP!*

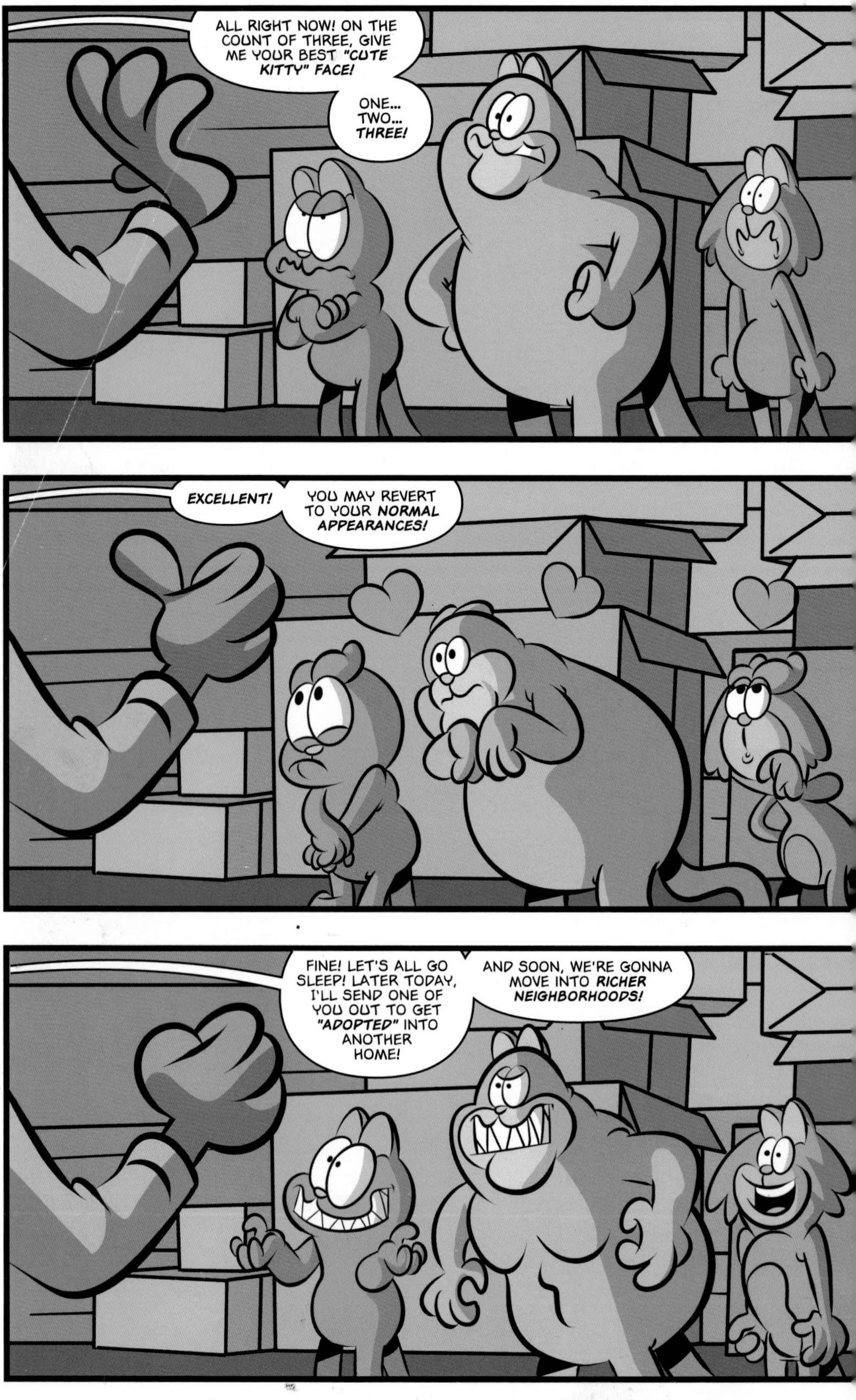
ALL RIGHT NOW! ON THE COUNT OF THREE, GIVE ME YOUR BEST "CUTE KITTY" FACE!
ONE... TWO... THREE!
EXCELLENT!
YOU MAY REVERT TO YOUR NORMAL APPEARANCES!
FINE! LET'S ALL GO SLEEP! LATER TODAY, I'LL SEND ONE OF YOU OUT TO GET "ADOPTED" INTO ANOTHER HOME!
AND SOON, WE'RE GONNA MOVE INTO RICHER NEIGHBORHOODS!

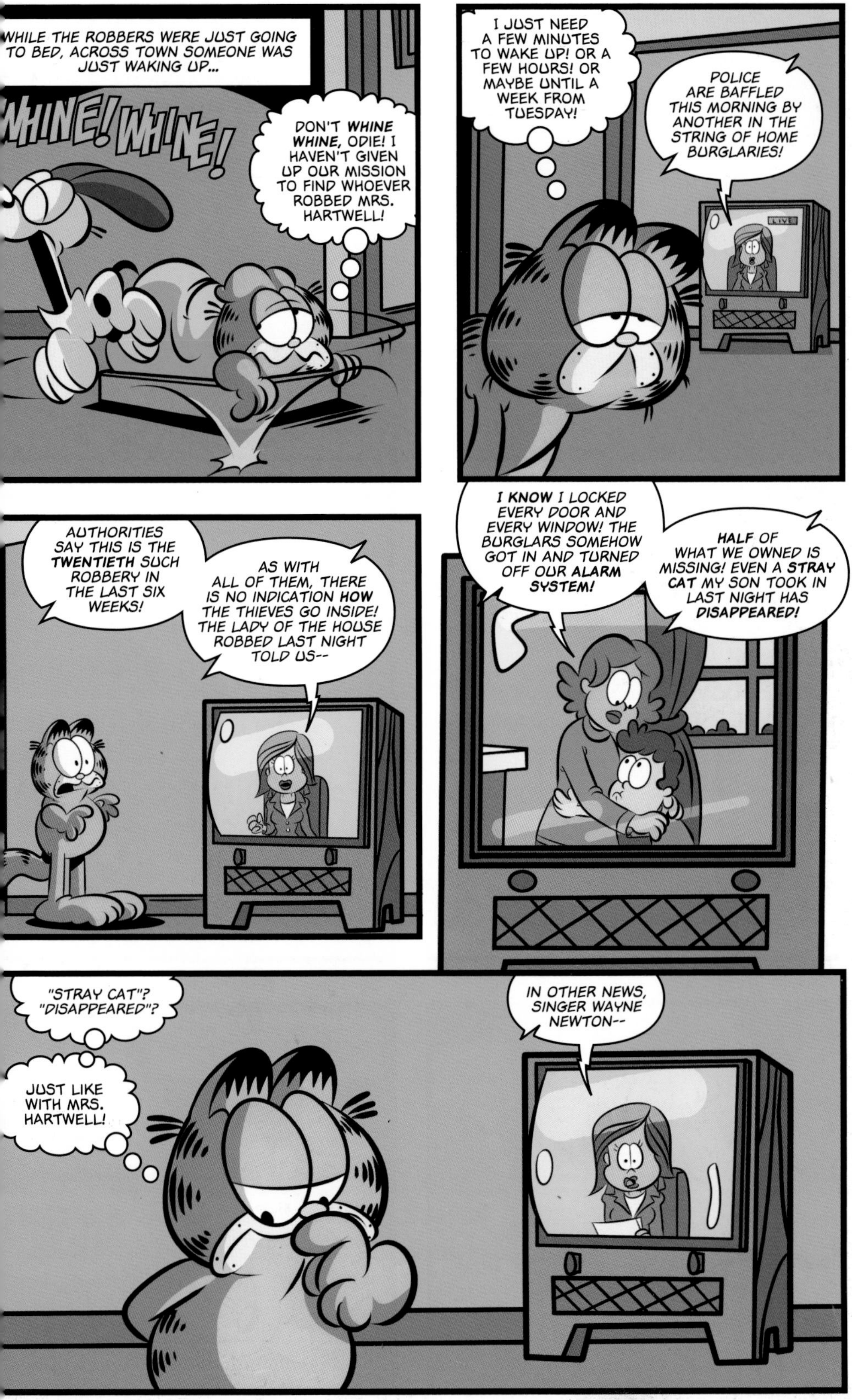

WHILE THE ROBBERS WERE JUST GOING TO BED, ACROSS TOWN SOMEONE WAS JUST WAKING UP...
WHINE! WHINE!
DON'T WHINE WHINE, ODIE! I HAVEN'T GIVEN UP OUR MISSION TO FIND WHOEVER ROBBED MRS. HARTWELL!
I JUST NEED A FEW MINUTES TO WAKE UP! OR A FEW HOURS! OR MAYBE UNTIL A WEEK FROM TUESDAY!
POLICE ARE BAFFLED THIS MORNING BY ANOTHER IN THE STRING OF HOME BURGLARIES!
LIVE
AUTHORITIES SAY THIS IS THE TWENTIETH SUCH ROBBERY IN THE LAST SIX WEEKS!
AS WITH ALL OF THEM, THERE IS NO INDICATION HOW THE THIEVES GO INSIDE! THE LADY OF THE HOUSE ROBBED LAST NIGHT TOLD US--
I KNOW I LOCKED EVERY DOOR AND EVERY WINDOW! THE BURGLARS SOMEHOW GOT IN AND TURNED OFF OUR ALARM SYSTEM!
HALF OF WHAT WE OWNED IS MISSING! EVEN A STRAY CAT MY SON TOOK IN LAST NIGHT HAS DISAPPEARED!
"STRAY CAT"? "DISAPPEARED"?
JUST LIKE WITH MRS. HARTWELL!
IN OTHER NEWS, SINGER WAYNE NEWTON--

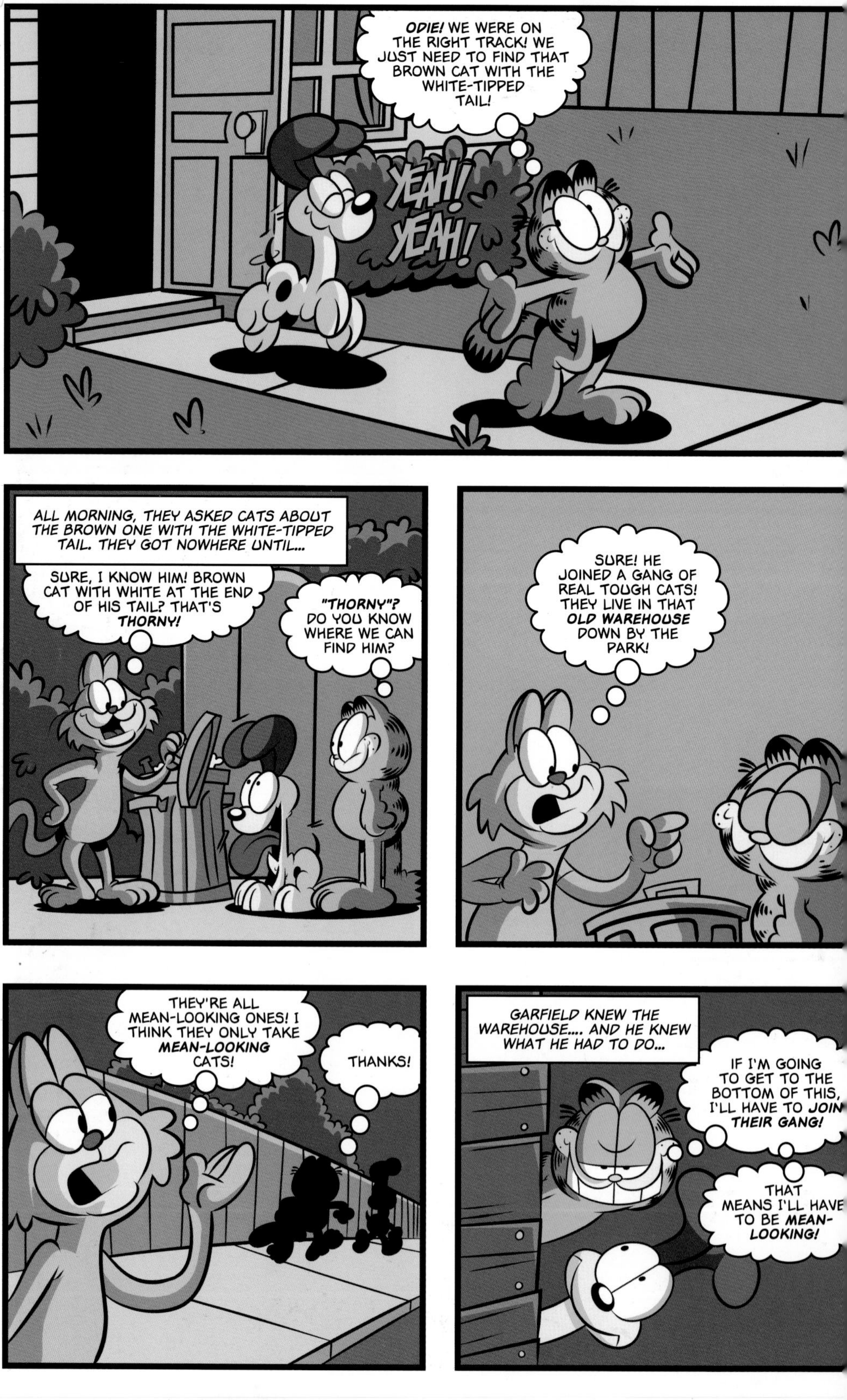
ODIE! WE WERE ON THE RIGHT TRACK! WE JUST NEED TO FIND THAT BROWN CAT WITH THE WHITE-TIPPED TAIL!
YEAH! YEAH!
ALL MORNING, THEY ASKED CATS ABOUT THE BROWN ONE WITH THE WHITE-TIPPED TAIL. THEY GOT NOWHERE UNTIL...
SURE, I KNOW HIM! BROWN CAT WITH WHITE AT THE END OF HIS TAIL? THAT'S THORNY!
"THORNY"? DO YOU KNOW WHERE WE CAN FIND HIM?
SURE! HE JOINED A GANG OF REAL TOUGH CATS! THEY LIVE IN THAT OLD WAREHOUSE DOWN BY THE PARK!
THEY'RE ALL MEAN-LOOKING ONES! I THINK THEY ONLY TAKE MEAN-LOOKING CATS!
THANKS!
GARFIELD KNEW THE WAREHOUSE.... AND HE KNEW WHAT HE HAD TO DO...
IF I'M GOING TO GET TO THE BOTTOM OF THIS, I'LL HAVE TO JOIN THEIR GANG!
THAT MEANS I'LL HAVE TO BE MEAN-LOOKING!

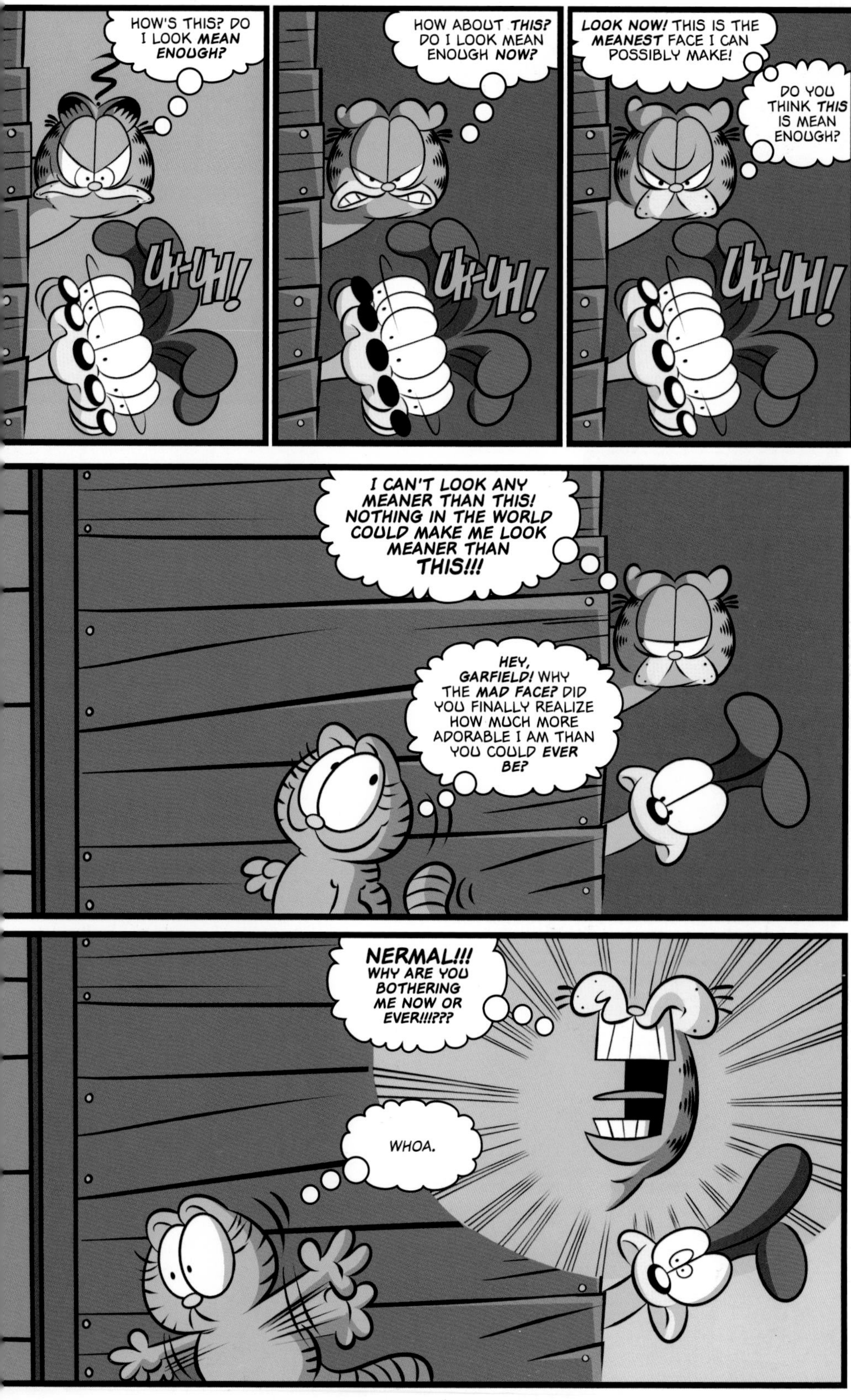
HOW'S THIS? DO I LOOK MEAN ENOUGH?
UH-UH!
HOW ABOUT THIS? DO I LOOK MEAN ENOUGH NOW?
UH-UH!
LOOK NOW! THIS IS THE MEANEST FACE I CAN POSSIBLY MAKE!
DO YOU THINK THIS IS MEAN ENOUGH?
UH-UH!
I CAN'T LOOK ANY MEANER THAN THIS! NOTHING IN THE WORLD COULD MAKE ME LOOK MEANER THAN THIS!!!
HEY, GARFIELD! WHY THE MAD FACE? DID YOU FINALLY REALIZE HOW MUCH MORE ADORABLE I AM THAN YOU COULD EVER BE?
NERMAL!!! WHY ARE YOU BOTHERING ME NOW OR EVER!!!???
WHOA.

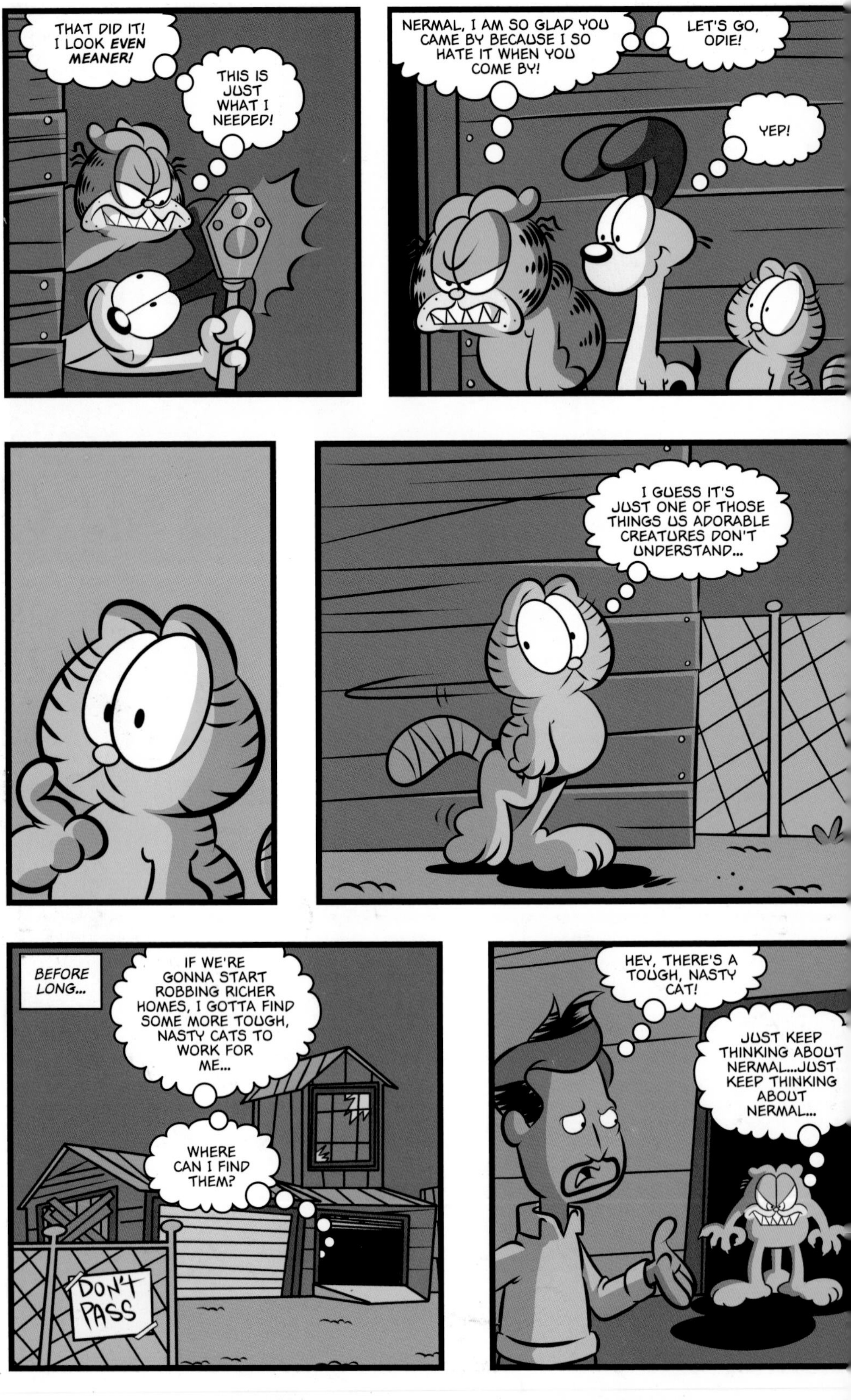
THAT DID IT! I LOOK *EVEN MEANER!*
THIS IS JUST WHAT I NEEDED!
NERMAL, I AM SO GLAD YOU CAME BY BECAUSE I SO HATE IT WHEN YOU COME BY!
LET'S GO, ODIE!
YEP!
I GUESS IT'S JUST ONE OF THOSE THINGS US ADORABLE CREATURES DON'T UNDERSTAND...
BEFORE LONG...
IF WE'RE GONNA START ROBBING RICHER HOMES, I GOTTA FIND SOME MORE TOUGH, NASTY CATS TO WORK FOR ME...
WHERE CAN I FIND THEM?
DON'T PASS
HEY, THERE'S A TOUGH, NASTY CAT!
JUST KEEP THINKING ABOUT NERMAL...JUST KEEP THINKING ABOUT NERMAL...

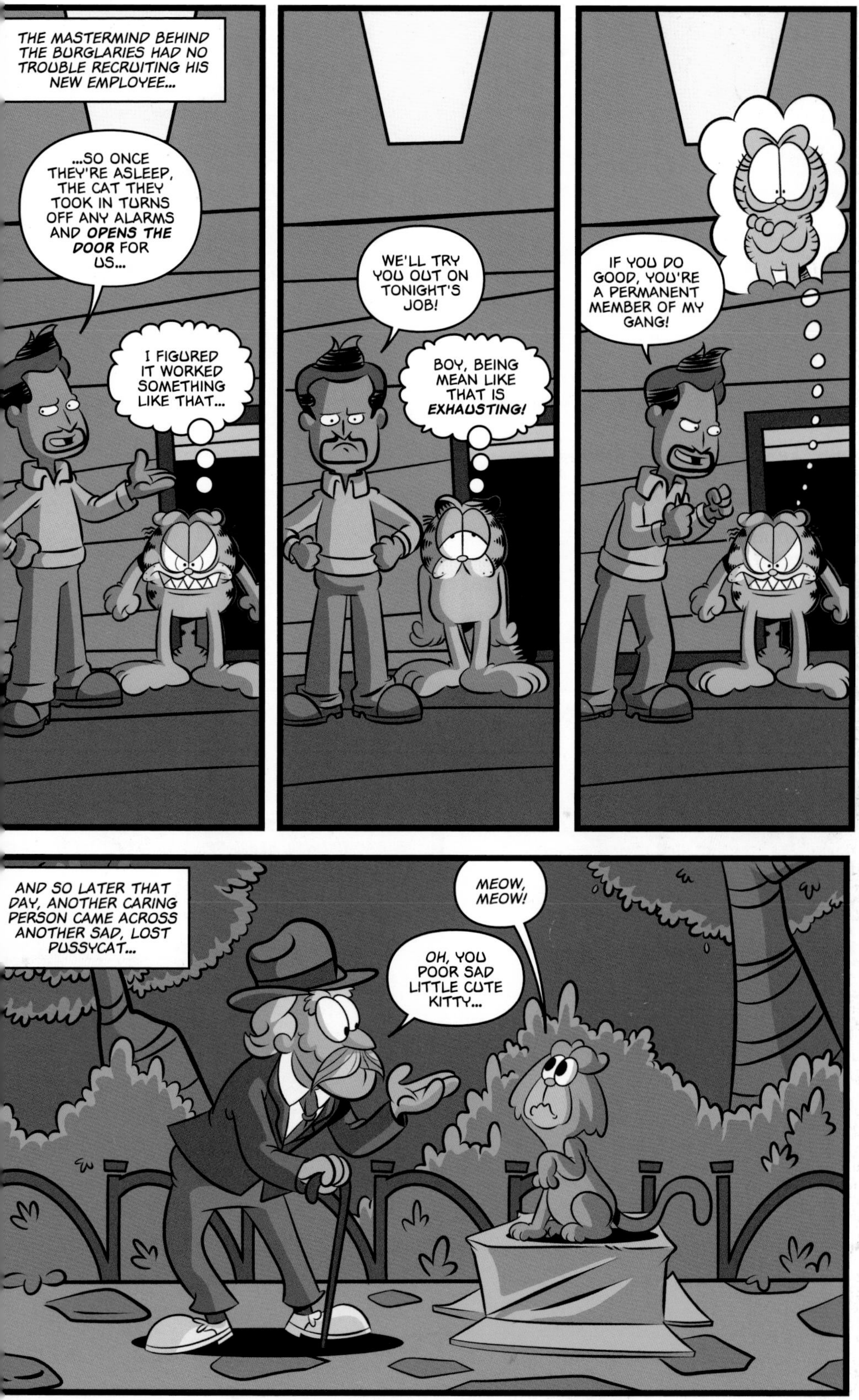
THE MASTERMIND BEHIND THE BURGLARIES HAD NO TROUBLE RECRUITING HIS NEW EMPLOYEE...
...SO ONCE THEY'RE ASLEEP, THE CAT THEY TOOK IN TURNS OFF ANY ALARMS AND OPENS THE DOOR FOR US...
I FIGURED IT WORKED SOMETHING LIKE THAT...
WE'LL TRY YOU OUT ON TONIGHT'S JOB!
BOY, BEING MEAN LIKE THAT IS EXHAUSTING!
IF YOU DO GOOD, YOU'RE A PERMANENT MEMBER OF MY GANG!
AND SO LATER THAT DAY, ANOTHER CARING PERSON CAME ACROSS ANOTHER SAD, LOST PUSSYCAT...
MEOW, MEOW!
OH, YOU POOR SAD LITTLE CUTE KITTY...

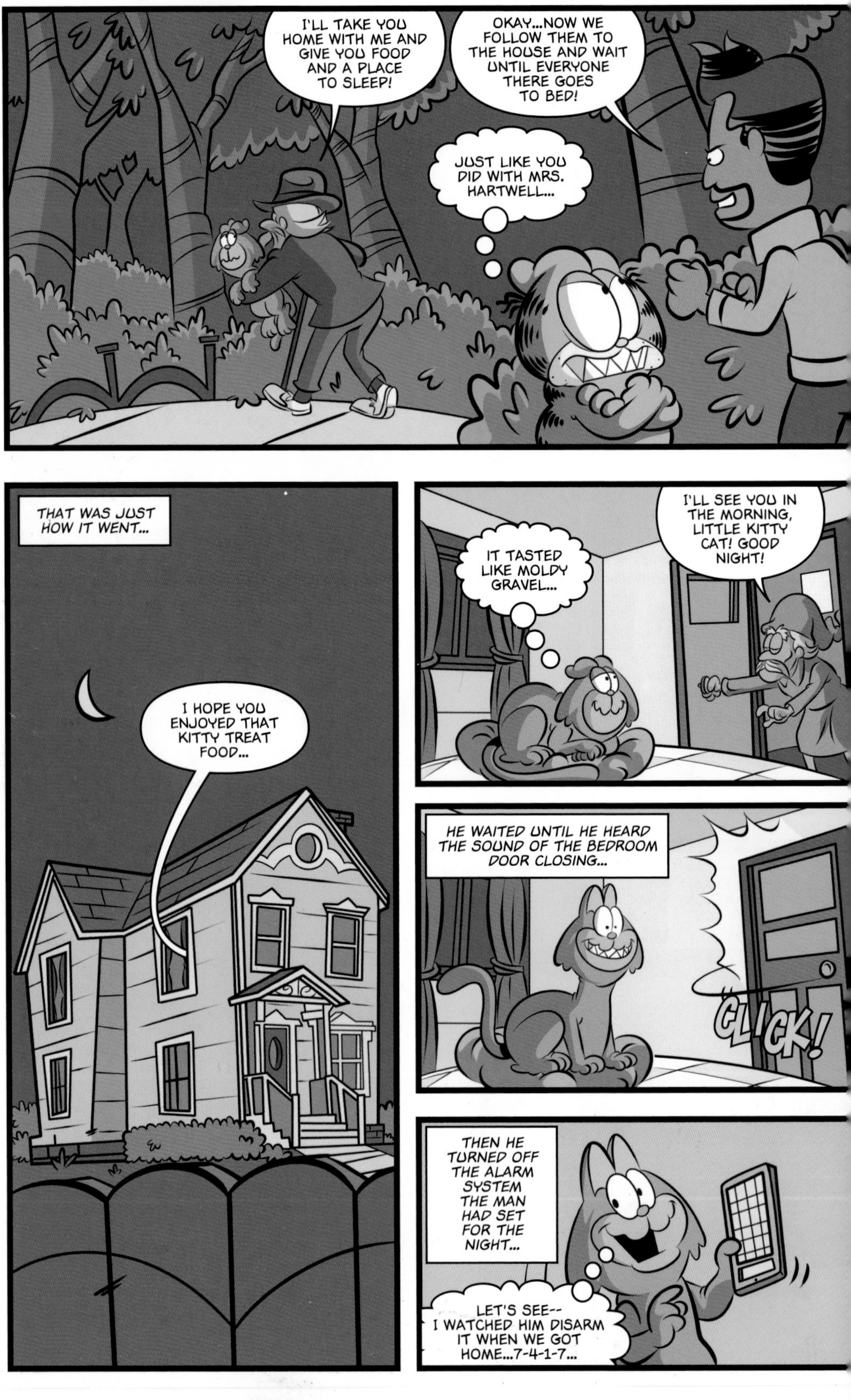
I'LL TAKE YOU HOME WITH ME AND GIVE YOU FOOD AND A PLACE TO SLEEP!
OKAY...NOW WE FOLLOW THEM TO THE HOUSE AND WAIT UNTIL EVERYONE THERE GOES TO BED!
JUST LIKE YOU DID WITH MRS. HARTWELL...
THAT WAS JUST HOW IT WENT...
I HOPE YOU ENJOYED THAT KITTY TREAT FOOD...
IT TASTED LIKE MOLDY GRAVEL...
I'LL SEE YOU IN THE MORNING, LITTLE KITTY CAT! GOOD NIGHT!
HE WAITED UNTIL HE HEARD THE SOUND OF THE BEDROOM DOOR CLOSING...
CLICK!
THEN HE TURNED OFF THE ALARM SYSTEM THE MAN HAD SET FOR THE NIGHT...
LET'S SEE-- I WATCHED HIM DISARM IT WHEN WE GOT HOME...7-4-1-7...

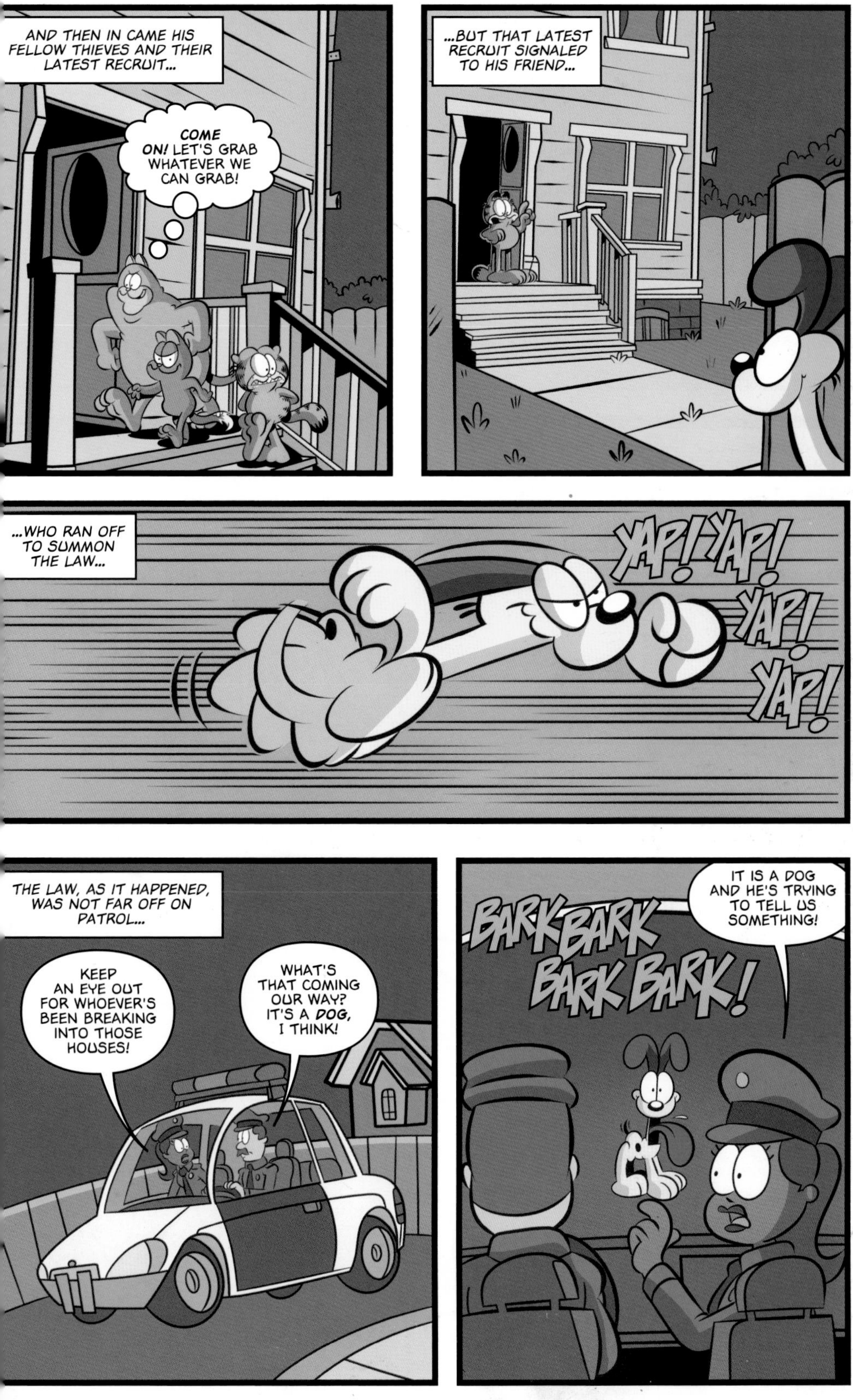
AND THEN IN CAME HIS FELLOW THIEVES AND THEIR LATEST RECRUIT...
COME ON! LET'S GRAB WHATEVER WE CAN GRAB!
...BUT THAT LATEST RECRUIT SIGNALED TO HIS FRIEND...
...WHO RAN OFF TO SUMMON THE LAW...
YAP! YAP! YAP! YAP!
THE LAW, AS IT HAPPENED, WAS NOT FAR OFF ON PATROL...
KEEP AN EYE OUT FOR WHOEVER'S BEEN BREAKING INTO THOSE HOUSES!
WHAT'S THAT COMING OUR WAY? IT'S A DOG, I THINK!
BARK BARK BARK BARK!
IT IS A DOG AND HE'S TRYING TO TELL US SOMETHING!

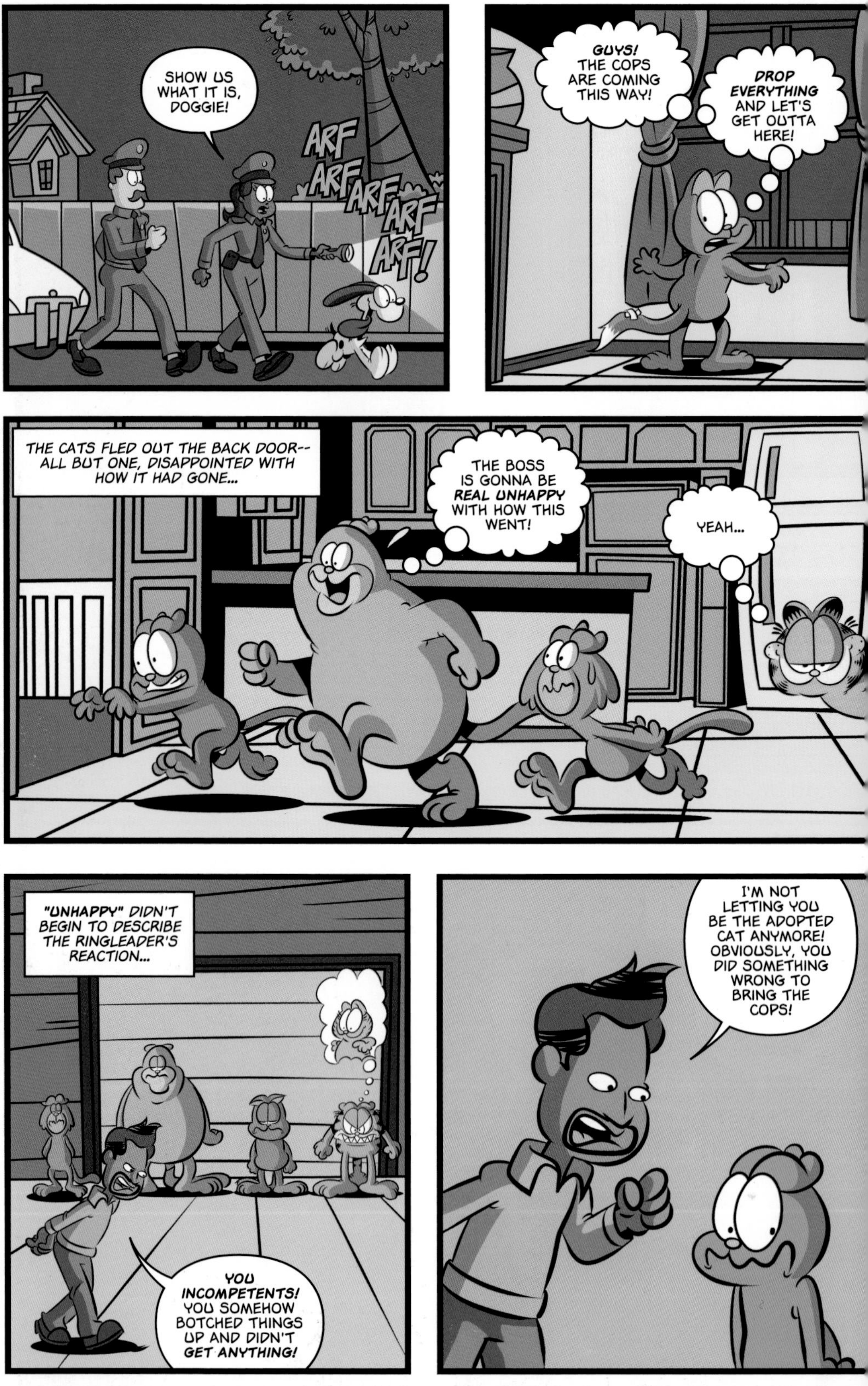
SHOW US WHAT IT IS, DOGGIE!
ARF ARF ARF ARF ARF!
GUYS! THE COPS ARE COMING THIS WAY!
DROP EVERYTHING AND LET'S GET OUTTA HERE!
THE CATS FLED OUT THE BACK DOOR-- ALL BUT ONE, DISAPPOINTED WITH HOW IT HAD GONE...
THE BOSS IS GONNA BE REAL UNHAPPY WITH HOW THIS WENT!
YEAH...
"UNHAPPY" DIDN'T BEGIN TO DESCRIBE THE RINGLEADER'S REACTION...
YOU INCOMPETENTS! YOU SOMEHOW BOTCHED THINGS UP AND DIDN'T GET ANYTHING!
I'M NOT LETTING YOU BE THE ADOPTED CAT ANYMORE! OBVIOUSLY, YOU DID SOMETHING WRONG TO BRING THE COPS!

MAYBE I'LL TRY THE *NEW CAT* OUT!

HOW ABOUT IT? CAN YOU MAKE A REAL SWEET *"CUTE KITTY"* FACE?

PERFECT!

THAT AFTERNOON, GARFIELD AND ODIE FOLLOWED A MAN HOME FROM HIS JOB...

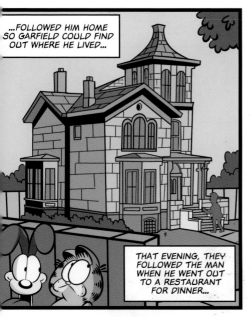

...FOLLOWED HIM HOME SO GARFIELD COULD FIND OUT WHERE HE LIVED...

THAT EVENING, THEY FOLLOWED THE MAN WHEN HE WENT OUT TO A RESTAURANT FOR DINNER...

WHEN HE CAME OUT, HE FOUND A SAD CUTE KITTY OUTSIDE THE RESTAURANT...

OH, YOU *POOR LOST LITTLE KITTY!* I'LL TAKE YOU HOME WITH ME!

GREAT! THAT GUY LOOKS LIKE HE REALLY HAS MONEY!

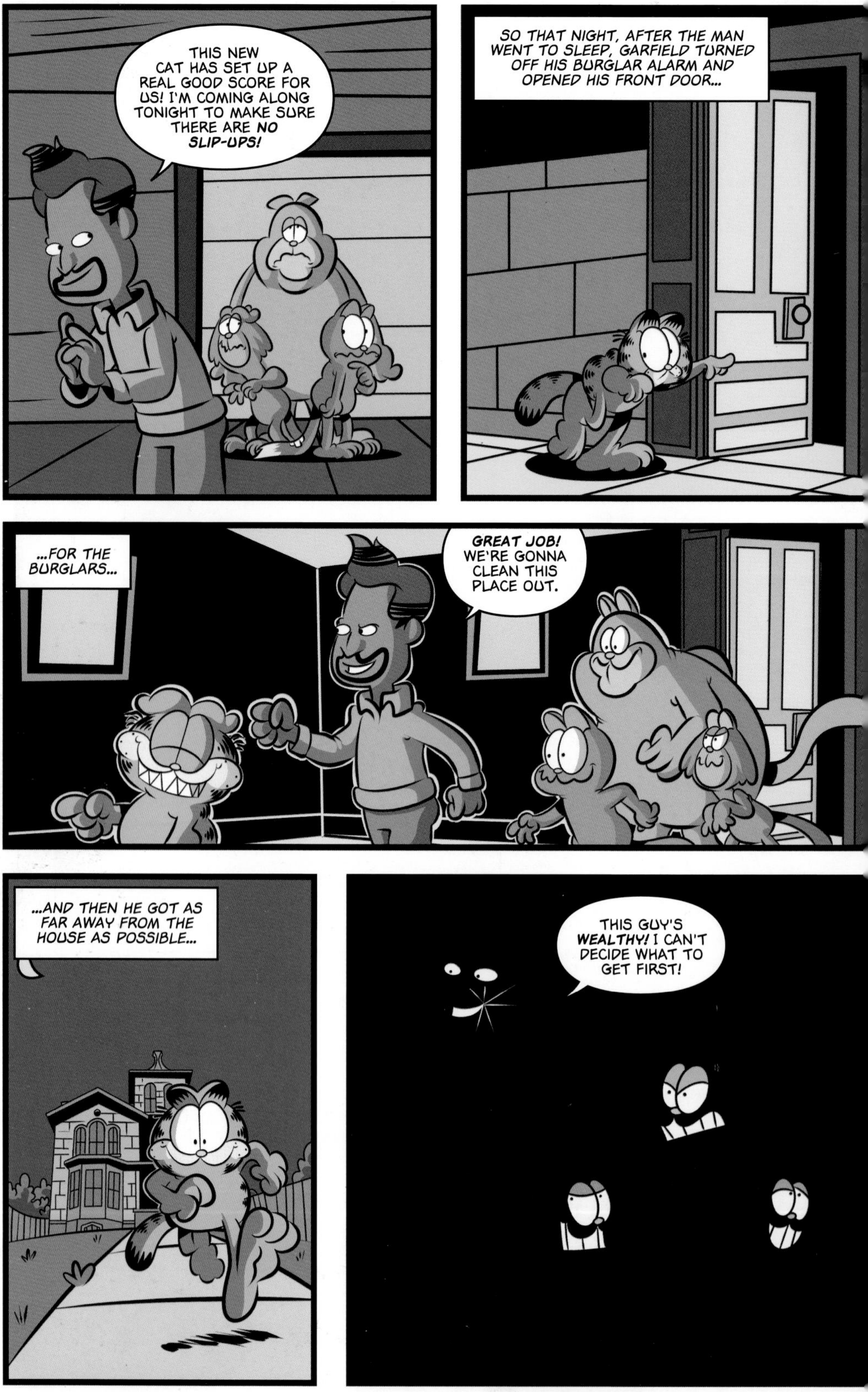
THIS NEW CAT HAS SET UP A REAL GOOD SCORE FOR US! I'M COMING ALONG TONIGHT TO MAKE SURE THERE ARE NO SLIP-UPS!
SO THAT NIGHT, AFTER THE MAN WENT TO SLEEP, GARFIELD TURNED OFF HIS BURGLAR ALARM AND OPENED HIS FRONT DOOR...
...FOR THE BURGLARS...
GREAT JOB! WE'RE GONNA CLEAN THIS PLACE OUT.
...AND THEN HE GOT AS FAR AWAY FROM THE HOUSE AS POSSIBLE...
THIS GUY'S WEALTHY! I CAN'T DECIDE WHAT TO GET FIRST!

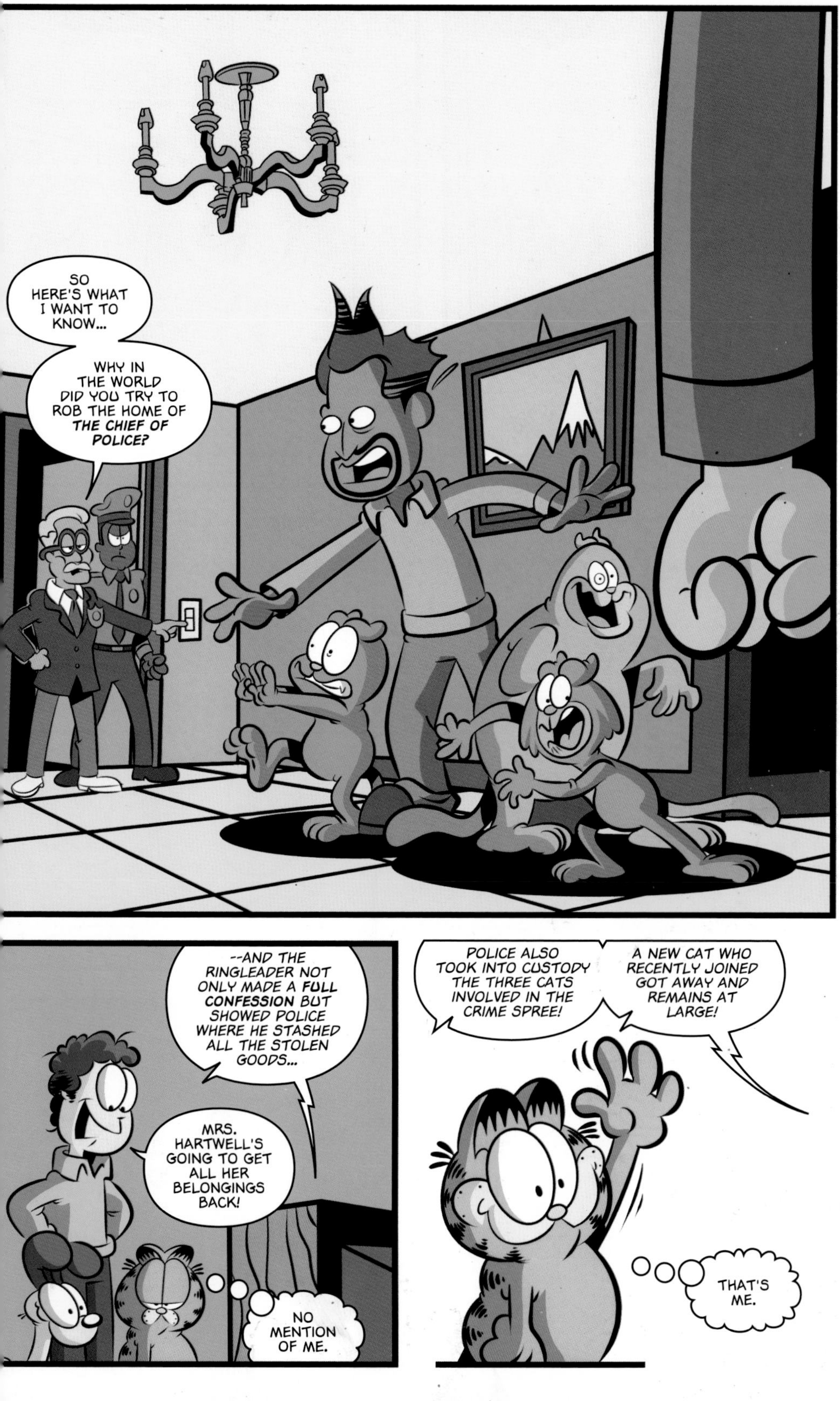
SO HERE'S WHAT I WANT TO KNOW...
WHY IN THE WORLD DID YOU TRY TO ROB THE HOME OF ***THE CHIEF OF POLICE?***
--AND THE RINGLEADER NOT ONLY MADE A **FULL CONFESSION** BUT SHOWED POLICE WHERE HE STASHED ALL THE STOLEN GOODS...
MRS. HARTWELL'S GOING TO GET ALL HER BELONGINGS BACK!
NO MENTION OF ME.
POLICE ALSO TOOK INTO CUSTODY THE THREE CATS INVOLVED IN THE CRIME SPREE!
A NEW CAT WHO RECENTLY JOINED GOT AWAY AND REMAINS AT LARGE!
THAT'S ME.

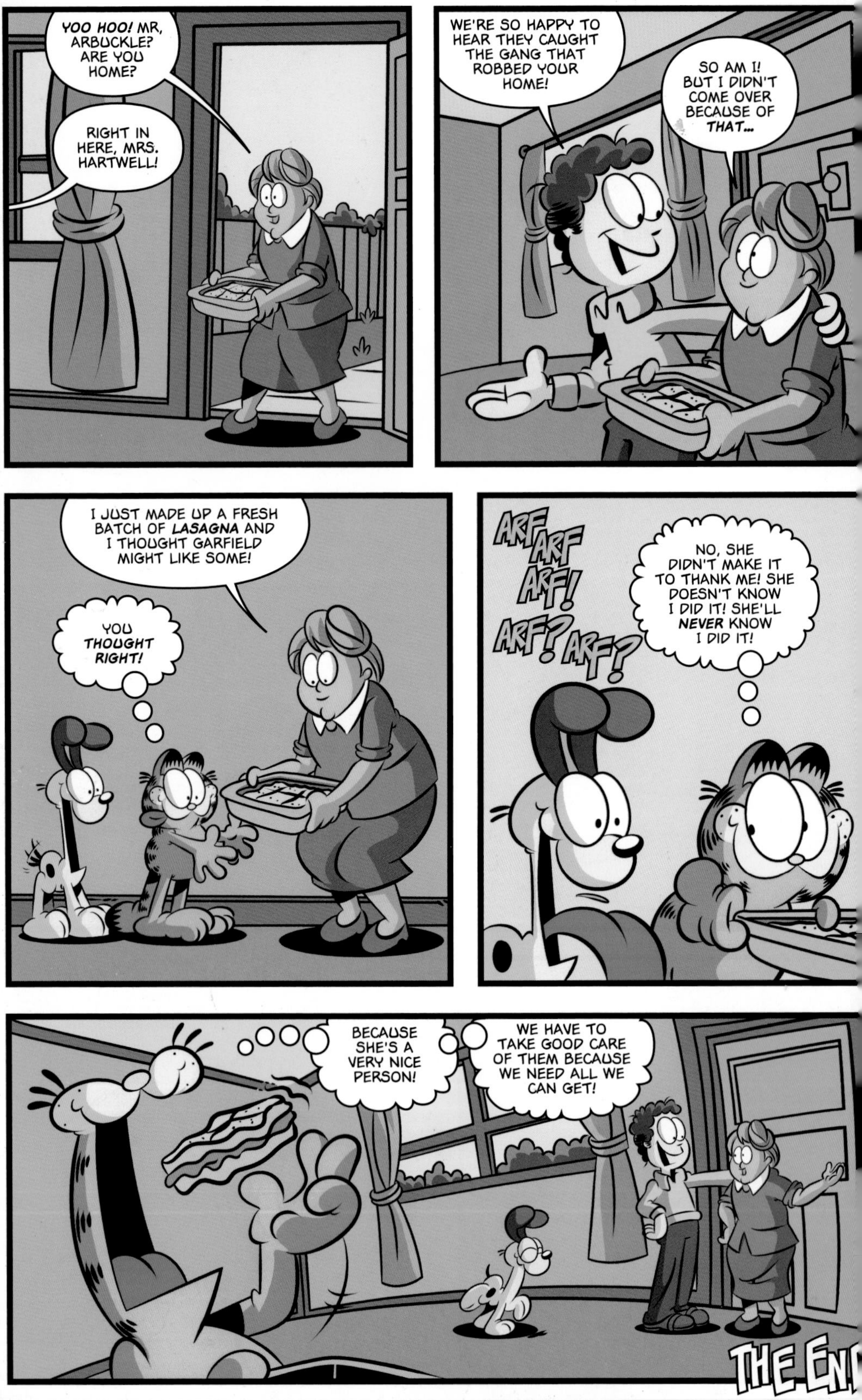
YOO HOO! MR, ARBUCKLE? ARE YOU HOME?
RIGHT IN HERE, MRS. HARTWELL!
WE'RE SO HAPPY TO HEAR THEY CAUGHT THE GANG THAT ROBBED YOUR HOME!
SO AM I! BUT I DIDN'T COME OVER BECAUSE OF THAT...
I JUST MADE UP A FRESH BATCH OF LASAGNA AND I THOUGHT GARFIELD MIGHT LIKE SOME!
YOU THOUGHT RIGHT!
ARF ARF ARF! ARF? ARF?
NO, SHE DIDN'T MAKE IT TO THANK ME! SHE DOESN'T KNOW I DID IT! SHE'LL NEVER KNOW I DID IT!
BECAUSE SHE'S A VERY NICE PERSON!
WE HAVE TO TAKE GOOD CARE OF THEM BECAUSE WE NEED ALL WE CAN GET!

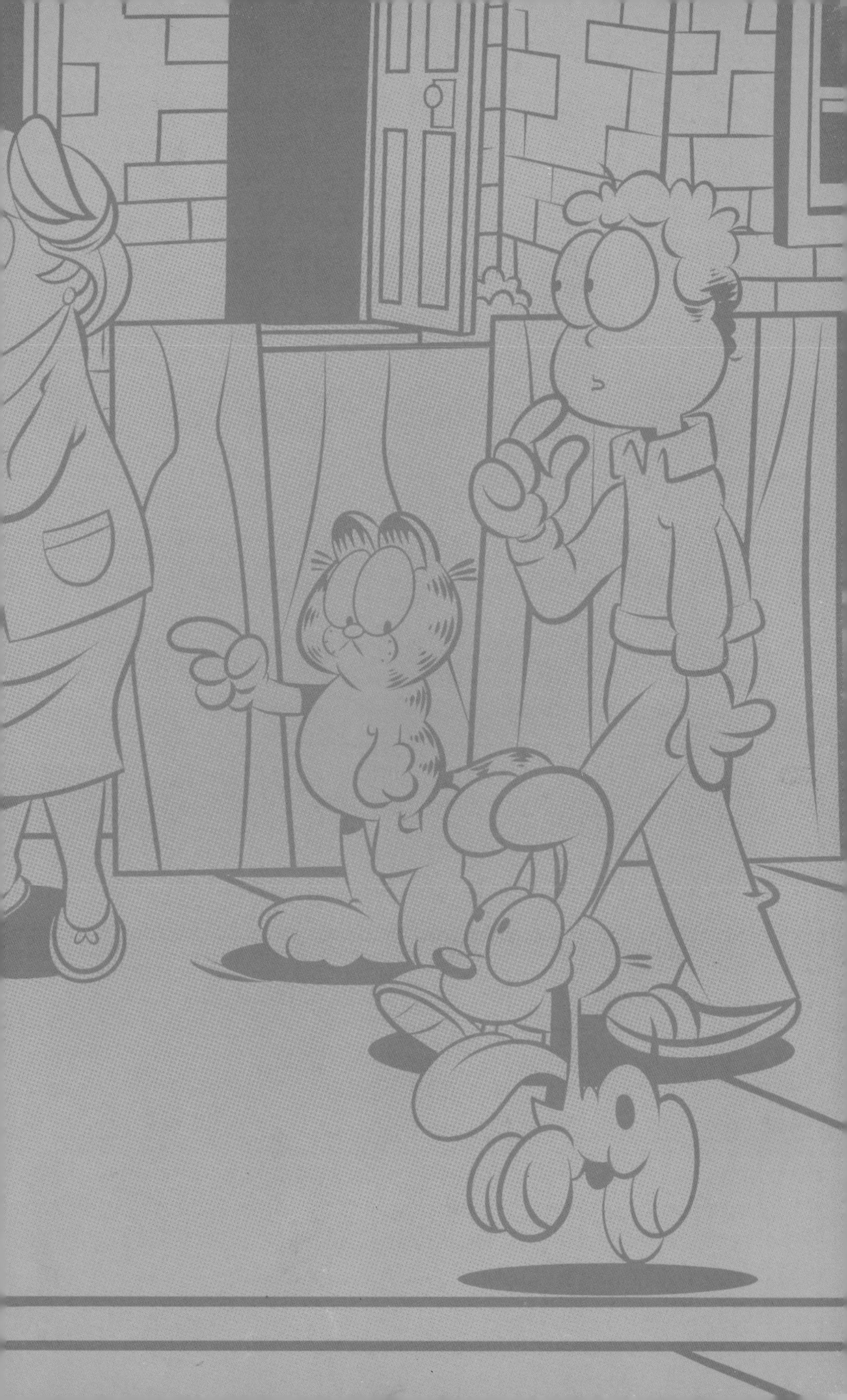

"DREAM BIG"

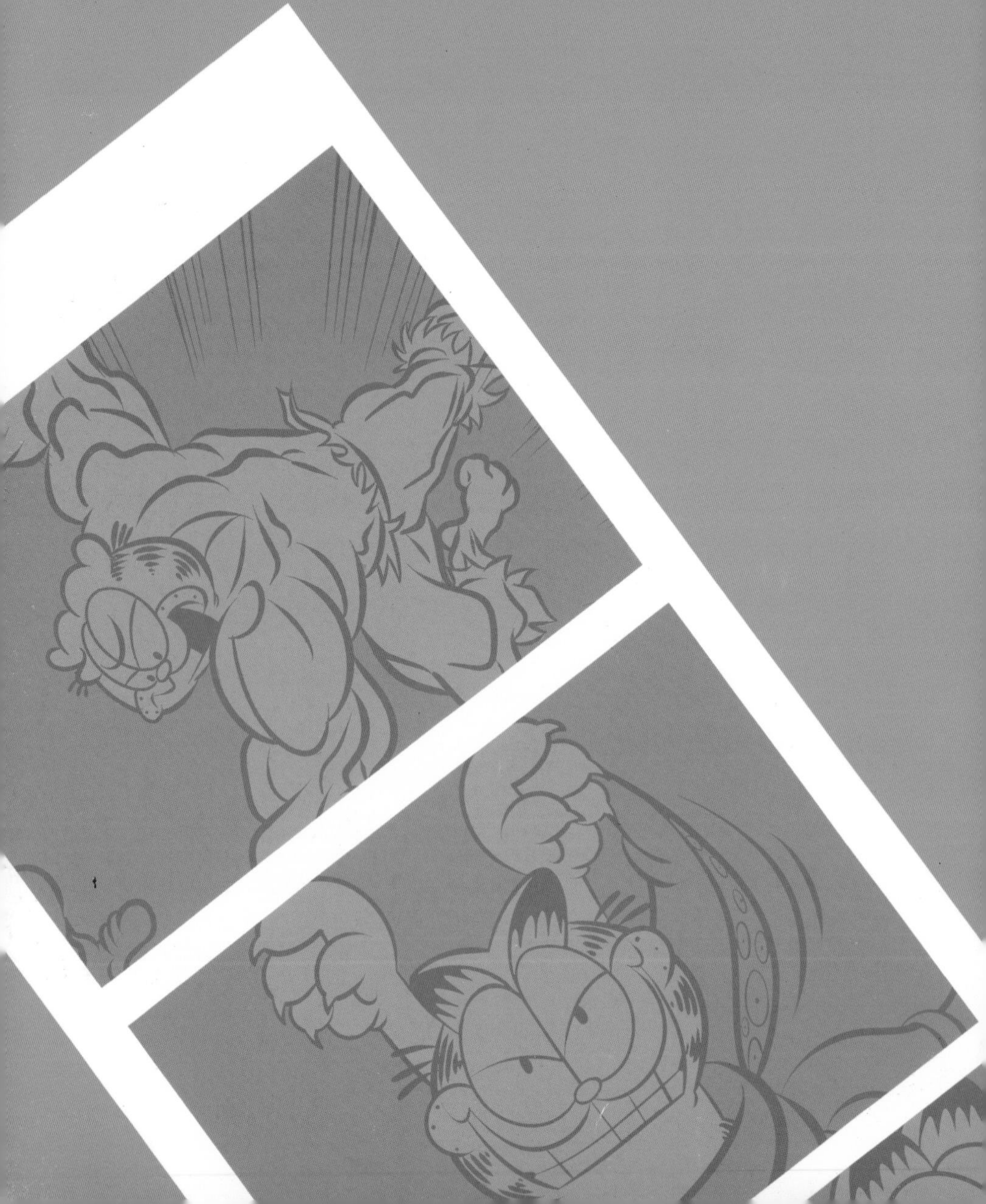

DREAM BIG

BY JUDD WINICK

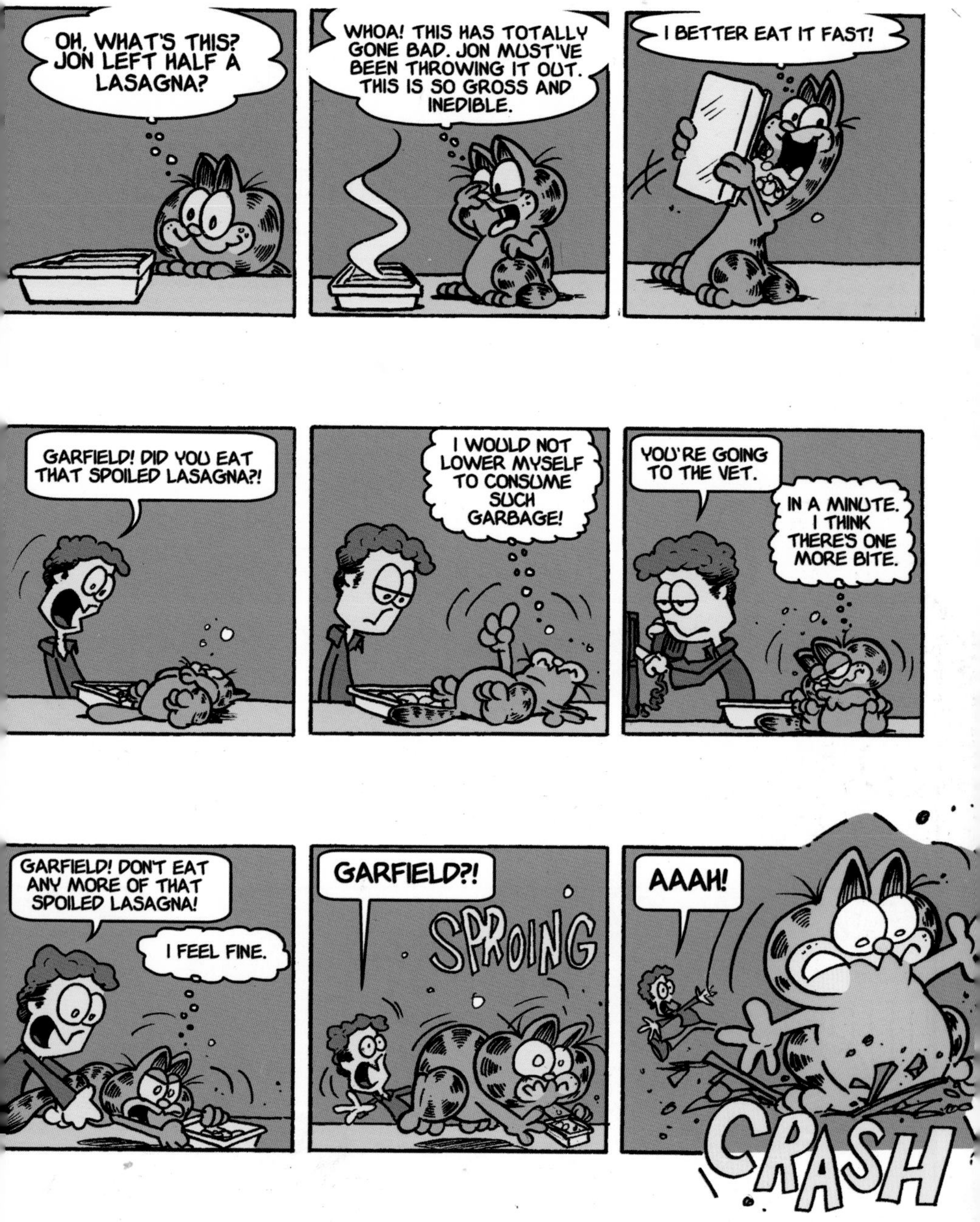

OH, WHAT'S THIS? JON LEFT HALF A LASAGNA?
WHOA! THIS HAS TOTALLY GONE BAD. JON MUST'VE BEEN THROWING IT OUT. THIS IS SO GROSS AND INEDIBLE.
I BETTER EAT IT FAST!
GARFIELD! DID YOU EAT THAT SPOILED LASAGNA?!
I WOULD NOT LOWER MYSELF TO CONSUME SUCH GARBAGE!
YOU'RE GOING TO THE VET.
IN A MINUTE. I THINK THERE'S ONE MORE BITE.
GARFIELD! DON'T EAT ANY MORE OF THAT SPOILED LASAGNA!
I FEEL FINE.
GARFIELD?!
SPROING
AAAH!
CRASH

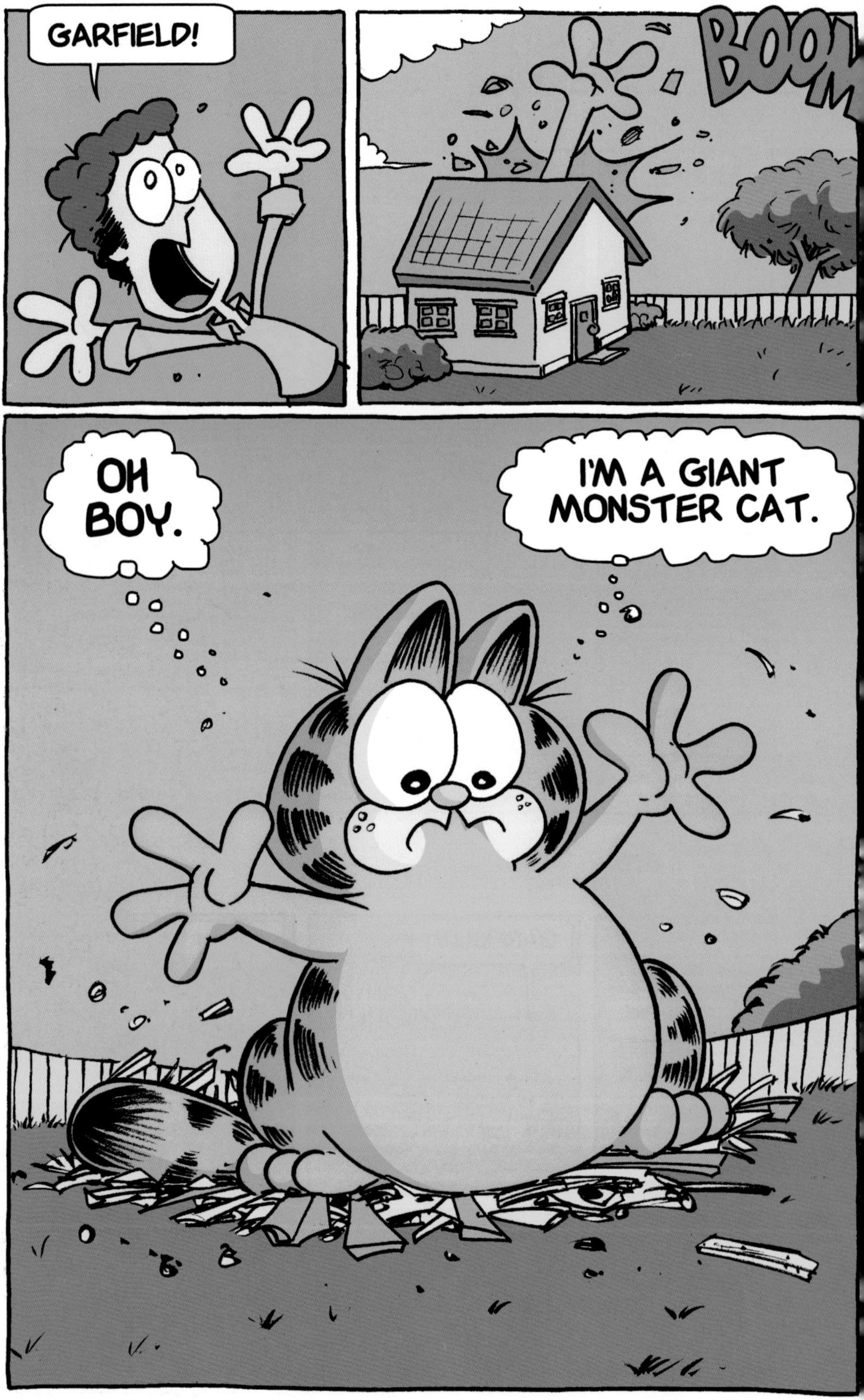
GARFIELD!
BOOM
OH BOY.
I'M A GIANT MONSTER CAT.

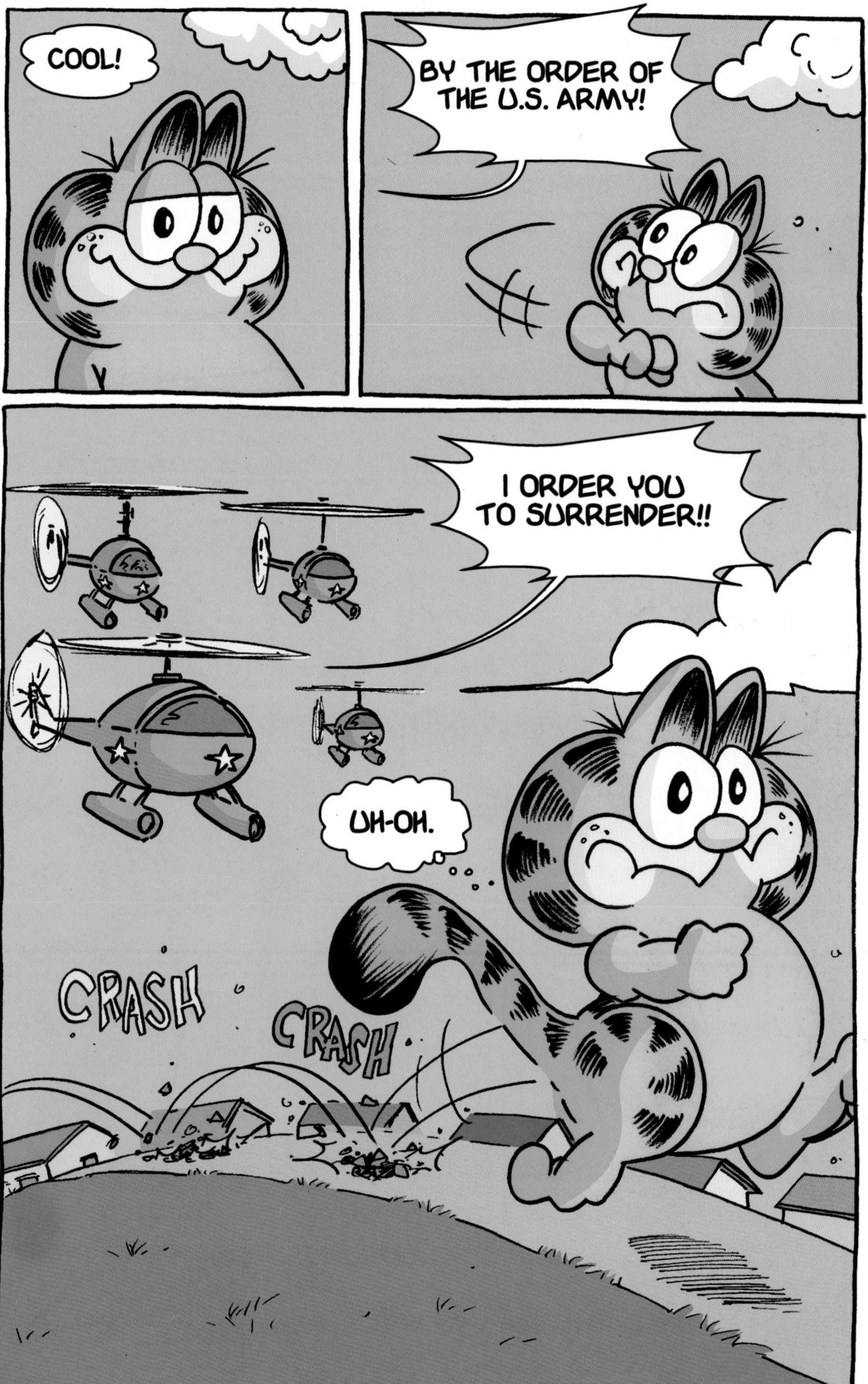
COOL!
BY THE ORDER OF THE U.S. ARMY!
I ORDER YOU TO SURRENDER!!
UH-OH.
CRASH
CRASH

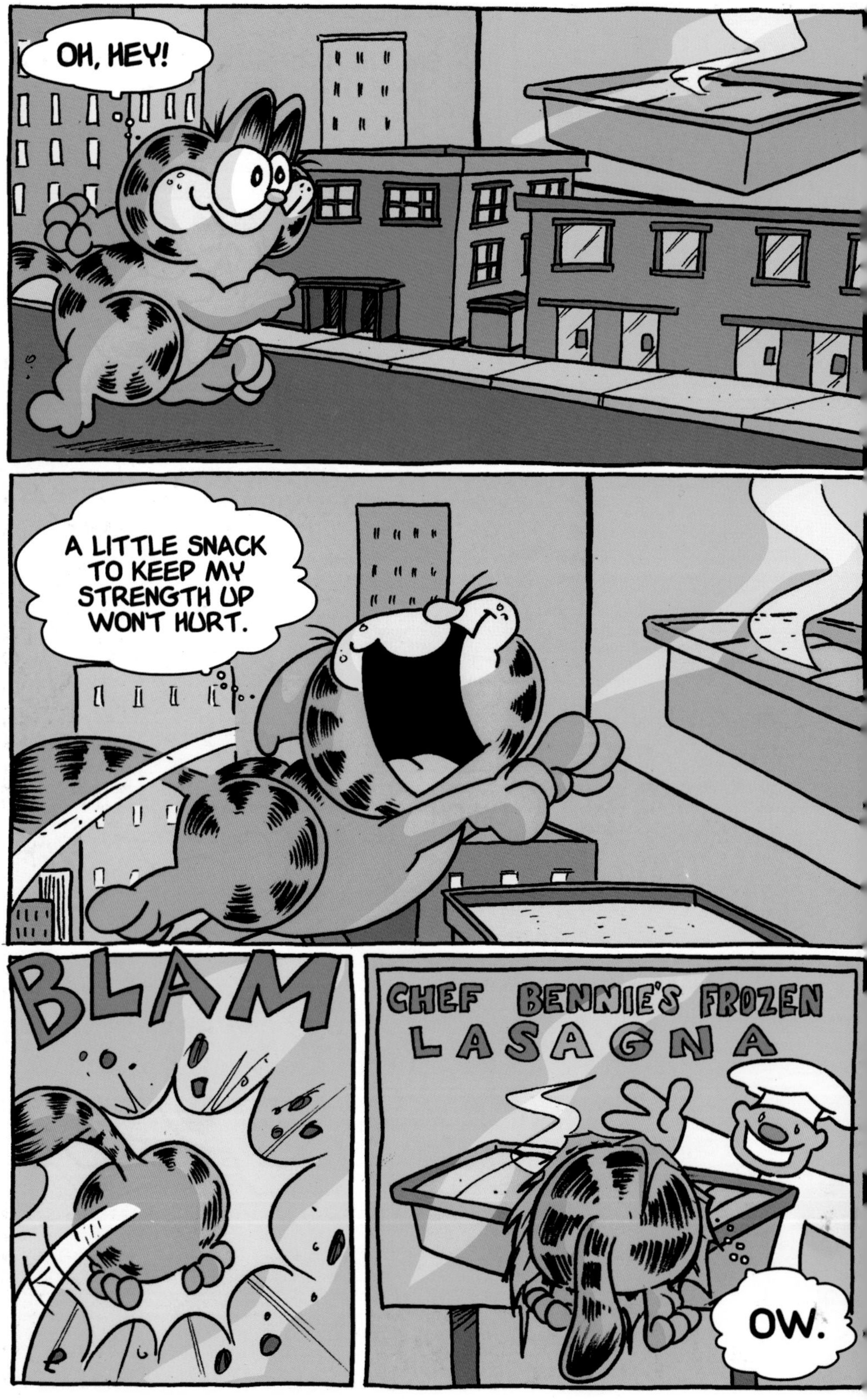
OH, HEY!
A LITTLE SNACK TO KEEP MY STRENGTH UP WON'T HURT.
BLAM
CHEF BENNIE'S FROZEN LASAGNA
OW.

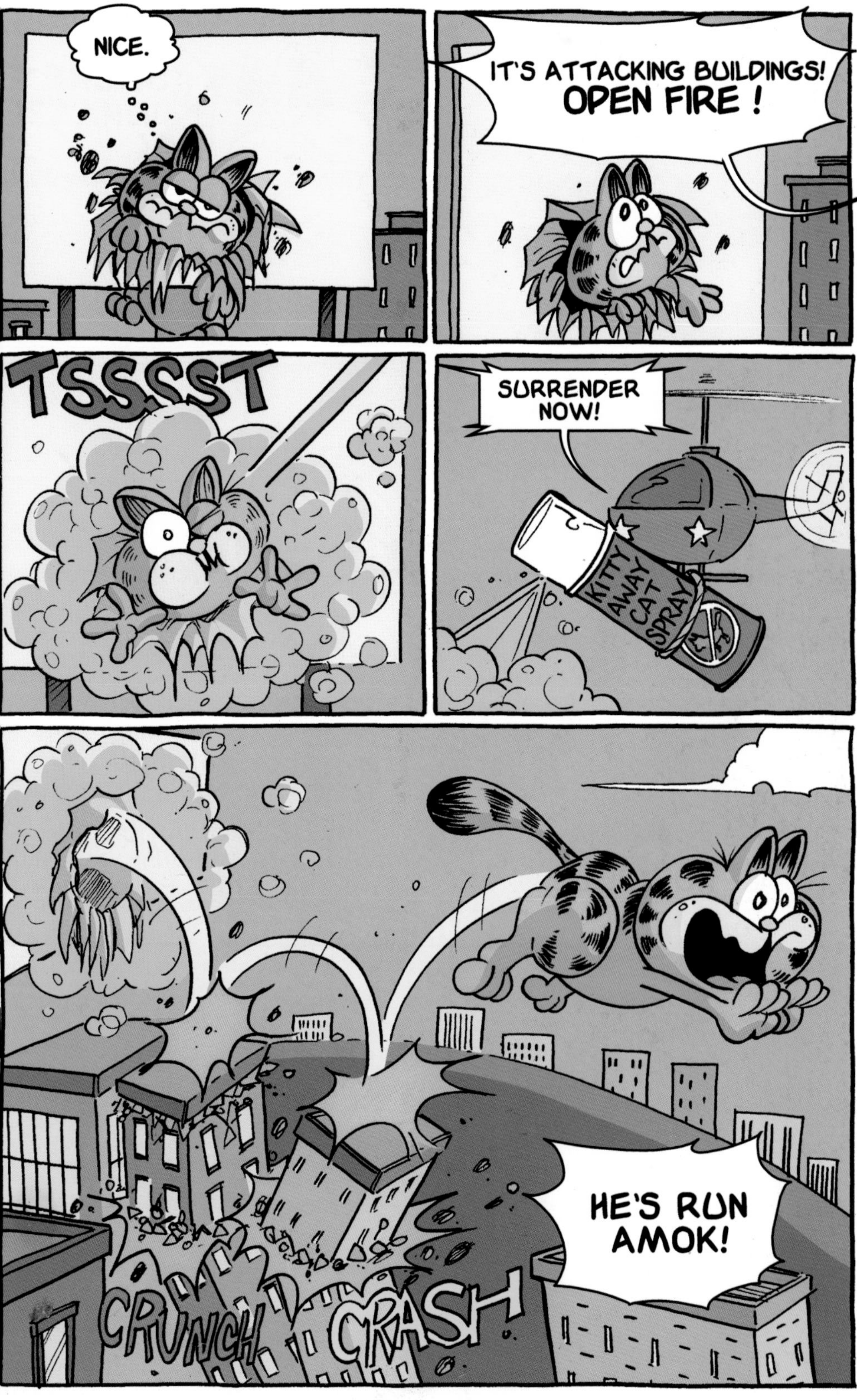
NICE.
IT'S ATTACKING BUILDINGS! OPEN FIRE !
TSSSST
SURRENDER NOW!
KITTY AWAY CAT SPRAY
HE'S RUN AMOK!
CRUNCH
CRASH

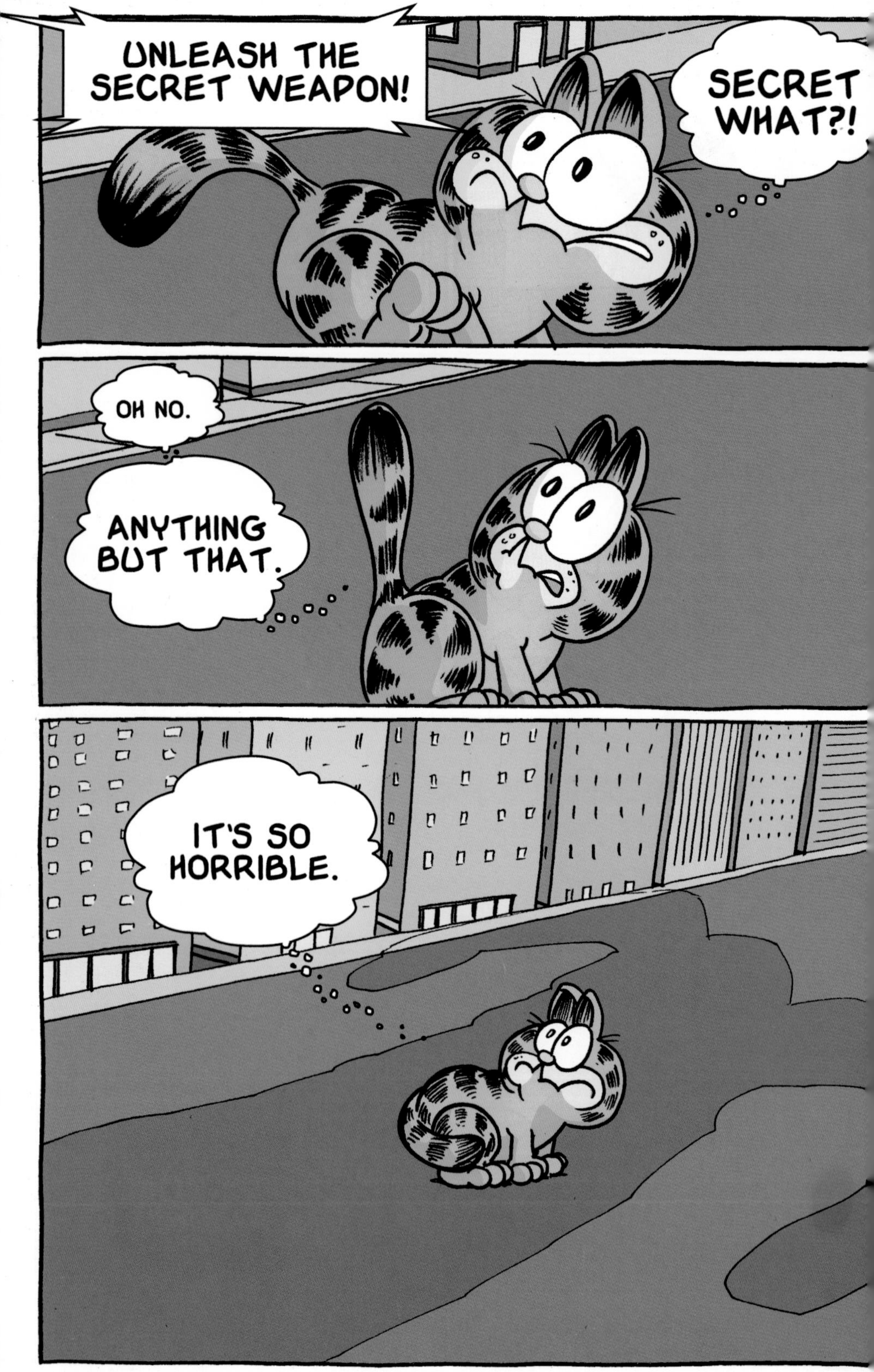
UNLEASH THE SECRET WEAPON!
SECRET WHAT?!
OH NO.
ANYTHING BUT THAT.
IT'S SO HORRIBLE.

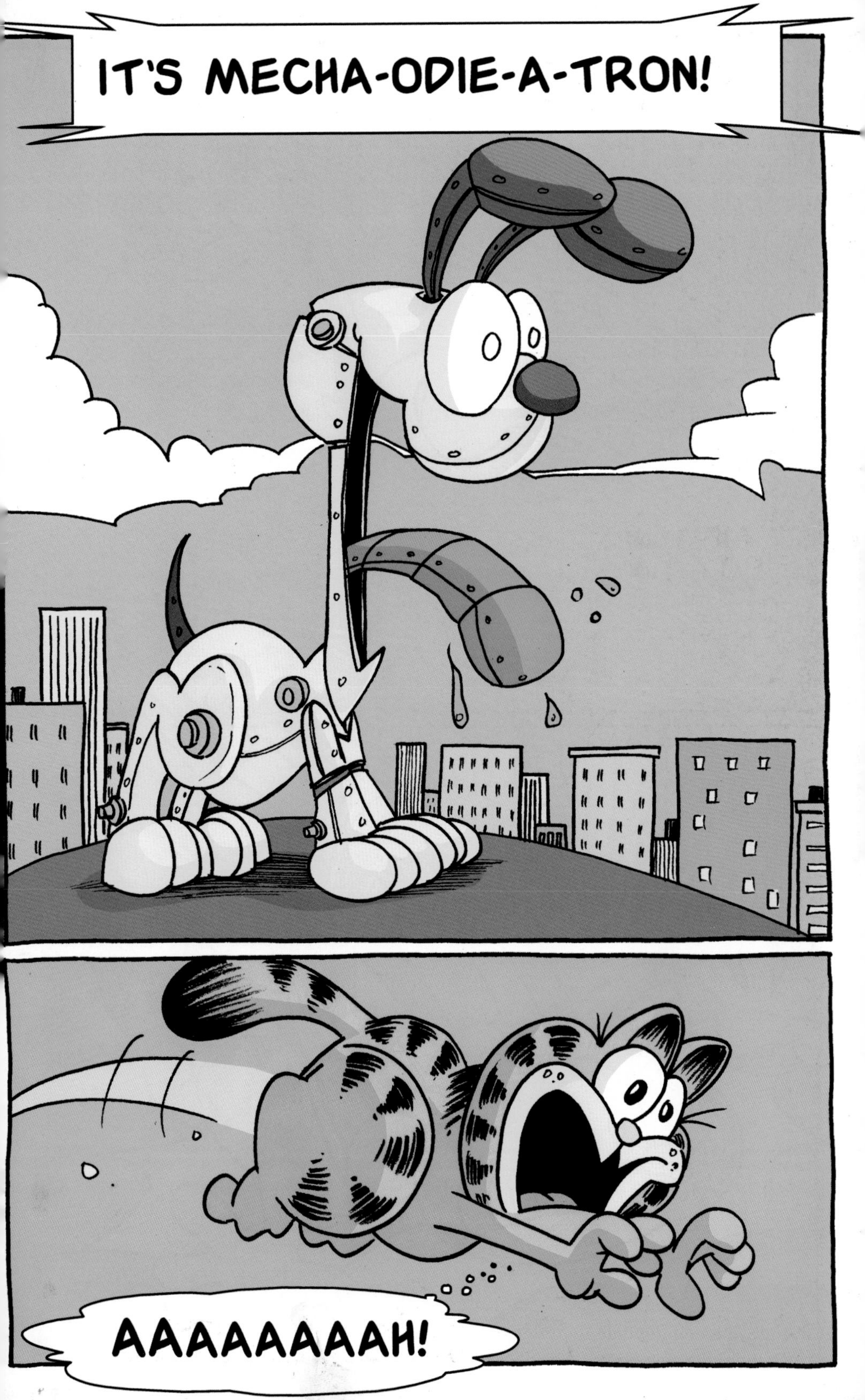
IT'S MECHA-ODIE-A-TRON!
AAAAAAAAH!

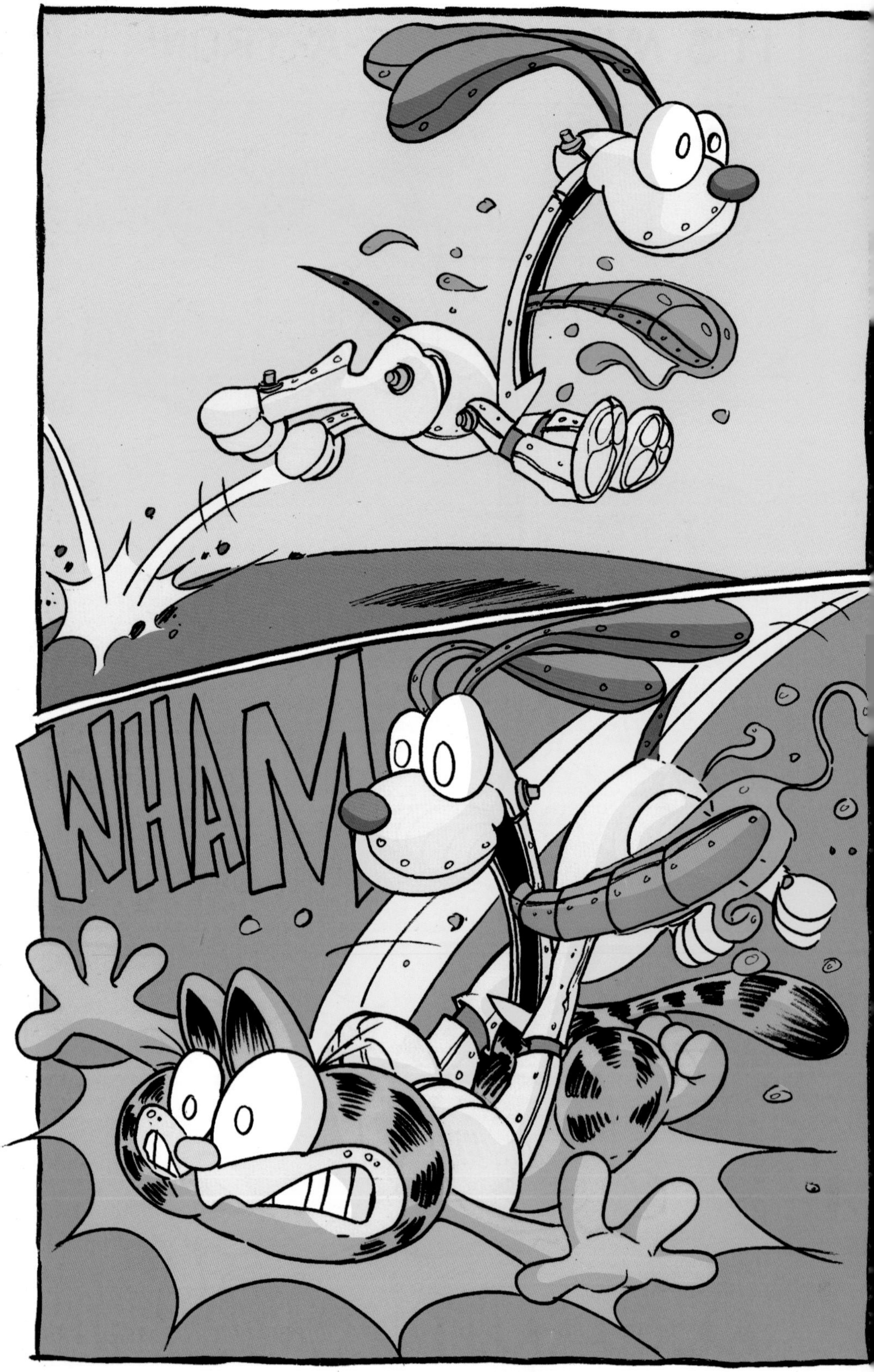
WHAM

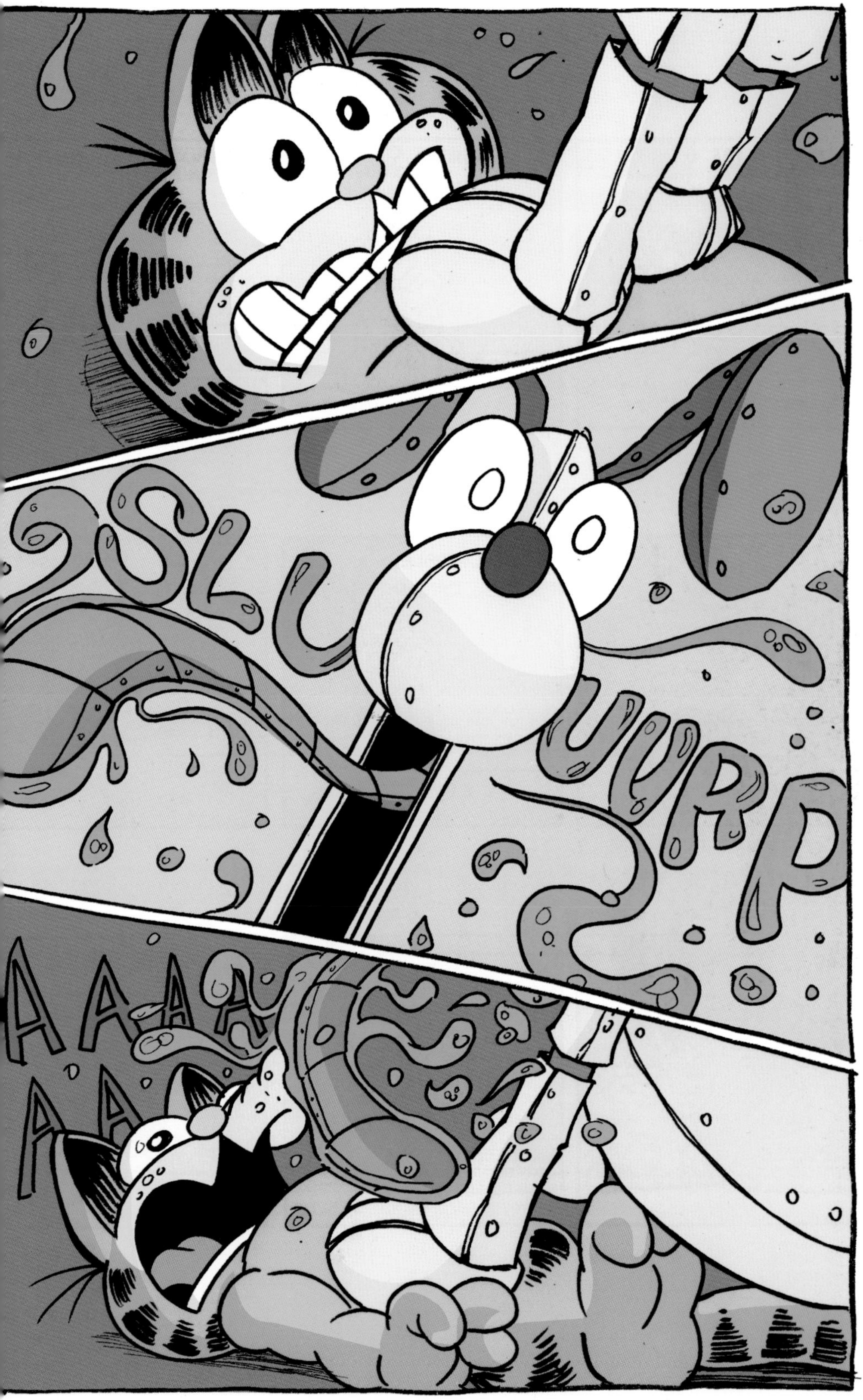
SLU
UURP
AAAA
AA

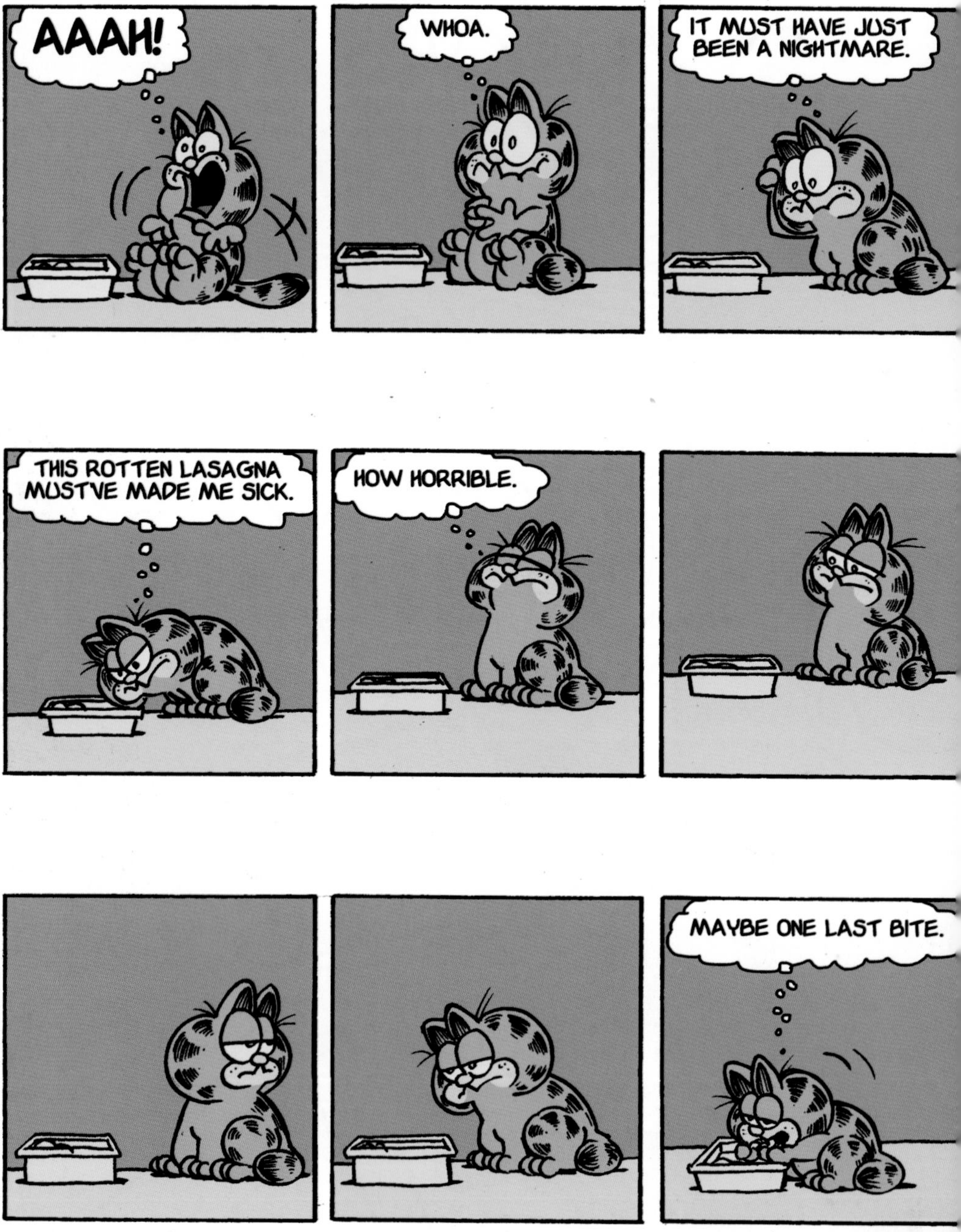
AAAH!
WHOA.
IT MUST HAVE JUST BEEN A NIGHTMARE.
THIS ROTTEN LASAGNA MUSTVE MADE ME SICK.
HOW HORRIBLE.
MAYBE ONE LAST BITE.

END

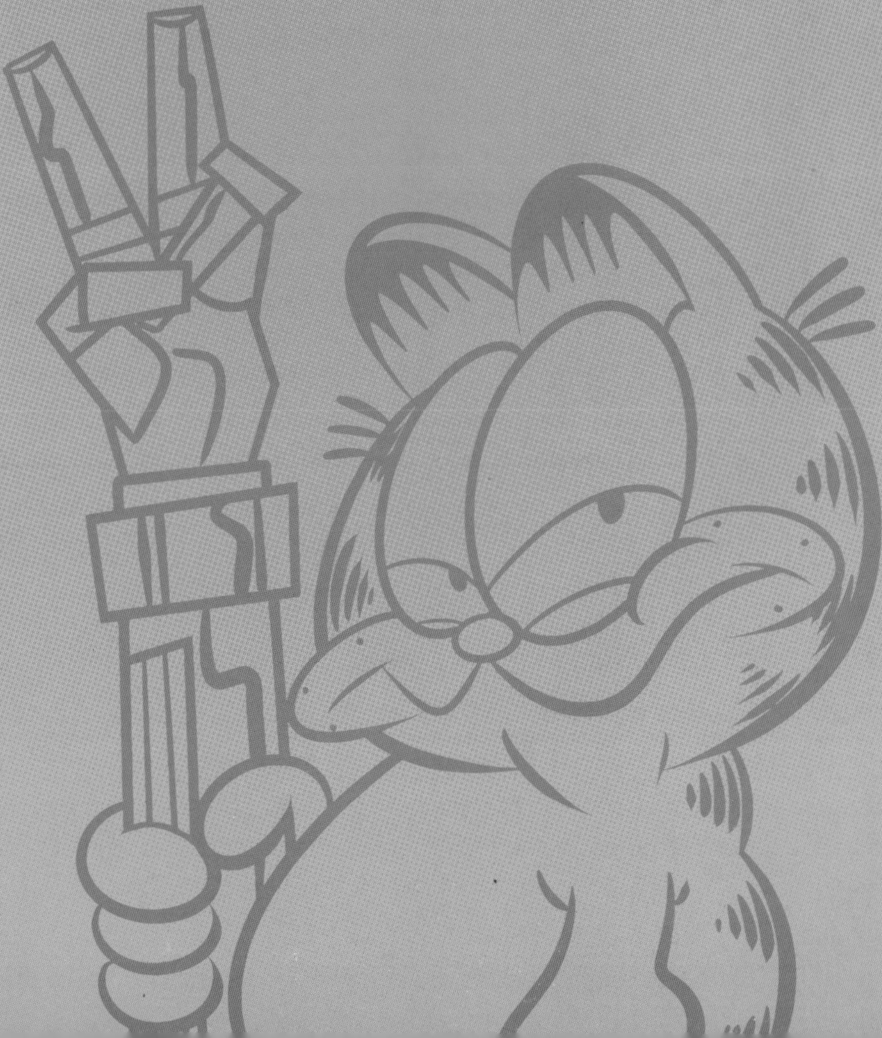

Vintage Attitude

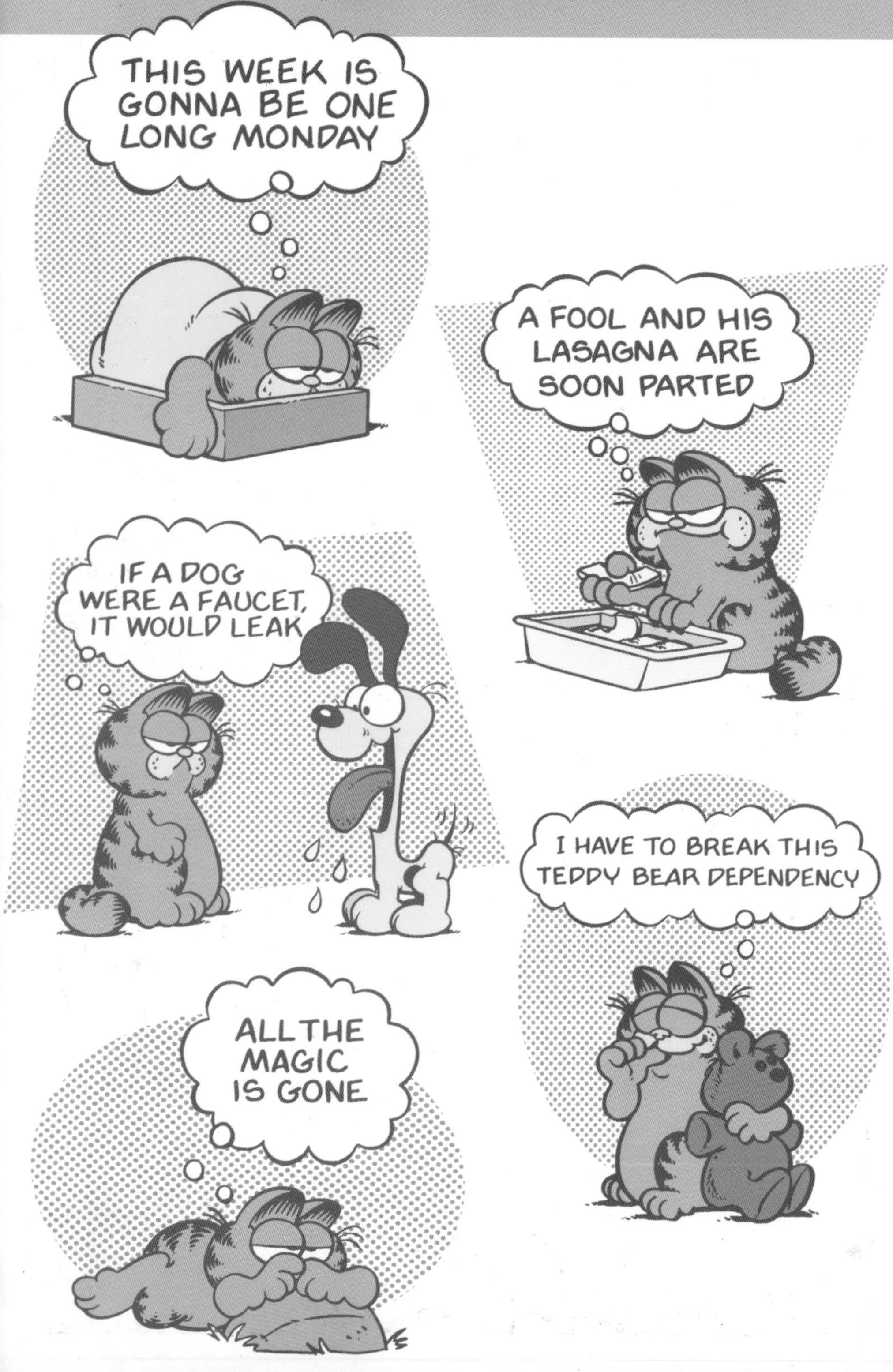
THIS WEEK IS GONNA BE ONE LONG MONDAY
A FOOL AND HIS LASAGNA ARE SOON PARTED
IF A DOG WERE A FAUCET, IT WOULD LEAK
I HAVE TO BREAK THIS TEDDY BEAR DEPENDENCY
ALL THE MAGIC IS GONE

TV Tabby

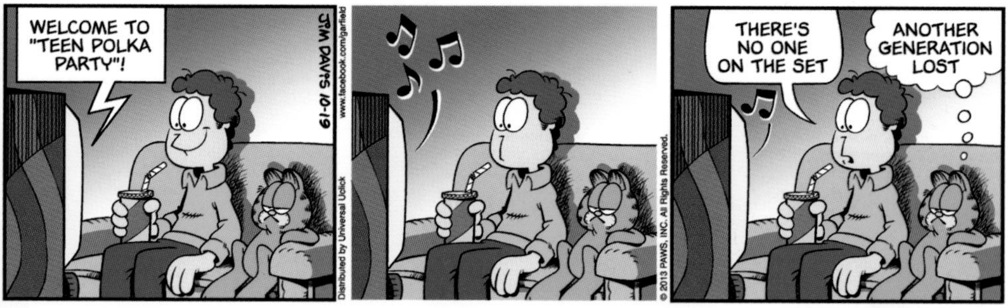

WELCOME TO "TEEN POLKA PARTY"!
JIM DAVIS 10-19
www.facebook.com/garfield
Distributed by Universal Uclick
THERE'S NO ONE ON THE SET
ANOTHER GENERATION LOST
© 2013 PAWS, INC. All Rights Reserved.

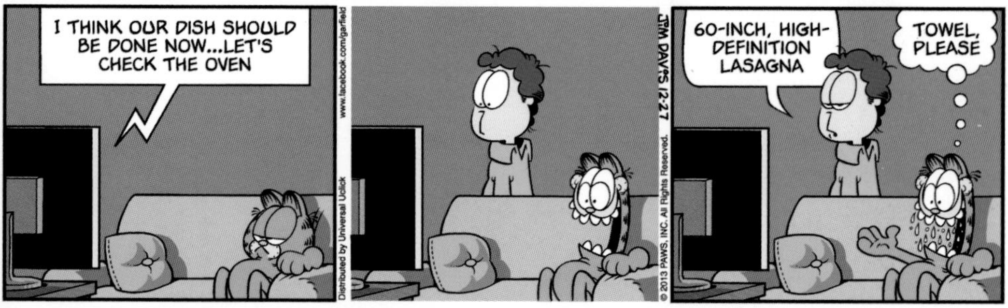

I THINK OUR DISH SHOULD BE DONE NOW...LET'S CHECK THE OVEN
www.facebook.com/garfield
Distributed by Universal Uclick
JIM DAVIS 12-27
© 2013 PAWS, INC. All Rights Reserved.
60-INCH, HIGH-DEFINITION LASAGNA
TOWEL, PLEASE

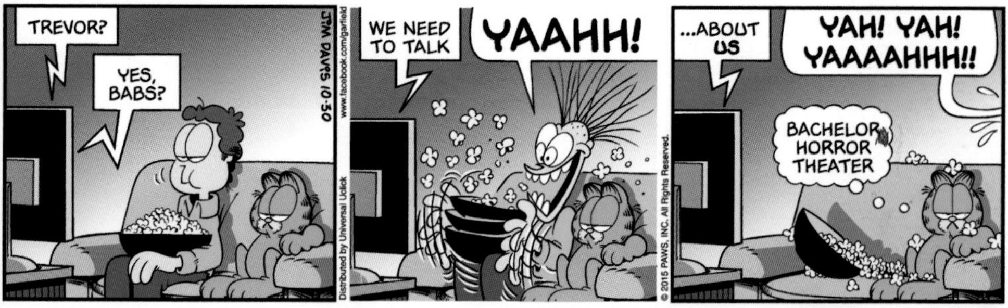

TREVOR?
YES, BABS?
JIM DAVIS 10-30
www.facebook.com/garfield
Distributed by Universal Uclick
WE NEED TO TALK
YAAHH!
© 2015 PAWS, INC. All Rights Reserved.
...ABOUT US
YAH! YAH! YAAAAHHH!!
BACHELOR HORROR THEATER

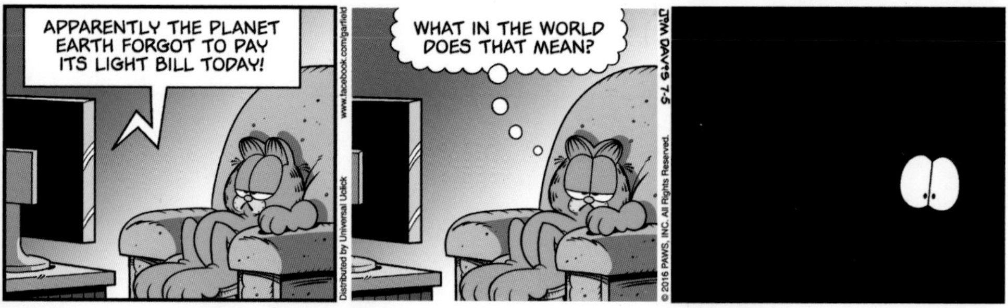

APPARENTLY THE PLANET EARTH FORGOT TO PAY ITS LIGHT BILL TODAY!
www.facebook.com/garfield
Distributed by Universal Uclick
WHAT IN THE WORLD DOES THAT MEAN?
JIM DAVIS 7-5
© 2016 PAWS, INC. All Rights Reserved.

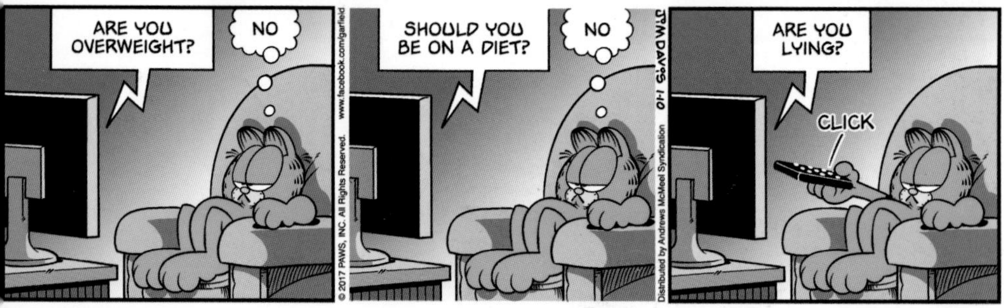

ARE YOU OVERWEIGHT?
NO
www.facebook.com/garfield
© 2017 PAWS, INC. All Rights Reserved.
SHOULD YOU BE ON A DIET?
NO
JIM DAVIS 1-10
Distributed by Andrews McMeel Syndication
ARE YOU LYING?
CLICK

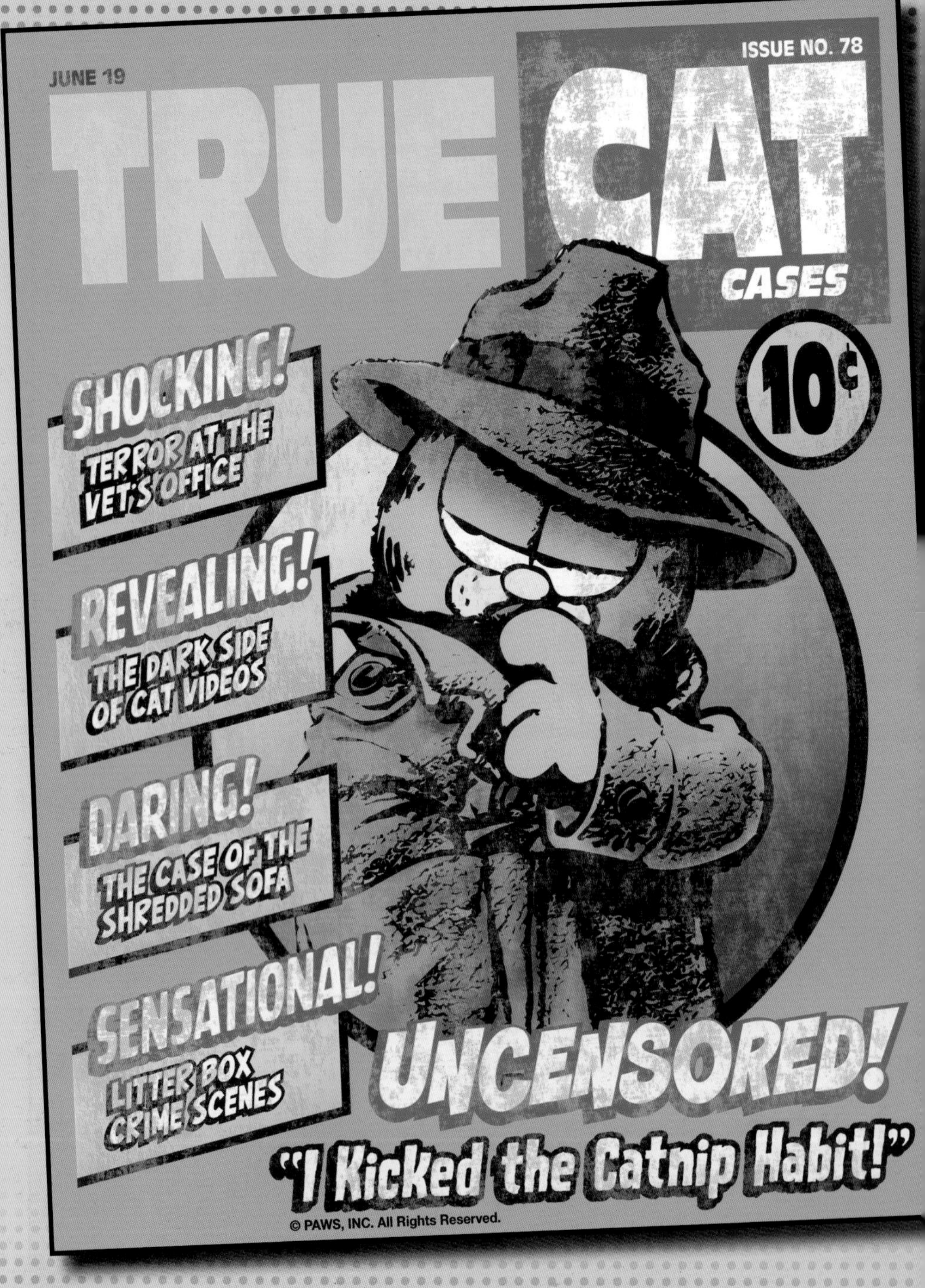

ISSUE NO. 78
JUNE 19
TRUE CAT
CASES
10¢
SHOCKING!
TERROR AT THE VET'S OFFICE
REVEALING!
THE DARK SIDE OF CAT VIDEOS
DARING!
THE CASE OF THE SHREDDED SOFA
SENSATIONAL!
LITTER BOX CRIME SCENES
UNCENSORED!
"I Kicked the Catnip Habit!"
© PAWS, INC. All Rights Reserved.

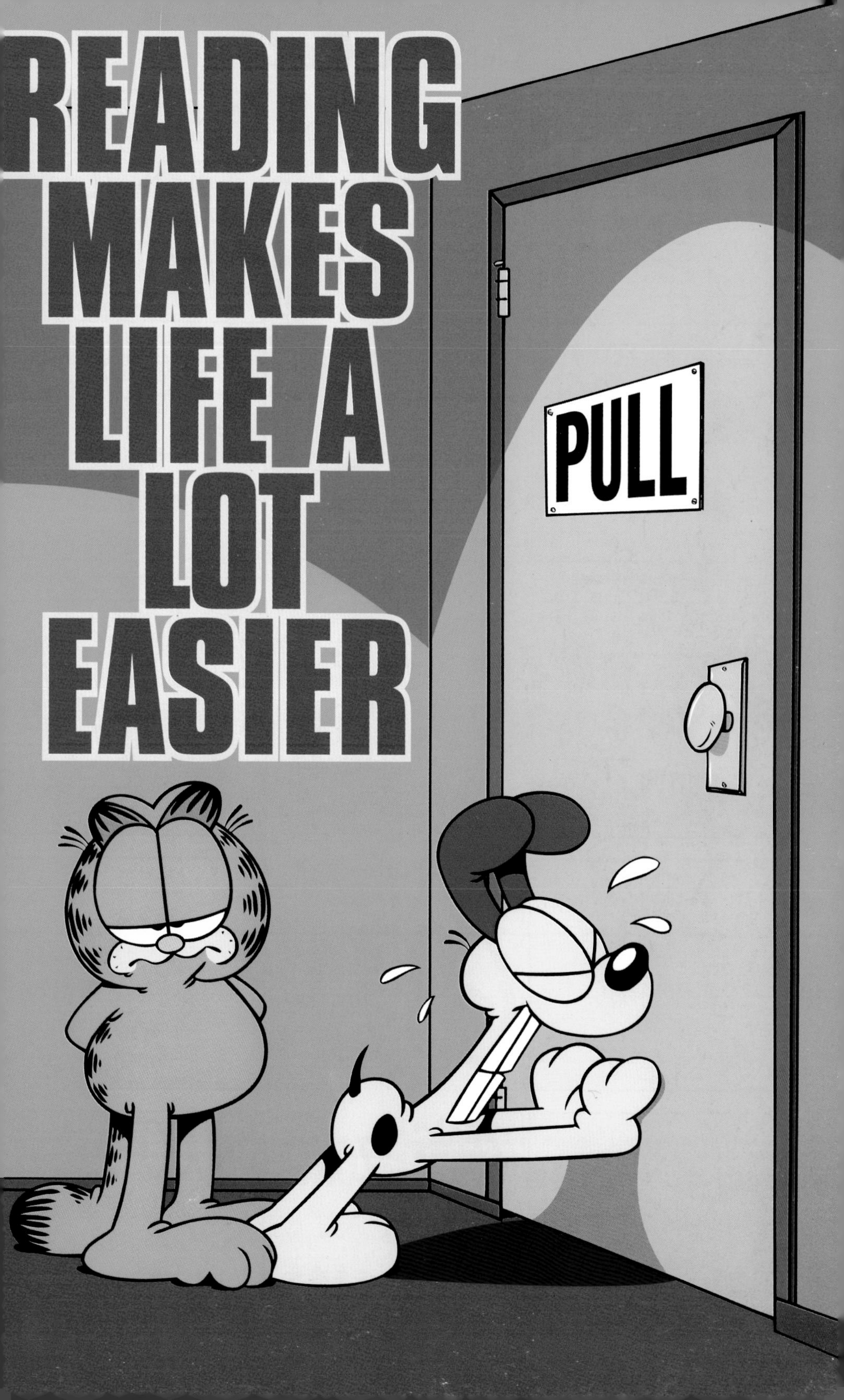
READING MAKES LIFE A LOT EASIER
PULL

Coffee Cat

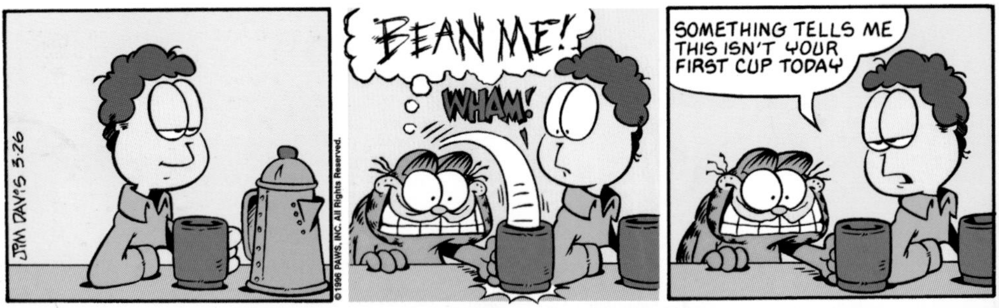
JIM DAVIS 5-26
BEAN ME!
WHAM!
© 1996 PAWS, INC. All Rights Reserved.
SOMETHING TELLS ME THIS ISN'T YOUR FIRST CUP TODAY

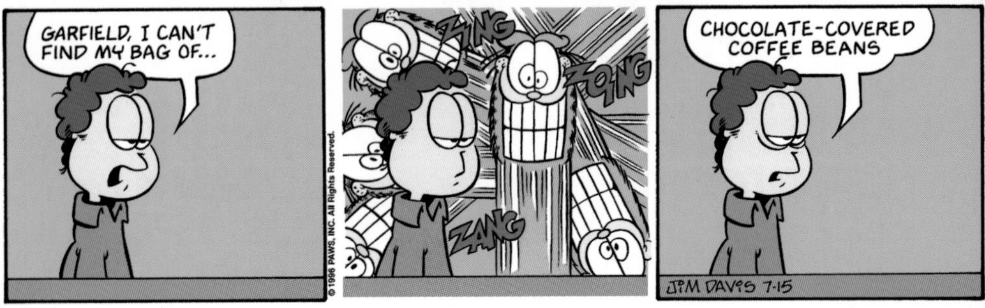
GARFIELD, I CAN'T FIND MY BAG OF...
© 1996 PAWS, INC. All Rights Reserved.
ZING
ZOING
ZANG
CHOCOLATE-COVERED COFFEE BEANS
JIM DAVIS 7-15

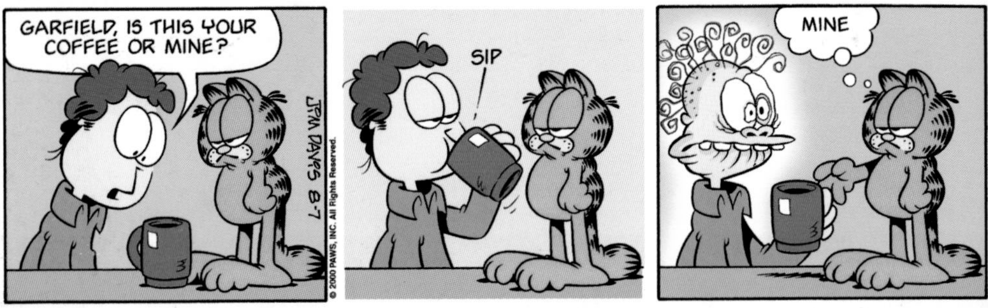
GARFIELD, IS THIS YOUR COFFEE OR MINE?
JIM DAVIS 8-7
© 2000 PAWS, INC. All Rights Reserved.
SIP
MINE

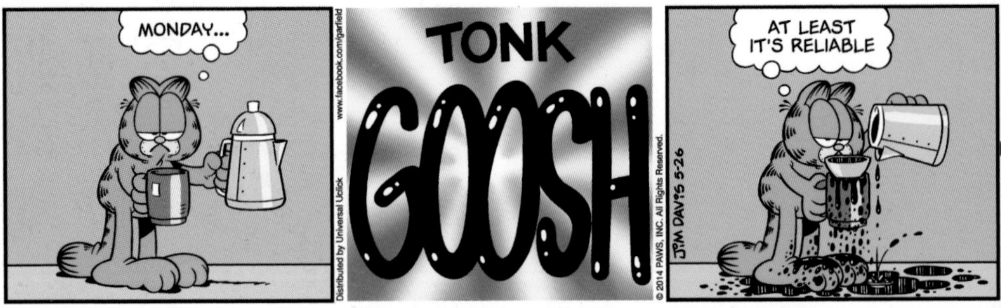
MONDAY...
www.facebook.com/garfield
Distributed by Universal Uclick
TONK
GOOSH
© 2014 PAWS, INC. All Rights Reserved.
JIM DAVIS 5-26
AT LEAST IT'S RELIABLE

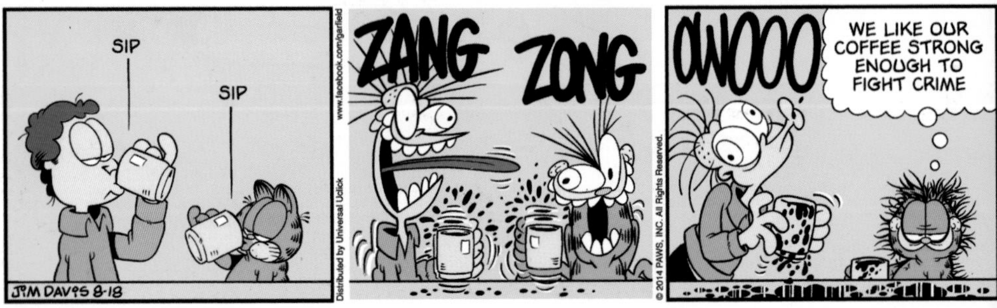
SIP
SIP
JIM DAVIS 8-18
www.facebook.com/garfield
Distributed by Universal Uclick
ZANG
ZONG
© 2014 PAWS, INC. All Rights Reserved.
OWOOO
WE LIKE OUR COFFEE STRONG ENOUGH TO FIGHT CRIME

Garfield Sunday Classics

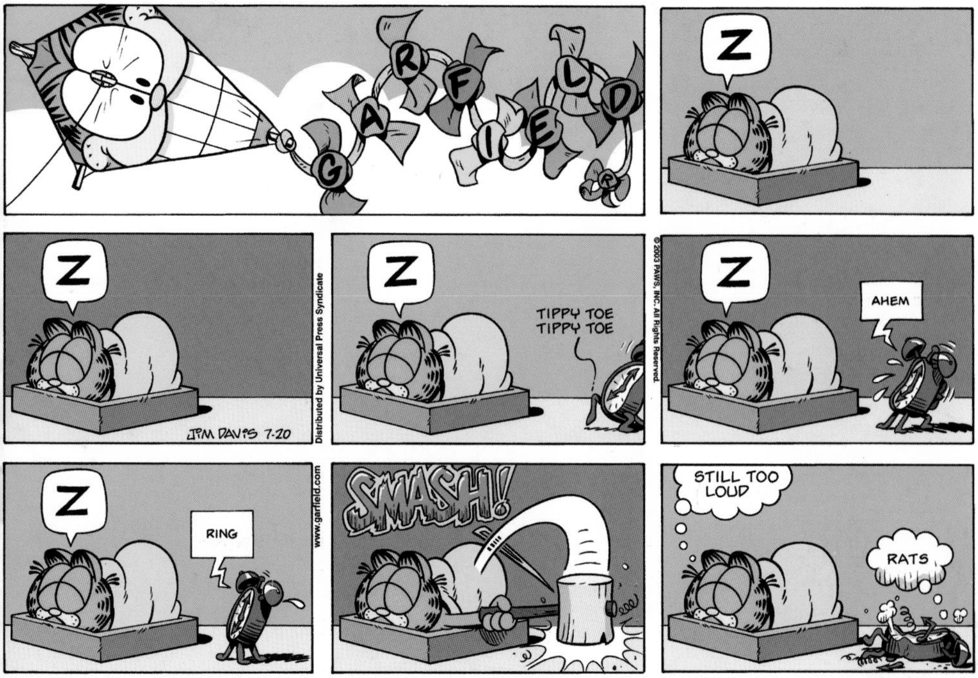
GARFIELD
Z
Z
JIM DAVIS 7-20
Distributed by Universal Press Syndicate
Z
TIPPY TOE
TIPPY TOE
© 2003 PAWS, INC. All Rights Reserved.
Z
AHEM
Z
RING
www.garfield.com
SMASH!
STILL TOO LOUD
RATS

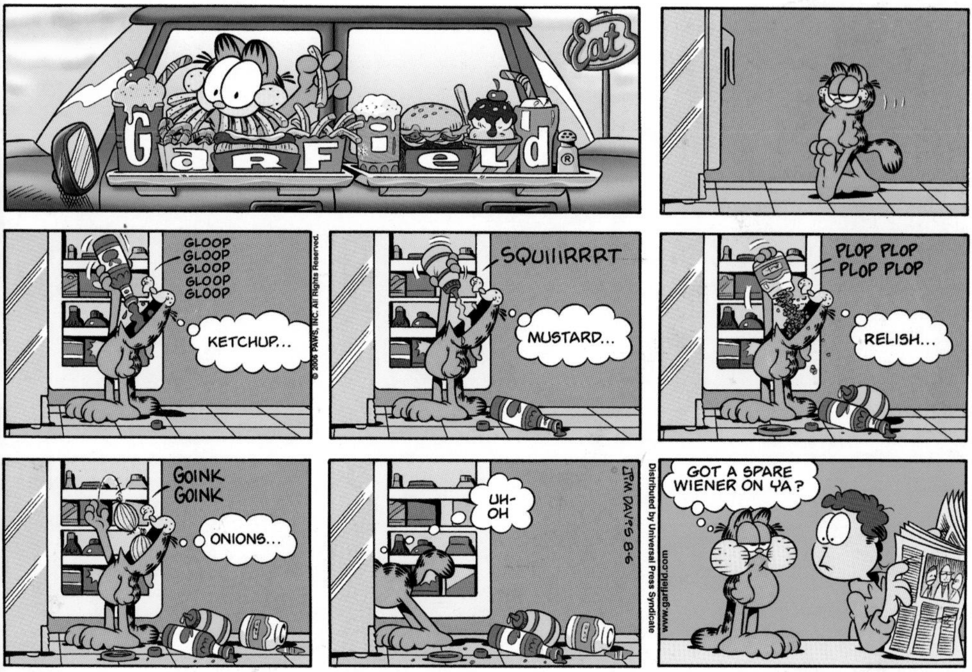
Eat
GLOOP
GLOOP
GLOOP
GLOOP
GLOOP
KETCHUP...
© 2003 PAWS, INC. All Rights Reserved.
SQUIIIRRRT
MUSTARD...
PLOP PLOP
PLOP PLOP
RELISH...
GOINK
GOINK
ONIONS...
UH-
OH
JIM DAVIS 8-6
Distributed by Universal Press Syndicate
www.garfield.com
GOT A SPARE
WIENER ON YA?

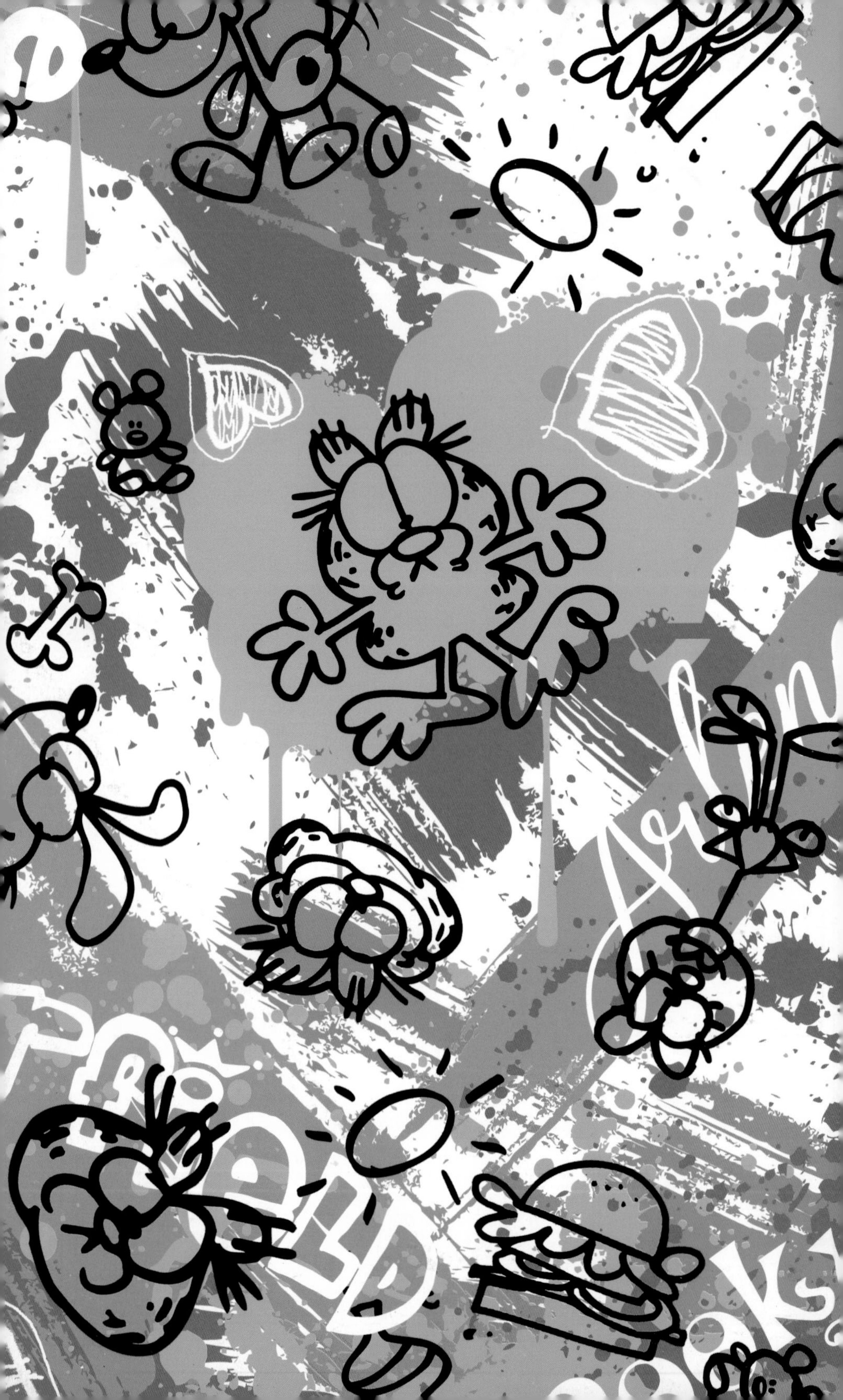

DISCOVER
EXPLOSIVE NEW WORLDS

AVAILABLE AT YOUR LOCAL COMICS SHOP AND BOOKSTORE
To find a comics shop in your area, call 1-888-266-4226
WWW.**BOOM-STUDIOS**.COM

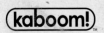

Adventure Time
Pendleton Ward and Others
Volume 1
ISBN: 978-1-60886-280-1 | $9.99
Volume 2
ISBN: 978-1-60886-323-5 | $14.99 US
Adventure Time: Islands
ISBN: 978-1-60886-972-5 | $9.99

Regular Show
J.G. Quintel and Others
Volume 1
ISBN: 978-1-60886-362-4 | $14.99
Volume 2
ISBN: 978-1-60886-426-3 | $14.99

Regular Show: Hydration
ISBN: 978-1-60886-339-6 | $12.99

The Amazing World of Gumball
Ben Bocquelet and Others
Volume 1
ISBN: 978-1-60886-488-1 | $14.99
Volume 2
ISBN: 978-1-60886-793-6 | $14.99

Over the Garden Wall
Patrick McHale, Jim Campbell and Others
Volume 1
ISBN: 978-1-60886-940-4 | $14.99
Volume 2
ISBN: 978-1-68415-006-9 | $14.99

Steven Universe
Rebecca Sugar and Others
Volume 1
ISBN: 978-1-60886-706-6 | $14.99
Volume 2
ISBN: 978-1-60886-796-7 | $14.99

Steven Universe &
The Crystal Gems
ISBN: 978-1-60886-921-3 | $14.99

Steven Universe:
Too Cool for School
ISBN: 978-1-60886-771-4 | $14.99

Peanuts
Charles Schultz and Others
Volume 1
ISBN: 978-1-60886-260-3 | $13.99

Garfield
Jim Davis and Others
Volume 1
ISBN: 978-1-60886-287-0 | $13.99